MYSTERIES
SEA MONSTERS

Monstrous Sea-Serpent as Described by Sailors. (*Earth, Sea and Sky* by Henry Davenport Northrop, 1887)

MYSTERIES & SEA MONSTERS

Thrilling Tales of the Sea

Volume Four

GRAHAM FAIELLA

The History Press

First published 2021

The History Press
97 St George's Place, Cheltenham,
Gloucestershire, GL50 3QB
www.thehistorypress.co.uk

British Library Cataloguing in Publication Data.
A catalogue record for this book is available from the British Library.

ISBN 978 0 7509 9087 5

Typesetting and origination by The History Press
Printed and bound in Great Britain by TJ International Ltd.

Trees for LYfe

CONTENTS

PREFACE

'Strange things indeed are seen in the sea world ...'
('The Nature of the Siren', poem by the ninth-/tenth-
century Old English poet Cynewulf)

The sea is an inherently mysterious place. Ships and seafarers have gone missing there, often without a clue about
why, since ships (and seafarers) first sailed away from sight
of land. For thousands of years, some ships have simply
gone, disappeared, and then come back, derelicts, without a
soul on board. Or, occasionally, with the remnants of what
was a well-found ship of souls as a skeleton ship of soulless
bones or corpses – or, indeed, as a phantom ship of ghosts.
These have become the mystery ships of legend, of sailors'
yarns that splice some strands of reality (sometimes) with
salt-seasoned imagination. They survive in sea lore because
they are good stories; they are dramatic, sometimes ghoul-
ish; they thrill to the thrall of sea mystery.

As for sea monsters: who knew how many there could be?
US Navy Lieutenant Fletcher Bassett knew; he chronicled
dozens of them in his *Legends and Superstitions of the Sea
and of Sailors – In all Lands and at all Times* (1885): 'monsters

of the deep are alluded to in many places in the Bible ... Classical authority has bequeathed us many [sea] monsters ... In Hindoo legend, Krishna slew a monster that lived at the bottom of the sea ... Scandinavia abounded in these monsters ... Icelandic legends tell of a monster called there Skrimsi, living in a fjord at Grimsey, who bit off the heads of seals, and wrecked ships.' And on and on – and on.

Of all these oceanic 'monsters', two in particular have protagonised the annals of cryptozoology – the pseudo-scientific 'search for and study of animals whose existence or survival is disputed or unsubstantiated' – as well as of legend, saga, lore, myth and, latterly, their perusal and inspection by naturalists and scientists: the sea serpent, and the kraken.

The kraken, for its part, has evolved from an ancient mythical creature of the northern seas, of immense size and equally terrifying ferocity, to a more rational assessment, in the nineteenth century, as a 'gigantic calamary': *Architeuthis dux*, the giant squid.

Sea serpents – much more benign creatures – have filled reams of narrative by first-hand witnesses of them. They have been claimed variously as other marine phenomena including long streamers of seaweed, large seals, extant prehistoric fossils, parades of porpoises, and other things besides the marine ophidian (snake-like) monsters recorded by observers of them and their kin.

The most intriguing nature of such mysteries, of ships and sea monsters alike, has been our human interaction and connection with them as essentially human stories that conflate some peculiarity of reality with legend or superstition or fear or horror. Because, as truth or fiction, or something in between, the mysteries of our ocean and seas, and ships thereupon or monsters therein, are, in their narrative form, quite simply ripping good yarns – thrilling tales of the sea.

MYSTERY SHIPS

One of the greatest of all sea mysteries concerned the discovery of the brigantine *Mary Celeste* near the Azores in mid-Atlantic, by another brigantine, the *Dei Gratia*, in December 1872. When three of the *Dei Gratia* crew boarded the *Celeste* they found her to be deserted: her master, Capt. Benjamin Briggs, his wife Sarah and their young daughter Sophia, and her seven crew had apparently jumped ship, suddenly and with no obvious cause. Why 'a perfectly seaworthy ship' (*Mary Celeste: The Greatest Mystery of the Sea*, by Paul Begg, 2005) was abandoned, and, moreover, while still under sail, has ever since been a complete mystery that has nurtured numerous speculative notions in books, magazine articles and other media, as well as some darker anecdotal postulates.

But why did that one derelict vessel so fabulously, so wondrously drift into such a prime position in the mythology of mystery ships? After all, thousands of deserted derelict vessels littered the seas in the age of sail. The difference was that the *Mary Celeste* was so well-found, so 'perfectly seaworthy' when her crew left her ('we genuinely have no idea why the captain and crew abandoned a perfectly seaworthy ship'), compared with the rag-tail un-shipshape condition of other ocean derelicts that had obviously been overwhelmed by some cataclysmic disaster. Amongst the multitude of mundanely mysterious fates of other ships, her dereliction defied any plausible explanation of a catastrophic cause.

The *Mary Celeste* and Other Mystery Ships

Mystery ships and their diversely true or fictitious – or both – stories have been confabulated by legend. *Mary Celeste* has proved amongst the most enduring, though by no means the only one from a flotilla of other mystery derelicts enshrouded in her wake:

> *Mysteries of the Ocean – The* Marie *[sic –* Mary*]* Celeste *and Others*
> Everyone knows that sailors get the credit of spinning yarns so tough that no one will believe them except the Marines, who are popularly supposed to be gullible enough to swallow anything. But it is doubtful if the toughest sailor's yarn ever conceived could possibly be one whit more amazing or credible than are many well attested facts.

> *The* Marie Celeste
> Take for instance the gruesome and mysterious story of the *Marie Celeste*. This vessel sailed from New York in November 1872, bound for Genoa with a cargo of oil [*sic* – her cargo was denatured alcohol for use in fortified wines]. There were thirteen souls on board of her all told, including Captain Brigg's wife and child [*sic* – there

were ten 'souls': Capt. Benjamin Briggs, his wife Sarah, their two year old daughter Sophia, and seven seamen]. She was sighted on the 4th December by the barque *Deo* [*sic – Dei*] *Gratia*, who signalled her, and receiving no response, suspected that something was wrong.

When a boat was sent off to investigate, the *Marie Celeste* was found to be absolutely deserted. Not a living thing was to be seen on her. Everything seemed in perfect order fore and aft, and the vessel was holding her course exactly as though she were under control. From that day to this not the faintest clue has been obtained as to what happened to her crew, or why, or even how they left her. The hull and cargo were intact, the rigging and spars were sound, and the sails were set for a light breeze such as was blowing at the time. The boats were every one at the davits, and there were no signs of either mutiny or bloodshed.

In the cabin a half-eaten breakfast for four was on the table, and a bottle of cough medicine, with a dose measured out in a tumbler, was beside a plate, where the captain's wife sat. A sewing-machine, with a child's gown under the needle, was against the bulkhead, just as the user had left it to have breakfast. In the galley the crew's food was cooked but not served out; and nothing in the forecastle gave any signs of coming trouble. The men's kits were in their usual places, and the weekly wash was hung up on the upper deck.

The log-book, posted to within 48 hours of being sighted by the *Deo Gratia*, showed the voyage to have been favourable, the last entry being the ship's position, and 'slight wind from S.E.' and it was quite clear that no rough weather had overtaken her in the interval. Everything appeared to be going on as usual up until the

The *Mary Celeste*.

moment that the crew had been spirited away by some mysterious agency which has never been revealed.

The *Marie Celeste* was towed into Gibraltar and a fresh crew put on board of her. But misfortune seemed to dog her through her whole career. Strange superstitions were connected with her. Crew after crew asserted that the ship was haunted, and that the lost crew were still on board and interfering with the working of the vessel. Finally she was alleged to have been deliberately cast away on the coast of South America, for which action her captain had to stand trial on a charge of barratry [misconduct injurious to a vessel or its cargo].

The Case of the Resolven

A case in many respects similar to the *Marie Celeste* was that of the brig *Resolven*, which left St. John's, Newfoundland, on a voyage to Labrador in August, 1884, with a crew of eleven all told. Early in the morning of the third day after leaving port she was discovered by H.M. gunboat *Mallard* quite deserted. The commander of the *Mallard* had his attention drawn to her owing to the strangeness of her behaviour.

On hailing her and getting no reply, a boat was sent to board her. So far as could be seen everything was in proper order. Her log-book was posted to within six hours of being sighted by the gunboat. The galley fire was alight, and both the binnacle lamp and side lights were burning. Her sails were set, but owing to the helm not being under control she was steering a very erratic course. No sign of disorder appeared anywhere. A bag of gold which was intended for the purchase of cargo, was found in a locker in the captain's cabin.

Why the crew abandoned her is one of the mysteries of the sea that will probably never be cleared up. At first it was thought that they had only left her temporarily for some purpose, though it is a little difficult to understand why they should have done so with all sail set. The *Mallard* remained in the vicinity of the spot where she fell in with the *Resolven* for a couple of days, but failed to get any indication of the fate of the crew, and then towed the abandoned vessel into the harbour.

The Gruesome Ocean Queen

A far more gruesome story than either of the above was that of the *Ocean Queen*, a clipper barque which sailed from Rangoon with a general cargo early in May 1876, bound for Melbourne. Her crew numbered nineteen all told, of whom more than one-half were foreigners of various nationalities. In addition to these there were some passengers, probably about a dozen in all. From the time of her leaving Rangoon nothing was heard of her until she was picked up on July 27th by H.M.S. *Orontes* about 400 miles east of the Seychelles group.

When the boat's crew of bluejackets boarded her their first impression was that there had been a mutiny or that the *Ocean Queen* had been attacked by pirates. No fewer than twenty-seven bodies in every stage of decomposition were scattered about the deck. Some of them had only been dead a few days, others again were reduced to skeletons. Some were clad in their every day clothes, others were naked.

In the cabin was the skeleton of a woman and two children. The youngest was a mere baby, and it was evident that the mother had died while nursing it; the other had died hugging its doll to its little breast. None of the bodies showed any signs of violence, nor were there any arms lying about.

So far as the vessel itself was concerned there was absolutely nothing to account for this extraordinary state of things. No attempt whatever had been made to either broach the cargo or rifle the cabins, in which there was a considerable amount of money. It was fairly evident that she had experienced some rough weather, but when the well was sounded there was found to be only six inches or so of water in it.

Everything of importance appeared to be intact, and the *Ocean Queen* was in good seaworthy condition, and well equipped with provisions and water. The log-book, however, was missing, and so also was the manifest.

On the chart the course was marked up for about three weeks after the vessel left Rangoon, the last mark being made at lat. 18 deg. 35 min. S., 64 deg. 28 min. E. – that is to say, in the neighbourhood of Rodriguez [Rodrigues] Island [just east of Mauritius], which would be a considerable distance out of her course. Assuming this to be correct, where did the vessel pass the intervening eight weeks or so which must have elapsed between the making of the last mark on the chart and her being picked up by the *Orontes*? It is hardly likely that she could have passed all that time in the track of ships to and from India and China without once being sighted.

Conjectures have been offered, but there is so much that is inexplicable about the whole thing that it would only be foolish to repeat them here.

The *Orontes* sent a party on board of her to clear up the decks and dispose of the bodies, afterwards leaving a crew to work her to Colombo. Four days after the vessels parted company, the *Ocean Queen* was spoken to [i.e. encountered] by one of the Messageres Maritimes boats, and this was the last that ever was heard of her. She vanished off the face of the ocean, and carried her secrets with her. Had she reached port, where she could have been more thoroughly examined, it is probable that some at least of the mystery surrounding her would have been cleared up. But it was decreed otherwise.

The Tale of the Foxdale

The story of the schooner *Foxdale* is perhaps as curious as any recorded of the sea. On October 13, 1891, this vessel left the Tees in ballast for Helsingfors [Helsinki, Finland]. On the second day out she was caught in a squall, and capsized, completely turning turtle. After drifting about for a couple of days in this condition, a warship was sent out to sink her, as she was a danger to other vessels.

When the warship sighted the derelict, the commander of her ordered up the gun's crew for practice, using the capsized schooner as a target. As soon as the smoke of the first discharge had cleared away, the commander, looking through his glasses, was amazed to see two men frantically waving to him from the bottom of the upturned craft, while a third was struggling in the water. Proceeding to the spot with all possible speed he succeeded in rescuing the whole party, and then learned an almost incredible story.

It appears that at the time the squall struck and capsized the *Foxdale*, there was only one man on deck, while two men and a boy were below. So suddenly was the vessel overturned that the air had not time to escape from between decks. As soon as the crew recovered their senses sufficiently to realise the situation, they saw that there was no immediate danger, for they had both food and water beside them, and the air might last for a week or more.

It was on the fourth day of their imprisonment that they were released under such strange circumstances. Immediately after the shot from the warship ripped open the planking, one of them ran to the hole and was almost lifted off his feet by the rushing out of the imprisoned air. The other two quickly followed suit.

It may be that sailors are superstitious and cling to a belief in the supernatural. Who can blame them when there are so many mysterious and inexplicable things happening to those who go down to the sea in ships ... (*Wanganui Chronicle* [New Zealand] (from *The Scotsman*), 14 March 1914)

Phantom Ships

On 22 January 1909 the Cardiff *Evening News* published an article titled 'The Phantom Schooner'. The narrator, an Englishman, was voyaging on board 'the clipper ship *Toreador*' to Australia for 'purer air and a milder climate'. During the voyage he struck up a friendship with the mate, Jim, who told him a yarn, 'one night, in the North-East trades' as they were 'leaning over the taffrail enjoying our evening smoke'. The story went that when 'Jim' was on a steamship bound across the Atlantic for Boston she collided with and apparently sank a schooner off the Isles of Scilly. On the return voyage, coming up to the English Channel, they again struck a schooner that was 'careering along, every sail full', though it was a perfectly calm night. The name of the schooner, the *Amitie*, was the same as the name of the schooner they hit on the outward voyage – and, in the mate's fevered imagination, she, too, sank.

It was a good yarn – but a fiction: the heading above the title in the *News* was 'To-day's Short Story'. Trying to separate fact from fiction in seafaring stories often smudges the two conceits together. The good yarn is often an amalgam of some kind of trope of truth spliced and braided and plaited with some fragmented memory of a real event by a creative imagination: real derelicts did drift, unmanned, around the seas, to be encountered occasionally by other vessels and, sometimes, storified as 'phantom' ships by awe-struck crews with fertile minds.

As Mark Twain, a journalist of record and fictionist of renown, is said to have written, 'The truth should never get in the way of a good story' (most likely an apocryphal attribution, but it does have the ring of a genuine Twain-ism). It is more of a truism that 'a good story', however chimerical, often shines and even gathers lustre long after any shades of truth in it have dimmed, flickered, sighed a final breath and expired.

And, indeed, that some mysteries of some real ships are, actually, real.

Le Vaisseau-Fantôme
('The Phantom Ship').
(*Le Petit Journal*,
5 March 1911)

The Legend of the Phantom Ship

It is a somewhat singular fact that there is not a single European nation whose mariners do not share in the picturesque and romantic superstition that certain parts of the ocean are haunted by the Spectre of a Ship. The tradition is quite the best known among the lore of the sea … Nor can we be permitted to doubt that such an ocean Phantom really does exist. For did not two royal princes see her with their own eyes as short a time ago as the 11th July 1881? Such testimony is not to be disputed by any loyal British subject … (*Chamber's Journal*, 16 June 1894)

The incident was picked up and reported by the press of the day:

The Flying Dutchman

To the two sailor sons of the Prince of Wales [Princes
Albert Victor and George] has been vouchsafed a glimpse
of that far-famed vessel the *Flying Dutchman*; the first
sight of her that has been seen, or at any rate reported, for
many a long year. Vanderdecken [the *Flying Dutchman*'s
captain] has apparently succeeded in doubling the Cape
[of Good Hope], since he has made his appearance on
the coast of New South Wales. In their 'Journal,' which
has just been published under the editorial supervision
of the Rev. John N. Dalton, appears under the date of
July 11 (1881):

'At 4 a.m. the *Flying Dutchman* crossed our bows [on
HMS *Baccante*]. A strange red light, as of a phantom ship
all aglow, in the midst of which light the masts, spars,
and sails of a brig 200 yards distant stood out in strong
relief as she came up. The lookout man on the forecastle
reported her as close on the port bow, where also the
officer of the watch from the bridge clearly saw her, who
was sent forward at once to the forecastle; but on arriving
there no vestige nor any sign whatever of any material
ship was to be seen either near or right away to the horizon; the night being clear and the sea calm.

'Thirteen persons altogether saw her, but whether it
was Van Diemen or the *Flying Dutchman*, or who else,
must remain unknown. The *Tourmaline* and *Cleopatra*,
who were sailing on our starboard bow, flashed to ask
whether we had seen the strange red light.

'At a quarter to 11 a.m. the ordinary seaman who had
this morning reported the *Flying Dutchman* fell from the
foretopmast cross-trees, and was smashed to atoms. At a
quarter past 4 p.m., after quarters, we hove-to with the

head yards aback, and he was buried in the sea. He was a smart royal-yardman, and one of the most promising young hands in the ship, and everyone feels quite sad at his loss. At the next port we came to the admiral also was smitten down.' (*Grey River Argus* [Greymouth, New Zealand], 6 August 1886)

The Legend of the Phantom Ship (continued)
... There are many versions of the famous legend of the *Flying Dutchman* ... Perhaps the story has been nowhere better told than by Captain [Frederick] Marryat in the novel which he founded upon it [*The Phantom Ship*, 1839]. Cornelius Vanderdecken, a sea-captain of Amsterdam, coming home from Batavia [Jakarta], is much troubled by head-winds when off the Cape of Good Hope. Day after day he goes on struggling against the baffling winds without gaining a foot of ground. The sailors grow weary, the skipper impatient. Still the bleak sou'-wester continues to blow this old galliot [galleon] steadily back.

For nine dreary weeks this goes on; then a terrible fit of passion seizes Vanderdecken. He sinks down upon his knees, and raising his clenched fists to the heavens, curses the Deity for opposing him, swearing that he will weather the Cape yet in spite of the Divine will, though he should go on beating about until the Day of Judgment. As a punishment for this terrible impiety, he is doomed to go on sailing in the stormy seas east of Agulhas [Cape Agulhas, east of the Cape of Good Hope] until the last trumpet shall sound, for ever struggling against head-winds in a vain effort to double the South African Cape.

Such, in brief, is the legend of the *Flying Dutchman*, as it has been accepted by English-speaking sailors for many generations past ...

Dutch Phantoms

Bechstein, in the 'Deutsches Sagenbuch' gives the Dutch version of the phantom ship, which is totally dissimilar from our own, both as regards the name of its evil-minded hero, and the sin for which he was condemned to wander.

'Falkenberg,' he says, 'was a nobleman who murdered his brother and his bride in a fit of passion; and was therefore condemned to wander for ever towards the north. On arriving at the seashore he found awaiting him a boat, with a man in it, who said, 'Expectamus te.' He entered the boat, attended by his good and his evil spirit, and went on board a spectral barque in the harbour. There he yet lingers, while the two spirits play at dice for his soul. For six hundred years has the ship been wandering the seas, and sailors still see her in the German Ocean [the North Sea] sailing northward, without helm or steersman. She is painted gray, has coloured sails, a pale flag, and no crew. Flames come forth from her masthead at night.'

Another Dutch account of the old legend says that the skipper of the phantom ship was a native of Amsterdam, one Bernard Fokke, who lived in the seventeenth century. He was a daring, reckless seaman, who had the masts of his ship encased with iron to strengthen them and enable him to carry more sail. It is recorded that he sailed from Holland to the East Indies in ninety days; and in consequence of having made many wonderful voyages, came at last to be reputed a sorcerer, in league with the devil. In one voyage he disappeared for a while, having been spirited away by Satan, and on his return was condemned – the legend does not say by whom – to sail for ever the ocean between the southern capes with no other crew than his boatswain, cook, and pilot.

Many Dutch seamen believe that his vessel is still to be fallen in with in the Southern Ocean, and that, when he sights a ship, he will give chase for the purpose of coming alongside to ask questions. If these are not answered, all is well; but should those hailed be so injudicious as to make any reply, ill-luck is certain to befall them ...

A Spanish Phantom ... and Its 'Fiendish Crew'

In a volume of a German 'Morgenblätter' [morning newspaper] for the year 1824 is contained another story of a phantom ship. A lookout man sights and reports a vessel. When questioned concerning her, he says he saw a frigate in a faint haze of light, with a black captain, and a skeleton figure with a spear in its hand standing on the poop. Skeleton shapes noiselessly handled the cobweb-like sails and ropes. The only sound which he heard as the mysterious craft glided past was the word 'water.' The history of this strange ship seemed to be known to one of the sailors on board, who recounted it as follows:

'A rich Spaniard of Peru, one Don Lopez d'Aranda, dreamed he saw his son, Don Sandovalle, who had sailed with his bride for Spain, on board his ship with a ghastly wound in his head, and pointing to his own form, bound to the mainmast of the vessel. Near him was water, just beyond his reach, and the fiendish crew were mocking him and refusing him drink. The crew had murdered the young couple for their gold; and the curse of the wandering Dutchman had descended upon them. They are still to be seen cruising off the entrance to the Rio de la Plata.'

A Purgatorial Phantom

The French version of the time-honoured legend is given by Jal, in his 'Scènes de la Vie Maritime.' He says: 'An

The Phantom Ship, drawn by Frank Brangwyn. (*The Graphic*, 15 July 1893)

unbelieving Dutch captain had vainly tried to round Cape
Horn against a head gale. He swore he would do it; and
when the gale increased, laughed at the fears of his crew,
smoked his pipe, and drank his beer. He threw overboard
some of them who tried to make him put into port. The
Holy Ghost descended on the vessel; but he fired his pistol
at it, and pierced his own hand and paralysed his arm. He
cursed God; and was then condemned by the apparition to
navigate always, without putting into port, only having gall
to drink, and red-hot iron to eat, and eternally to watch.

'He was to be the evil genius of the sea, to torment and
punish sailors, the spectacle of his tempest-tossed barque
to presage ill-fortune to the luckless beholder. He is the
sender of white squalls, of all disasters, and of storms.

Should he visit a ship, wine on board turns sour, and all food becomes beans – the sailors' particular aversion. Should he bring or send letters, none must touch them, or they are lost. He changes his appearance at will, and is seldom beheld twice under the same circumstances. His crew are all old sinners of the sea, marine thieves, cowards, murderers, and so forth. They toil and suffer eternally, and get but little to eat and drink. His ship is the true purgatory of the faithless and idle sailor.'

The Italian Version
The Italian legend is a local one, as old as the year 1339, when Venice was first wedded to the Adriatic by the ceremony of a ring being dropped over the prow of a gondola into its limpid blue waters. During a tempest, a fisherman was bid to row three mysterious men first to certain churches in the city, then out to the entrance of the port. The boatman with terror beheld a vast Saracen galley rushing in before the wind, crowded with most fearful-looking demons. The three men in his boat, however, caused her to founder before she could get near the city, thus saving the city.

When they stepped ashore again, one of them handed the waterman a ring, by means of which these three strangers were discovered to be St Mark, St Nicholas, and St George. Giorgione has painted this phantom vessel, with her crew of spectral demons leaping overboard, affrighted by the saints; and the picture may still be seen in the Venetian Academy ...

Instances of traditions and superstitions founded upon the idea of a phantom ship might be multiplied until this article assumed the dimensions of a stout volume; but want of space forbids that the list should be further extended. It is not difficult to conceive the paternity of the romantic old legend. The sudden disappearance of a distant ship through some subtle, imperceptible wreathing of mist upon the horizon, would be sufficient to suggest the notion of a spectral vessel.

Herman Melville, in his admirable work 'Typee,' has a quaint idea, out of which might easily grow a tradition of a phantom ship. 'I heard,' he says, 'of one whaler which, after many years' absence, was given up for lost. The last that had been heard of her was a shadowy report of her having touched at some of those unstable islands in the far Pacific whose eccentric wanderings are carefully noted in each edition of the South Sea charts. After a long interval, however, the *Perseverance* – for that was her name – was spoken somewhere in the vicinity of the ends of the earth, cruising along as leisurely as ever, her sails all bepatched and bequilted with rope-yarns, her spars all fished [tied together] with old pipe-staves, and her rigging knotted and spliced in every possible direction.

'Her crew was composed of some twenty venerable Greenwich pensioner-looking old salts, who just managed to hobble about deck. The ends of all the running ropes, with the exception of the signal-halyards and poop-downhaul, were rove through snatch-blocks, and led to the capstan or windlass, so that not a yard was braced or a sail set without the assistance of machinery. Her hull was encrusted with barnacles, which completely encased her ... What eventually became of her, I never learned; at any rate, she never reached home.'

Nor is the belief in the *Flying Dutchman* a superstition of the past. Sailors in this age give just as great credence to the ancient legend as they did a couple of centuries ago. Indeed, no race is more persistent in credulity than seamen. They continue to cling to traditions that have come down from mariners of a date when the ocean was still shrouded in mystery and romance. Friday's sailing is as unlucky as ever it was; the St Elmo's Fire is yet full of significance; and a Finn amongst the crew ruins the prospects of a voyage at the very outset. It will take many generations, even in this prosaic age of iron and steam, for the sailor to abandon his old beliefs; and it may be safe to predict that the very last fragment of superstition he will be willing to give up will be the legend of the Phantom Ship. (*Chamber's Journal*, 16 June 1894)

Sally G.'s Encounter with the *Flying Dutchman*

In April 1881 an American vessel, the barque *Sally G.*, en route from Sicily to New London, Connecticut, encountered an anonymous Dutch brig in mid-Atlantic. The *Sally G.*'s master, Capt. Prodgers, went on board the stranger where he found 'a weather-beaten old man in command of her'. Communication was unintelligible to both men. Could it have been *the*, or at least *a* 'Flying Dutchman'? Capt. Prodgers was in no doubt:

The Flying Dutchman

There can be little doubt that Captain Prodgers, of the American barque *Sally G.*, has actually met the *Flying Dutchman*. On the arrival of *Sally G.*, at New London [Connecticut] last Wednesday [6 May 1881], from Palermo, with fruit to consignee, her captain told the following remarkable story:-

On the 11th of April last, and at about 10 o'clock in the morning, the barque being then in latitude 42° 18', and about fifteen hundred miles from Montauk Point [north-east tip of Long Island; *Sally G.* was just north of the Azores] – there being a light breeze from the south-south-east, and the barque running dead before it with all her square sails set, and the mate having just ordered the studding-sails booms to be rigged out – a sail was reported a little on the starboard bow. In due time the *Sally G.* came up with what proved to be a Dutch brig, so far as could be judged from her spars and green deck-house, which backed her maintop-sail and launched a boat.

It was evident that her captain wanted to speak to the *Sally G.*, and accordingly the latter was hove to, her captain being a humane man and not being in any particular hurry. The brig was old-fashioned, and from her appearance had been at sea a long time, so long that her name had faded from her stern, unless, of course, it had been designedly scraped off. Still, she seemed to be in good enough condition, and Captain Prodgers naturally wondered what the Dutchman could want.

The latter's boat hooked on to the main chains – there being very little sea at the time – and the man in charge of her boarded the *Sally G.*, and made a long speech to the captain in an unknown tongue. The gallant American crew of the *Sally G.* consisted of eighteen men, among whom were eight Irishmen, three Scotchmen, two Englishmen, a Swede, and four 'Dagos,' who were either Portuguese, Spaniards, or Italians. The word was passed forward for some one of the crew to come aft, and act as an interpreter, but it was found that there was not a man on board who could understand what the alleged Dutchman wanted.

In these circumstances Captain Prodgers told the mate, Mr. Anderson, that he had better take a boat and board the brig and find out what was the matter. The mate promptly launched the quarter-boat and pulled to the brig. He found a weather-beaten old man in command of her, who seemed greatly pleased to see him, but to all Mr. Anderson's questions, although they were asked in the loudest and clearest voice the latter could command, the captain replied at great length, but in perfectly unintelligible words.

When the mate chalked the latitude and longitude on the after-hatch, thinking that the brig's chronometer might be out of order, the Dutch captain shook his head with great emphasis. Mr. Anderson then sounded the well to find if the brig leaked, looked into the harness cask and into the steward's pantry to see if there was any sign that provisions were low; searched through the cabin and forecastle, thinking that perhaps the cholera had broken out among the crew, and satisfied himself that the water-casks on deck were reasonably full.

With all his efforts he could not find that there was anything wrong about the brig or her people, and when he said to her captain, 'So far as I see, there ain't nothin' the matter no more than what a sailor-man would expect to find aboard a Dutchman,' the latter smiled serenely and began another long speech, after which Mr. Anderson thanked him, and said it wasn't worth mentioning, and so returned to the *Sally G*. Both vessels then filled away and stood on their respective courses, the Dutchman steering about south-east, as if he were making for the Bermudas or, say, the Spanish Main [i.e. northern South America].

It is Captain Prodgers' firm belief that this mysterious Dutch brig was the genuine *Flying Dutchman*. He was strengthened in that belief by the fact that within eighteen hours after leaving her he experienced a violent hurricane from the westward, which drove him more than a hundred miles out of the course. What the Dutchman wanted will forever be a profound mystery. If the captain of the brig was really a live man, it is inconceivable that he should induce an American barque to heave to merely in order to make polite speeches in unknown tongues. If, on the contrary, he was the *Flying Dutchman*, he would naturally do all sorts of mysterious things.

Other vessels will do well to keep a look-out for a strange Dutch brig with single topsail yards and stump royal masts, and ascertain, if possible, her true character. (*The New Zealand Herald*, 30 July 1881)

A 'Queer Yarn'

An old sea-dog of 'an advanced age' – a marine pilot, as it happened – steadily filling his sea-boots with rum until 'his face gradually began to assume a carmine tint' lubricated his storytelling faculties such that 'his companions knew that a yarn was coming'. And so it did. About an old derelict ship that fired his imagination of a close encounter with the *Flying Dutchman*.

Saw the Flying Dutchman – *The Queer Yarn Spun by an Old Sailor When Off Duty*

A group of bronzed pilots sat in an office lately testing the age and qualities of a bottle of rum. One was a retired [marine] pilot, whose advanced age rendered him unfit for the perilous life, but it did not seem to impair in the least his powers for consuming rum, as a greater portion found its way into his glass and his face gradually began to assume a carmine tint. The continued effects of the hot rum and the fire gradually got in their work, and from the sparkle in his eyes his companions knew that a yarn was coming.

'It's a long time ago, when I was on the old Blunt,' he said, 'that I saw for the first time that terror to all sailors, the *Flying Dutchman*. Many and many a night around the galley fire, when I was a boy, I had listened open-mouthed to the tales told of the ghostly craft. One night in June, somewhere around the '6os, I had the last turn on the Blunt, and had just turned in when the boat-keeper sung out that there was a ship in sight. I went on deck, and sure enough, heading our way, about two miles to leeward, was a full-rigged ship with all sail set. That in itself was peculiar, as we had just an occasional puff, while the ship seemed to be holding a twenty-knot breeze; but I was so anxious to get it that I did not notice it at the time, but jumped into the cabin to dress.

'We gave her a torch [i.e. signalled her] and she answered us that she wanted a pilot, and in a few moments I was in the yawl with two boys pulling toward her. She was a deep ship and I saw a cool two hundred [dollars] in her [to pilot her], and while the boys bent their backs to the oars I took a good look at her. There was certainly something uncanny in the look of her, and, look as hard as I could, I could not see a soul aboard, not even a man at the wheel.

'All of a sudden the wind seemed to leave her, her sails dropped and she appeared to be still in the sea. Well, we pulled, and we pulled for nearly an hour, but she was still as far off as at first, and I was about to turn back when she seemed to get a breeze head on and began to sail backward. That was enough for the boys, and as quick as a wink they turned about and we pulled like blazes for the Blunt. We made sail and turned tail, but as sure as I live we could not shake her off. There she was all night, first alongside, then ahead and then astern, and I will never forget her as long as I live. Just at daybreak she seemed to fade away, and finally disappeared.' (*Aspen Daily Times* [Colorado], 2 December 1888)

The *Marlborough*

The *Flying Dutchman* was probably the most famous ghost ship that (probably) never was. The *Marlborough* was one of the most famous (including the *Mary Celeste*) that most definitely was. In January 1890 *Marlborough* left Lyttelton, New Zealand, for England, commanded by Capt. W. Hird. She carried one passenger (Mrs W.B. Anderson, of Dunedin, New Zealand), a crew of around thirty (possibly thirty-three), and a cargo of '10,362 carcases of mutton and 969 carcases lambs' as well as '1,981 bales wool and two bales skins'. By the middle of that year she had been posted missing by Lloyd's, presumed lost.

The Missing Ship Marlborough

There is now very slight doubt indeed but that the missing Shaw-Savill ship *Marlborough*, bound Home from this colony, has gone down with all hands in the Southern Ocean, leaving not a soul to tell the tale. She is now 184 days out from Lyttelton for London, and has long been posted at Lloyd's as missing. Like the ill-fated ship *Trevelyan*, nothing more will be heard in all probability of the *Marlborough*.

The *Marlborough*, a fine iron ship of 1,174 tons, set out from Lyttelton for London on January 12th last. She had on board a valuable cargo of frozen mutton, etc., and was expected to make the voyage in 100 days. Nearly double that period has elapsed and no tidings have come to hand of the vessel, and the agents have long since given out that they believe that she has been lost with all hands. (*Auckland Star*, 15 July 1890)

The last sight of the *Marlborough* was when she was two days out from Lyttelton and spoke to (encountered) the ship *Falkland Hill*. A full twenty-three years afterwards, a story came to light in 1913 that a sea captain who had been wrecked near Cape Horn many years before had discovered another wreck nearby. He claimed that it was the long-lost *Marlborough* – and her 'crew' …

Strange Story of the Sea – Fate of Missing Ship
– Twenty Skeletons

Dunedin, This Day

A well-known Dunedin shipping man to-day received from the skipper of one of the Shaw, Savill, and Albion liners this letter:-

'Just a hurried line to tell you something in which New Zealand people may take an interest. A month ago Captain McArthur, in command of one of Alfred Holt's Blue Funnel steamers trading to Seattle, via China and Japan, came into the London office and stated he had met in Seattle a pilot who told him, in the course of conversation, that he was once wrecked off Cape Horn, that most of the crew got ashore, and that all decided to part company, and to go two by two in different directions to look for the Mission Station.

'He and his companion, who he believes, were the only survivors in this search for the station, which they eventually reached, came upon a large painted-port ship wrecked in a cove, and he distinctly saw the name *"Marlborough."* There were three large tents erected and big heaps of shell-fish, which had been consumed by the survivors, but they were all dead, and there were twenty skeletons.

'Young Hird, son of the captain, is in the office of Law, Leslie And Co., Leadenhall-street, and is in communication with this pilot, who has the exact latitude and longitude. Is it not a strange story of the sea?' (*Evening Post* [Wellington, New Zealand], 26 September 1913)

Capt. S. Burley, the Puget Sound pilot from Seattle, elaborated on his story, which Basil Lubbock included in his account of the *Marlborough* mystery in *The Last of the Windjammers* (Brown, Son & Ferguson, 1927):

'On July 23, 1890 [*sic* – 1888], I was wrecked on Tierra del Fuego in the barque *Cordova* (iron barque, 521 tons, owners Parry, Jones & Co. of Liverpool). The whole crew succeeded in reaching the shore, landing in a bay named Thetis Bay [near Cabo San Diego, the easternmost point of Tierra del Fuego]. After spending about two weeks there and suffering terribly on account of the extreme cold, it being the dead of winter, and, further, becoming nervous on account of a wandering band of Fuegians who had attached themselves to us, the mate and second mate and seven of the crew took the boat with the idea of reaching Staten Island [20 miles away across the Straits of Le Maire] and procuring assistance, but unfortunately perished on the way. [In fact they did reach the lighthouse at the eastern extremity of the island. There they met a group of surviving castaways from another ship wrecked near Thetis Bay, the *Glenmore*.]

'This left the captain and four, including myself. One night at camp somebody remarked that there were always whalers in Good Success Bay [just around the other side of Cabo San Diego], which was to the southward of where we were camped, boiling out their oil; and, as two of our party were nearly gone, one other and myself volunteered to endeavour to reach Good Success Bay by tramping along the beach.

'We left next morning at daylight which was nearly 10 o'clock, but the travelling was so difficult that by four we had not travelled far. We passed the wreck of a barque, named *Godiva*. I cannot recall whether she belonged to Glasgow or Greenock, but the after end was high on the rocks, the forward end having disappeared, and her cargo, coal, was scattered along the beach.

'I never saw any signs of the *Marlborough*, but a few miles to the southward of the wreck of the *Godiva*, was a boat marked "*Marlborough* of London." It was a square stern gig with teakwood thwarts, and had brass knees and a grating made of teakwood in the after end. The boat was pulled up out of reach of the seas and the oars were all there. It also contained a water beaker, the same being either oak or teak, and had a stand and was bound with brass hoops.

'Up above the boat in a sheltered part of the rocks we found a tent, made from the belly of a square sail, and I am inclined to believe that the survivors of the boat from the *Marlborough* had obtained the same from the *Godiva*, although the camp in question was several miles to the southward of the wreck.

'In the tent were seven skeletons and outside was a pile of a sort of mussel shells, which they had apparently subsisted on. I am inclined to believe that they had perished from exposure and ptomaine poisoning. One of the skeletons had on a Welsh grey flannel shirt with the initials worked in red on a piece of tape, sewn on a piece down the front – the initials were either W.R.J. or W.J.R., which I cannot recall. It was growing dark at the time, and, being in the condition we were, you can readily understand our feelings when we ran across that gruesome sight.

'We two started back to our camp, having given up the idea of reaching Good Success Bay; and we camped that night not far from that spot. After suffering untold hardships, we survivors were picked up on August 23 by a barque named *Banco Mobiliario* and landed at Coquimbo [Peru], after having been cast away 33 days.

'I would state that there were signs of a wreck right below where the camp was, but there were no means of identifying what ship it was.'

It was a good story: shipwrecked near Cape Horn, finding the vestiges of another shipwreck including her skeletal crew, and being rescued by a passing ship. Although the details of the *Cordova* castaways were approximately true, it had one major flaw with regard to the missing ship *Marlborough*: the *Cordova* was actually wrecked on Tierra del Fuego in July 1888, two years *before* the *Marlborough* sailed from Lyttelton. The *Marlborough*, moreover, was from Glasgow, not 'of London'.

The Skeleton Ship Story
A second account of the 'discovery' of the remains of the *Marlborough* and her crew was circulated around the same

Un Vaisseau Fantome — the supposed 'ghost ship' *Marlborough*. The following caption, translated from a French newspaper in 1913, does nothing to clarify the mystery of the *Marlborough*'s disappearance: 'An English ship on her way to Lyttelton has made, at Punta Arenas (near Cape Horn), a macabre discovery. A ship was seen that appeared to be disabled. The English ship signalled her but there was no response, and so she came up to her and some sailors went on board. There they found twenty human skeletons. The vessel showed the name *Marlborough*, from the port of Glasgow. Now, in 1890 a ship of that name sailed for Chile [*sic*] and was last seen near the Magellan Straits, since which time nothing has been heard of her and she was posted lost.' (*Le Petit Journal*, 19 October 1913)

time as Capt. Burley's 25-year-old mis-memoir. It included the gothic detail of a crew of skeletons on board the vessel where she reportedly lay 'in one of the rocky coves near Punta Arenas in the Magellan Straits' of which there are, indeed, many.

Crew of Skeletons – Missing Ship Reported after Twenty-Three Years – A Weird Story

... A day or two ago another British sailing ship arrived in Lyttelton with the story that she had found the *Marlborough* and the skeletons of twenty of her crew in one of the rocky coves near Punta Arenas (Sandy Point), in the Magellan Straits. The captain is quoted as telling the story in the following words:

'We were off the rocky coves near Punta Arenas, keeping near the land for shelter. The coves are deep and silent, the sailing difficult and dangerous. It was a weirdly wild evening, with the red orb of the sun setting on the horizon. The stillness was uncanny. There was a shining green light reflected on the jagged rocks on our right. We rounded a point into a deep cleft cove. Before us, a mile or more across the water, stood a sailing vessel with the barest shreds of canvas fluttering in the breeze. We signalled and hove to. No answer came. We searched the 'stranger' with our glasses [binoculars]. Not a soul could we see, not a movement of any sort. Masts and yards were picked out in green – the green of decay. The vessel lay as if in a cradle. It recalled 'The Frozen Pirate,' a novel that I read years ago [probably *The Frozen Crew of the Ice-Bound Ship*, in 1868].

'At last we came up. There was no sign of life on board. After an interval our first mate, with a member of the crew, boarded her. The sight that met their gaze was thrilling. Below the wheel lay the skeleton of a man. Treading warily on the rotten deck, which cracked and broke in places as they walked, they encountered three skeletons in the hatchway. In the mess-room were the remains of ten bodies, and six were found, one alone, possibly that of the captain, on the bridge.

'There was an uncanny stillness around and a dank smell of mould which made the flesh creep. A few remnants of books were discovered in the captain's cabin, and a rusty cutlass. Nothing more weird in the history of the sea can ever have been seen. The first mate examined the still faint letters on the bows, and after much trouble read *"Marlborough"*.' (*The Straits Times* [Singapore], 27 October 1913)

Another good if somewhat melodramatic *Marlborough* story. But also one with mysterious flaws, the first being the question of why a British ship (the one that apparently came across the derelict wreck of the *Marlborough*, in the captain's story above), on her way from, presumably, Britain or Europe bound for Lyttelton, New Zealand, would be anywhere near Cape Horn. Unless she was heading to the west coast of South America first and then on to New Zealand (very unlikely), any sailing vessel outward-bound going direct from Europe or North America to Australia or New Zealand would go eastwards round the Cape of Good Hope, running *with* the strong westerly winds rather than head-butting *against* them going west. The return *east-bound* passage, driven by the following westerlies, would be via Cape Horn, but not the outward passage pummelling against those head-winds.

Why, too, was the supposed *Marlborough* in the Magellan Straits at all? Her natural route homeward-bound from New Zealand would certainly be eastwards towards the

Horn. But sailing ships wanted plenty of open sea to stay safe, even in the worst weather. Land-bound rocky inlets, coves and enclosed watercourses with treacherous currents (and weather) like the Straits of Magellan would have been more dangerous than the greybeard-strewn open seas south of the Horn, even in the iceberg-littered Southern Ocean.

So, how and why had she apparently got in amongst those rock-bound waters? Perhaps 'keeping near the land for shelter', like the vessel that 'found' her – which was, in any case, mysteriously well away from the usual route that a vessel outward-bound for New Zealand would have taken around the southern tip of *Africa*, not the southern tip of South America. If she *was* the *Marlborough*, that is.

The *Dunedin*

On 19 March 1890, two months after the *Marlborough* left Lyttelton, the *Dunedin*, 1,320 tons, Capt. Roberts, a sister ship to the *Marlborough* in the Shaw, Savill & Albion Line, left Oamaru, on the South Island of New Zealand, bound for London. She was spoken once in the Southern Ocean, and then, like the *Marlborough*, never heard from again. It was supposed that she probably struck ice and sank somewhere in the Southern Ocean, taking with her into the deep her thirty-four crew; the captain's daughter was also on board.

Unlike her sister *Marlborough*, the *Dunedin*, like many thousands of other vessels lost for one or other of a myriad possible calamities natural to the seafarer's way, never resurfaced in the annals of sea mysteries that remain forever unresolved. There was nothing unusual in her disappearance. Ships and their crews went missing all the time.

And the sea, with a sigh, surged. Silent. And she soon forgot.

The *Glenalvon*

Disaster, most probably tempestuous, had rendered the brig *Glenalvon* a 'dreary sepulchral hull' by the time another vessel, the schooner *Lancaster*, came across her in August 1872. The *Lancaster*'s Capt. Martin took a handful of his crew, 'and a Mr. Dugan, a passenger', on board the derelict to have a closer look. It was a sadly horrific scene that ended with a commitment to the deep of the *Glenalvon*'s crew, such as they were, by the end of that day. Mr Dugan later wrote an account of the incident.

*Horrible Story from the Sea – A Skeleton Crew
– Ghost Ship* Glenalvon

The *Lancaster*, whilst bound to Sydney, Cape Breton [Nova Scotia], from Charlestown, Prince Edward's Island, on the 18th August, fell in with a dismasted vessel, which was apparently deserted. The master of the *Lancaster*, Captain Martin, with several of his crew, and a Mr. Dugan, a passenger, boarded the wreck. Mr. Dugan gives the following account of what he and his companions saw on boarding the wreck, which we extract from the *New York Times*:-

'Splintered spars entangled in canvas and rigging gear, and the planks of a boat torn asunder by the wind and sea were scattered around in sad confusion. More dismal still were the scenes which further investigation brought to light. Below a heap of motley rigging, and broken by the weight of a spar which lay across it, were the bones of a human being – a skeleton. The skull and ribs had been crushed almost on a level with the deck. Shreds of canvas trousers and a Guernsey frock were found among and near the bones. Further search revealed five other skeletons. A slight covering of crisped flesh remained on four of the skeletons, showing that they had died more recently than the other two.

'Many of the utensils of the galley were found, and Captain Martin made a strict search among them to assure himself whether there had been any food on board at the time of the death of these men. Not a single remaining pot or vessel of any nature in the cooking department of the ill-fated craft contained the least particle of food. This discovery seemed to satisfy the captain that all on board had perished from hunger, having failed, after months of eager expectation and short allowance, to meet with any helping hand.

'The spectacle on board the dreary sepulchral hull was at least appalling. It was ascertained that the vessel had been rigged a brig. The hull bore no name on its sternpost. On the bowsprit the word "*Glenalvon*" was barely legible. In the forecastle, which was almost filled with water, a most unearthly stench was discovered, and only two men could be found to enter and remain long enough inside to report on what they had seen there. There were two corpses on the floor, and one stretched across a "bunk." These sad relics were removed on deck, and the nine bodies were arranged in line, and covered in canvas by the captain's order.

'The wheelhouse had been carried away, and the fastenings of the rudder broken. This, as the captain remarked, was the wreck of some tremendous sea. The foremast had been cut away to save the vessel from foundering – one of the extremest emergencies in a hurricane at sea. The jib-boom was gone, and the entire craft, as she then appeared, was the most complete wreck Captain Martin had seen or heard of in his nautical experience of nearly 40 years.

'Entering the cabin, a foul odour was discovered, but not intense enough to forbid a thorough investigation. Towards the end of the steps leading down to the cabin a foetid pool of water was seen, and the men had to wade through it in order to reach every portion of the cabin. Between a stationary table and a couch, the head of a corpse protruded from a berth in the wall, and when brought on deck it was found to be in a state of decay. A buttoned jacket of good material, blue pantaloons, a flannel shirt marked "T.F.," and one boot covered the corpse.

'The chronometer in the cabin pointed to half-past 4 o'clock, and on the stationary table was an open Bible turned downward, a revolver with two chambers loaded, and a bottle containing a piece of paper, upon which was written, "Jesus, guide this to some helper. Merciful God, don't let us perish." The words were detached, and a hiatus occurred between every two or three of them, which showed that the writer must have been either in the lowest stage of debility or driven to madness by hunger.

Captain's Last Words

'In the captain's store-room his corpse was found lying bent on the floor, as though he had fallen from weakness, while struggling with faint hope to save himself and men. On his bed were scattered books, papers, &c.; but one sheet attracted particular attention. It was dated –

Martinique, May 30, 1872.

Dear Kate – I will post this letter here, to assure you of my well-being; but do not attempt to hazard an answer to this port, as you will not find me here a week hence. I have kept all my strong promises to you, in spite of a thousand bad advices from my comrades. I drink a little beer, but that is all. Your precious photograph is a little silent angel – at least I think it so, and I read your letters over a hundred times and a hundred again. You say in yours, dated from 16, Hope-street, Liverpool, that the old man was altogether turned in my favor when he heard of my having passed the Board [Board of Trade examination]. Now mind and keep him so until I get home again, when everything will be comfortable and jolly. Write to Hal's address in St. John, New Brunswick; for should it not reach me there, Hal at least will know where I am.

Wishing you good health and cheerfulness and good fortune, my own darling Kate, I am for ever your own Robert.

Robert C. Hart.

'The ship's regular papers were not found open; but Captain Martin took in charge a neat writing-desk, found in the captain's trunk, and locked. There was a slate on the table in the cabin, which table was covered by guards, such as are used at meals in stormy weather. The slate, intended for taking down the log in rough, contained only figures and illegible writing. The captain's trunk contained numerous letters, which Captain Martin intends to give up to the authorities at Sydney.

'Towards 3 o'clock a dead calm prevailed, and the boat's company that went on board the dismal wreck rowed back to procure something to eat and drink. At 7 p.m., the calm continuing, Captain Martin proposed to set out for the ill-fated vessel again, to perform the sorrowful services of a burial at sea. For coffins a quantity of old canvas was brought, and rude bags were quickly formed out of the material. At half-past 8 o'clock, the pale moon shining solemnly over that lonely sepulchre of the sea, a long board was laid along a sound portion of the bulwarks, and two bags, to which weights were tied, were laid down, and rattled as they fell.

'A lamp was held by a sailor on each side of the temporary hearse, and after Captain Martin had read the usual service, the plank was lifted upward, whereupon the coffin bags and skeletons slid into the sea. The ceremony over, the party put back again for the *Lancaster*, happy to quit the gloomy craft that had harbored so many dead, heard so many dying groans, and such awful roaring of the wind and sea, that had caused all that death and destruction. Captain Martin has procured every possible clue, all of which he will give to the authorities at Halifax or Sydney, so that the true history of the *Glenalvon* may be learned.' (*The South Australian Advertiser* [Adelaide, South Australia], 28 December 1872)

A Skeleton Ship of 'Grinning Skulls'

In 1893 the steamship *Breidablick* came across a derelict and deserted barque, the *Vila*, adrift on the Atlantic. The mystery was why she had been abandoned at all; like the *Mary Celeste*, she 'was in a perfectly seaworthy condition' when a boarding party from the *Breidablick* went on her. But an altogether more ghastly, and ghostly, mystery appeared when they peered into her hold.

A Mystery of the Sea – A Ship Loaded with Arab Skeletons

Had the prize [i.e. salvage] crew of four which in September last brought the abandoned Austrian barque *Vila* into port at New York, known the nature of the cargo in her dark hold, they would have fled from the ship, filled with a feeling of dread which could not have been greater had the *Flying Dutchman* appeared off their port bow. Below the decks of the derelict were stored in bulk thousands of human bones and skulls, which had been collected on the deserts of Africa. Much rather would the four hardy sons of Neptune have preferred seeing a phantom ship bearing down upon them than they be aboard of the lonely and dismantled derelict with a knowledge that her hold contained hundreds of grinning skulls.

The *Vila* passed through the late storms which lashed the coast and tested the sea-going qualities of the stoutest vessels. The fate of her crew, including her gallant skipper, Captain George Stanos, may never be known. They left the ship, but when nobody knows. No scrap of paper was left behind which conveyed the slightest intelligence as to the fate of the men.

The craft was deserted when the prize crew went aboard. The cupboards and cabins had been looted of their contents. The sailors' clothing was gone, and even the bedclothing had been taken. By whom was the vessel stripped? Surely not by the *Vila*'s crew.

The superstitious mariners say that an evil spirit followed the *Vila* when she sailed from the ancient port of Alexandria, Egypt, for in her cargo were the bones of a famous Arab chief whose body, when once buried, his followers said should not be disturbed. The vandals who desecrated his grave they say would be followed by the Arabian curse. The bones of the Arab chief were exposed by a *simoon* [desert wind] and were carted, with the bones of a thousand other unfortunates who had perished on the desert, and in combats, to the holds of the *Vila*.

The mysterious derelict was sighted at sea by Captain Nelson, of the steamship *Breidablik.* The sails on the derelict foremost were spread to the brisk breeze, and she was bounding along at a lively rate. Captain Nelson could hardly believe his eyes. Not a soul was aboard in sight, and the wheel was unlashed [i.e. swinging freely].

Suddenly the abandoned craft luffed up in the breeze, her yards rattled, the spread of canvas fluttered and she was motionless. Captain Nelson sent a prize crew of four men aboard. The ship was found to be deserted. There was not a living thing aboard. Captain Nelson could not explain the mystery. She was in a perfectly seaworthy condition; her hull was as tight as a cork, and free from water.

The derelict was taken in tow, and the prize crew remained aboard. The *Vila* was successfully towed into port, and now she lies at her anchorage off Erie basin. Her prize crew has left her. When the hatches were opened, and the grinning skulls met their gaze, they had no further desire to remain on the *Vila*, and returned to their comfortable berths aboard the *Breidablik*. (*The Mercury* [Hobart, Tasmania], 30 October 1893)

A Curious Yarn

In 1885 an abandoned Norwegian sailing ship, the *Observant*, was found drifting derelict around the North Atlantic. The only living thing seen on her by a passing ship, the *Salus*, was 'a large black dog … on the poop' deck. It was never discovered whatever happened to her crew. Between 1891 and 1894 an American three-masted schooner, the *Fannie E. Wolston*, drifted three times back and forth across the Atlantic after her crew abandoned her when she was dismasted by a hurricane off Cape Hatteras in October 1891. 10,000 later she wrecked, apparently, on the coast of Scotland late in 1894.

Abandoned derelicts were common in sailing ship days (though not many that left a dog on board to fend for itself, alone, no doubt to perish eventually from hunger). Few derelict vessels, however, were encountered with a crew still aboard, like the Portuguese Goan brig that the Glen Line steamship *Glenearn* found drifting in the Indian Ocean in 1884. The story of the encounter was told by the chief engineer of the *Glenearn* to one of her passengers, Rev. Edwin Buttolph, an American clergyman who was returning home from China. The salient feature of the story was, at heart, an enigma shrouded in a mystery, echoes of the *Mary Celeste* found abandoned in the North Atlantic in 1872 – but with a gruesome twist.

A Mystery of the Sea – A True Story, by Edwin K. Buttolph

In the summer of 1884 I was coming across the Indian Ocean in the steamship *Glenearn*, homeward-bound from Shanghai with a cargo of tea. We had passed Ceylon, catching a glimpse of the distant island and a whiff of the spicy breeze offshore, and were nearing the treacherous chain of coral reefs known as the Maldive Islands, when I came up from the cabin after dinner for a stroll on deck. The evening sky glowed with the beauty of a rich sunset such as is rarely seen outside the tropics. The good ship rocked easily upon a long, smooth swell, and plowed her way into a sea of molten gold, turning it, as by the touch of a magician's rod, into blue depths of water beneath her keel. The vessel's wake, churned into foam and shot through with countless flashes of phosphorescence, stretched far astern like a silvery path leading to the very edge of the full moon which hung just above the horizon.

I found the chief engineer leaning against the rail and enjoying the glorious beauty of the evening. For some time neither of us spoke. At length he remarked in a meditative way:

'It was just here that we met the Portuguese brig when we were coming out.'

Now Nesbitt was a clear-headed Scot who had studied in one of the English universities and taken his degree; then, giving way to his passion for a roving life, he had gone to sea and spent twenty years afloat. He had doubled more than once the Horn and the Cape [of Good Hope], made a dozen voyages to China and Japan, and, as an engineer in the Portuguese navy, had visited the whole coast of Africa, and once crossed the Dark Continent on foot just below the equator. In short, he had seen much of the world, and taken good note of what he saw. The chief engineer, therefore, was a man who had in his head much material for a good story; and it was in the hope of getting a story now that I asked:

'Well, what about the Portuguese brig?'

He looked up in surprise. 'What! Haven't you heard of the adventure we had on the last trip out? No? 'Bout as curious a thing as I ever came within hail of. But it's a long yarn; so let's find some seat first, and then I'll spin it for you.' We took possession of a couple of steamer chairs on the after-deck, and forthwith the chief spun his yarn as follows:

'We came out in February loaded mostly with iron; had a rough time of it in the Bay of Biscay and the Mediterranean, but when we had gotten past those cussed Frenchmen on the Suez Canal [opened in 1869] our troubles for that voyage were over. Those canal pilots make an engineer swear more than a storm at sea.

'Well, just in this place, one day about noon, we passed a brig about four miles north of us. The sun was hot, there was not a breath of wind, and the brig lay rocking on the swell with all sail set and flapping. She showed no colors [signals of distress or request to communicate or for assistance], and failed to answer the signals which we made to her. The captain swore a little at her want of manners and we went on; but when we had passed her some distance, perhaps a couple of miles, I went on the bridge and found him still leveling his glass at her. As I came up he said, "I don't like the looks of that craft at all. She isn't ship-shape, and I am going to run over to her and find out what's wrong."

'He put the steamer's head for the brig, and soon we were as close as the swell would allow. We hailed her, but got no reply. Then the old man began to get excited, and ordered the mate to call away the crew of the cutter and investigate. When the mate came close alongside he hailed again. Still no reply. She lay with her starboard beam towards us. He pulled around her stern and found the port gangway open. A man in a red shirt and a pair of trousers sat there on the deck, his legs hanging over the side. He was leaning back upon a box under his left arm, and a red handkerchief trailed from his right hand across his lap. A loud hail at close quarters brought no movement or response, and a sudden awe fell upon the boat's crew.

'The man was dead!

'The mate pulled forward to the bow and climbed up the chains to the deck. He said afterward that nothing would have hired him to climb into the gangway beside that silent figure. Four men lay on the deck around the forward hatch. They had been dead a long time, and the burning sun poured down upon ghastly bodies which were almost skeletons, they were so thin. The crew of the cutter were ordered up, and they searched the ship from stem to stern. They found no one in the forecastle or the hold, and no one in the cabin; but in the galley they found

the Malay cook and the cabin-boy, both dead, the cook
lying upon his face with his fingers twisted in his long
black hair. All the men except the captain seemed to have
died in agony, for their bodies were writhed and twisted.

'There was plenty of food aboard – a cask of salt beef;
several hundred-weight of rice, and some flour. There were
plenty of coals for the galley fire. The ship was perfectly
sound, not a sail was split, not a halyard started; the masts
and spars were all secure, and the wheel and rudder in good
order. *But there was not a drop of water aboard.* Here was
the secret of the tragedy. Every water-cask was dry, every
butt had been upset and drained to the last drop. The little
cabin-boy lay with his head and shoulders inside one of the
overturned casks, and his stiff fingers grasped a tin cup into
which he had been trying to drain a few drops of water.

'The ship's papers and two or three hundred Mexican dol-
lars were in the despatch-box under the captain's elbow. I
translated the papers – they were in Portuguese – when they
were brought aboard the steamer. They showed that the
brig was Portuguese, registered at Goa. Her name was the
Santa Maria, and she had cleared from Goa three months
before for a trading voyage along the west coast of India.
Her master was also her owner; his name was signed to the
papers with a cross. There was not, as it seemed, a single man
on board who could write, for no log was found. There was
a compass and a crude chart of the Indian coast in the cabin,
but no sextant or chronometer and no signal-flags.

'So these poor wretches had probably been blown off
the coast by a storm, and once out of sight of land they
lost their bearings and could not find the way back again.
Their supply of water gave out, and they died. But judging
from the size of the brig, she required a crew of about fifteen men to handle her, and there were only seven bodies

on board. What became of the others no one can tell. They may have drunk salt water, gone mad, and jumped into the sea to end their misery. There were lots of sharks swimming about the brig when we found her.

'I said there was no log on board. Perhaps that is true and perhaps it is not. On the deck by the captain's side was a little heap of pebbles which had evidently been brought up from the ballast, and carefully piled in one corner of the despatch-box beside the ship's papers were seventeen of those same pebbles. It is not unlikely that each pebble represented a day of thirst and watching. It makes me shudder, even now – the picture of that red-shirted captain sitting in the waist of the ship watching for a sail, and seeing his crew, maddened by thirst or by salt water, jump down one by one into the jaws of the sharks waiting below. I always think of that captain as catching sight of some steamer on the horizon and raising himself to wave his red handkerchief; his only signal of distress, then, as the steamer keeps on her course, falling back in despair – to die!'

We sat for a long time in silence, while the steady throb of the steamer's iron heart drove her forward into the night. At length I asked: 'What did you do with her?'

'We could not take her into port, and it is against the law to leave a vessel adrift upon the high seas. So when the mate had come back with a white face and told his story the captain sent the crew over to the brig and dismantled her. We took out her stores, cordage, sails, and everything we could move. Then the carpenter went down and bored a lot of holes in her bottom. We put all the bodies in the cabin and laid the ship's flag over them. The captain read the prayer from the burial service. Then we locked the cabin-door and left her; and as we steamed away we could see her slowly settling down.

'We turned over everything belonging to her to the Portuguese consul at Singapore; and if you will ask the captain he will show you the letter of thanks he got from Portugal, with King Luis's own signature. At length they were sold and converted to the crown, for no living soul could be found who knew anything about the *Santa Maria* or her crew.' (*Century Magazine*, Vol. 41, No. 5, March 1891)

Ghost Ice Ships – The *Jenny* and Others

The story of the *Santa Maria* might just have been a good old sailor's yarn, spun to the thrall of a young listener on a balmy tropical night on the high seas. It might have been like many other seafarers' yarns that owed more to a salt-seasoned imagination than to the truth of an incident that could not be verified. Another kind of yarn that did the rounds of macabre story-telling of yesteryear was the encounter of a ship with another vessel which the former found frozen in the polar ice and manned by frozen-stiff … stiffs. There were various versions of the story, but the motif of the discovery of a frozen ship with a long-frozen dead crew was virtually the same.

The mystery was not only how the ghost ice ships and their frosty crews came to such a spine-chilling end, but where the stories came from in the first place. And whether they were based on fact or fiction.

At least one polar conundrum was indeed based on fact: the mystery, at the time, of what happened to the 129 men of the expedition led in 1845 by Sir John Franklin in two ships, *Erebus* and *Terror*, to find a so-called Northwest Passage across the frozen top of Canada from the Atlantic to the Pacific and Asia. The last of some forty search expeditions that went to look for survivors (if any) of Sir Franklin's calamitous journey, in the decade after his death (11 June 1847), and to resolve the mystery of what happened to it, was one that his widow Lady Jane Franklin sent, in 1857, commanded by Francis Leopold McClintock (1819–1907).

An Irishman from the Royal Navy with many years of Arctic exploration, McClintock eventually found traces of the Franklin expedition that seemed to confirm that, if not entirely how, all the expedition members had perished (including a note that recorded the date Sir John Franklin had died) – though the two ships themselves lay undiscovered until 2014 (*Erebus*) and 2016 (*Terror*). In September 1859 McClintock arrived back in England and wrote the report of what he had discovered about the tragic fate of the Franklin expedition. A summary of the report appeared in a German geographical journal, the *Globus*.

A Ship in the Ice of the Southern Polar Sea

We read MacClintock's report about the journey in search of Sir John Franklin with excited attention and not without emotion. The first written report of the missing seafarers was found at Cap Victoria, on the Northwest coast of King William Island, where Bad Bay lies, on 28 May 1847, and at that time everything was still good. But in the margins was a transcript according to which the ships *Erebus* and *Terror* were abandoned on April 22, 1848, after they had been trapped in ice since September 12, 1846. Franklin had already died on June 11, 1847, and the total loss of life already stood at 9 officers and 15 men from the rest of the crew. On April 26th the survivors wanted to leave for Bad Fish River.

On May 30, 1859, MacClintock found a large boat on the west coast of King William's Island not far from Cape Crozier (69 degrees 8' north latitude, 100 degrees, 8' west longitude) at a place where the coast makes a turn to the east, and which had been examined by his companion Hobson several days earlier. It had a length of 28 feet, was flat built, and apparently carefully prepared for a ride on the Big Fish river and stood on a very strong sled. In this boat lay two human skeletons; one had been torn into by wolves, the other still wrapped in clothes and furs. Next to these unfortunates lay five pocket watches, leaned against the side stood two double shotguns, each with one barrel loaded. Next to various devotional books was a copy of *The Vicar of Wakefield*. MacClintock also found an amazing amount of clothes, nails, files, all kinds of equipment, some tea, forty pounds of chocolate, some tobacco and firewood. Earlier the Eskimos had told us that many white men had fallen down on the way to the Big Fish river: at Cape Herrschel they had found a skeleton partly covered with snow. An old Eskimo woman said: 'They fell down and were walking dead.' (*Globus*, 1862)

This brings us to the other mystery, of the ghost ice ship and her frozen crew, within the same piece in the *Globus*.

MacClintock's report reminded us of another one we once read about a death ship in the Southern Arctic Ocean. It must be a terrible fate to be trapped by icebergs in the grey polar cold of the ice caps, to be held enclosed and to be worn out by cold, hunger, terror and despair, and to realize that one will disappear without a trace.

In September of the year 1840, the whaler *Hope*, under Captain Brighton, sailed beyond Cape Horn in icy southern seas. One night in September a storm drove him into ice fields and icebergs, which formed a wide circle in the sea, and half a nautical mile away, a seemingly never-ending chain of high, snow-capped mountain tops could be seen, everything was covered in ice and in every direction it seemed the Ocean was apparently frozen over. Within the wide ice-enclosed circle, however, the sea was calm and *Hope* was not in danger of being thrown against the ice coast. No icebergs floated around either, as they all formed a cohesive mass. Meanwhile the captain remained watchful and the crew was ready to take advantage of the first favourable wind, which usually rises at midnight in those latitudes in September. If you stayed in this ice port for too long, the worst case could happen: the icebergs would start moving, crowding together and wedging in the whaler either until mild weather arrived, or for eternity.

The wind really started rising at midnight and at the same time there was heavy snowfall. Soon after a sound of the rolling of thunder could be heard and the noise of a terrible crash of the icebergs filled the crew with terror and horror. The previously rigid masses of ice began to move. The floes also began to drift violently and bounce against the ship, and Brighton hardly dared hope for a way out of the undulating ice labyrinth.

The terrible night passed with feelings that could not be described. The storm subsided when the day arrived, and the crew breathed a sigh of relief when they saw that the ship was not substantially damaged. The ice masses, which had formed an impenetrable, mountainous main-land the evening before, had now dissolved into countless floating islets and formed a mobile archipelago, as it were.

A ship in sight! The watchful sailor shouted down from the crow's nest at around noon. The captain on deck could only see the tips of the masts because of the icebergs between the *Hope* and the ship the sailor had indicated, but soon the hull also appeared. The crew wondered about the strange condition of the rigging. The ship drifted before the wind against an iceberg and then remained stuck.

Now there was no doubt that it was abandoned by the crew. The captain lowered a boat to the sea and went over to the wreck. Soon it became clear how much it had suffered. On the upper deck there were drifts of high snow and no living creature to be seen; there was no answer to repeated calls. Brighton moored and boarded with three sailors. Not a soul moved. As he stepped into the cabin, what did he see? A man was sitting on a chair in front of a table with a logbook on it. Everyone's hair stood on end, for the man remained motionless and when they waved to him in greeting, there was no answer. The man was a frozen corpse. He held a pen in his hand and the last sentence in the logbook was: 'January 17, 1823. Today is the seventy-first day since we were locked in by the ice. Despite all our efforts, the fire went out yesterday. Captain's attempts to rekindle it failed. His wife died of hunger and cold this morning, five sailors died. No more hope!'

That was what they found in the helmsman's cabin. In the Captain's cabin, there was the body of a woman on the bed; her face still looked almost alive, only the convulsively contracted limbs hinted at her desperate fight with death. Next to her sat a man: on the floor next to him lay a steel flint, a stone and a lighter as well as burnt canvas. The hammocks held several dead sailors, a dead dog lay in front of the stairs and nowhere was there a trace of food.

The frights and superstitions of the sailors did not allow a more detailed investigation, but Captain Brighton took the logbook with him to bring back to the ship's owners.

The ship was called the *Jenny*, her home port the Isle of Wight; it had last been in the port of Callao de Lima and had been in Antarctic ice for a full seventeen years. Captain Brighton happily returned to Europe with the *Hope*. (translated from the original German by Karen Proff)

So: a derelict ship, the *Jenny*, found in September 1840 amongst the ice of Antarctic waters by a presumably British whaleship, the *Hope*, commanded by Capt. Brighton, with all the *Jenny*'s crew and her captain's wife (and a dog) frozen dead, and the captain's last words written by his hand in the logbook and dated 17 January 1823: a ghost ship icebound, that is, 'for a full seventeen years'.

That story was re-told virtually unchanged by the Australian author William (Bill) Alfred Beatty (1902–72) and published as 'The Phantom Schooner Jenny' in *The Sydney Morning Herald* on 12 October 1946. The main differences with the *Globus*'s story were: that the *Jenny*'s last log entry was 'May 4th, 1823' and so 'thirty-seven years before!' the *Hope* came across her 'on September 22, 1860'; that the log entry was a brief: 'No food for 71 days. I am the only one left alive'; and that the ghost ship was identified as 'the English schooner *Jenny*, which had left the port of Lima, Peru, half a human lifetime before'.

The *Octavius*

There had been a legend, like the *Flying Dutchman*, of a ghost ship schooner in the eighteenth century, the *Octavius*, that was said to have been found by a whaleship, the *Herald*, off the west coast of Greenland on 11 October 1875, with all the *Octavius*'s crew and (unnamed) captain and his wife frozen stiff for thirteen years after the last log entry of 11 November 1762 (and the captain himself with pen in hand, frozen at his desk).

The legend had it that the *Octavius* had sailed from England to the Far East in 1761. Her captain tried to return across the top of Canada by a 'North-West Passage'. But the ice to the north of Alaska gripped the ship in, and her crew froze to death. Her last position, apparently noted by her captain in the ship's logbook, was longitude 160° W, latitude 75° N, a few hundred miles north of what came to be named Point Barrow, Alaska. A ghost ship of corpses, she drifted across the Arctic polar sea before being boarded by the *Herald*'s men off Greenland thirteen years later in 1775.

The legend of the ghostly ice-ship *Octavius* has been persistent and long-lived, perhaps not surprisingly for its macabre ghost story character. It appeared in what was then a 'largely fictional news tabloid,' the Florida-based *Weekly World News*, as a story – 'Arctic death ship remains baffling seagoing mystery' – published on 14 April 1981. Including all particulars of the legend, the story detailed how Captain Warren of the Yankee whaling ship *Herald* came across the derelict off the west coast of Greenland: 'The ship was encrusted with ice but they could make out its name: "Octavius".'

And then there was the discovery of the frozen crew, including the rather colourful embellishment that the frozen female they found on a bed in the cabin was 'a lovely blonde woman'. And that the corpse of the small boy was crouched next to a sailor holding a flint and a steel, 'his face buried in the seaman's jacket as if he had huddled there in pathetic search for warmth'. And the final citation of the *Octavius*'s 'historic 13-year voyage' that 'the ghostly *Octavius* with her crew of frozen dead' had realised 'the dream of all mariners': to achieve a crossing, albeit unbeknownst to her crew, of 'the legendary Northwest Passage.'

So the *Octavius* was an *Arctic* vessel, not an *Antarctic* ghost ice ship like the 'schooner *Jenny*'. Other stories repeated that northern version of the ice ship and her frozen crew, in various iterations. One of the more accessible – meaning shorter – accounts was published in *The Ariel – A Literary and Critical Gazette*, from Philadelphia. In its Saturday, 13 December 1828 number it included the following story.

The Dangers of Sailing in High Latitudes – Awful Incident

One serene evening in the middle of August, 1775, Captain Warrens, the master of a Greenland whaleship, found himself becalmed among a vast number of icebergs in about 77 degrees north latitude. On one side, and within a mile of his vessel, these were of immense height and closely wedged together, and a succession of snow covered peaks appeared behind each other as far as the eye could reach, showing that the ocean was completely blocked up in that quarter, and that it had probably been so for a long period of time.

Captain Warrens did not feel altogether satisfied with his situation, but there being no wind, he could not move either one way or another, and he therefore kept a strict watch, knowing that he would be safe as long as the surrounding icebergs continued in their respective places.

About midnight the wind rose to a gale, accompanied by thick showers of snow, while a succession of tremendous thundering, grinding, and crushing noises gave fearful evidence that the ice was in motion. The vessel received violent shocks every moment, for the haziness of the atmosphere prevented those on board from discovering in what direction the open water lay, or if there was actually any at all on either side of them.

The night was spent in tacking as often as any cause of danger happened to present itself, and in the morning the storm abated, and Captain Warrens found to his great joy that his ship had not sustained any serious injury. He remarked with surprise that the accumulated icebergs which had on the preceding evening formed an impenetrable barrier, had been separated and disarranged by the wind, and that in one place a canal [channel] of open sea wound its course among them as far as the eye could discern.

The Ghost Ship

It was two miles beyond the entrance to this canal that a ship made its appearance about noon. The sun shone brightly at the time, and a gentle breeze blew from the north. At first, some intervening icebergs prevented Captain Warrens from distinctly seeing anything except her masts, but he was struck with the same manner in which her sails were disposed, and the dismantled aspect of her yards and rigging. She continued to go before the wind for a few furlongs, and then grounding upon the low icebergs, remained motionless.

Captain Warrens' curiosity was so much excited, that he immediately leaped into the boat with several seamen, and rowed towards her. On approaching, he observed that her hull was miserably weatherbeaten, and not a soul appeared upon the deck, which was covered with snow to a considerable depth. He hailed her crew several times, but no answer was returned. Previous to stepping on board, an open port hole near the main chains caught his eye, and on looking into it, he perceived a man reclining back in a chair, with writing materials on a small table before him, but the feebleness of the light made every thing indistinct. The party, therefore, went upon deck, and having removed the hatchway, which they found closed, they descended to the cabin.

They first came to the apartment which Captain Warrens had viewed through the port hole. A tremour seized him as he entered it. Its inmate retained his former position, and seemed to be insensible to strangers. He was found to be a corpse, and a green damp mould had covered his cheek and forehead, and veiled his eye balls. He held a pen in his hand, and a log book before him, the last sentence in whose unfinished page ran thus,

'11th Nov. 1762; We have now been enclosed in the ice seventy days. The fire went out yesterday, and our master has been trying ever since to kindle it again but without success. His wife died this morning. There is no relief –'

Captain Warrens and his seamen hurried from the spot without uttering a word. On entering the principal cabin, the first object that attracted their attention was the dead body of a female reclining on a bed in an attitude of deep interest and attention. Her countenance retained a freshness of life, and a stiff contraction of the limbs alone showed that her form was inanimate. Seated on the floor in one corner of the room, was the corpse of an apparently young man holding a steel in one hand and a flint in the other, as if in the act of striking fire upon some tinder which lay beside him.

In the fore part of the vessel several sailors were found lying dead in their berths, and the body of a dog was crouched at the bottom of the gangway stairs. Neither provisions nor fuel could be discovered any where, but Captain Warrens was prevented, by the superstitious prejudice of his seamen, from examining the vessel as minutely as he wished to have done. He therefore carried away the log book already mentioned, and returned to his own ship, and immediately steered to the southward, deeply impressed with [the] awful example which he had just witnessed, of the danger of navigating the polar seas, in high northern latitudes.

On returning to England, he made various inquiries respecting the vessel that had disappeared in an unknown way, and by comparing the results of these with the information which was afforded by the written documents in his possession, he ascertained the name and history of the imprisoned ship, and of her unfortunate master, and found that she had been frozen up seventeen years previous to the time of his discovering her among the ice.

'Capt. Warrens' might well have 'ascertained the name and history of the imprisoned ship'; pity he didn't reveal it to the *Ariel*'s readers! He did ascertain, by dubious arithmetic, that the ghost ice ship and her crew were 'frozen up seventeen years' from the master's last logbook entry of 11 November 1762. But by the intervening dates, from 1762 to 'One serene evening in the middle of August, 1775 ...', the ship had actually been 'frozen up' for thirteen years.

The *Gloriana*

The date of the logbook entry of the anonymous vessel did, however, coincide with the last entry in the logbook of another corpse-littered ice ship found in high northern latitudes by another, or possibly the same, 'Captain Warrens' of another (or possibly the same) Greenland whaleship in the same month of the same year, August 1775. But that whaleship *was* named, as was the frozen derelict, in a story titled 'A Frozen Crew' published in a book, *Wonderful Deeds and Adventures*, in 1893, compiled by 'Anonymous':

> It was in the middle of August, 1775 – I have cause enough to remember the date – that I, John Warrens, captain of the Greenland whaler *Try Again*, ran across the experience that I am going to tell, word for word, just as it happened. I can't say I expect to be believed, though reckoned a truthful man; but I'm growing accustomed to *that*. My private consolation is that I never had half the wits enough to invent it, so if you don't believe what I tell you for gospel, why, in a way, you're only paying me a compliment after all ...

Our Greenland whaling ship's captain 'John Warrens' related much the same as the *Ariel*'s narrative of an 'Awful Incident': that the events happened 'in about 77° north latitude'; that 'the wind fell dead calm, and left us to drift' among the ice-strewn sea; that, however, 'by midnight it was blowing half a gale'; that the ice around them 'creaked and groaned, crashed, thumped, and thundered, till our hearts jumped into our mouths – and stayed there'; and that 'towards morning the wind dropped again'.

The morning after the storm Capt. Warrens found his *Try Again* 'without an injury, even of the smallest'. Moreover, the ice had been 'driven asunder' such that he could steer southward through 'a regular canal of open water'. And then, as master and mate were contemplating the way down a bend in the 'canal':

> The mate was standing at my shoulder ... and says he – 'Now Heaven send the channel ain't closed down yonder!' I was just going to answer, when I stopped short, and caught him by the arm – 'Stop!, No, it isn't,

for look – look! What's that down yonder?' 'Bless my soul! It looks like a ship's masts.'

She was, indeed, another ship – 'a brig, sailing down the channel ahead of us.' As the *Try Again* chased down what the lookout had said appeared like 'a ghost', Capt. Warrens sensed something 'was desperately amiss':

Her rigging was just anyhow – torn, tangled, and drop-ping. Her sails were tattered and hung in strips from the yards. Whenever a puff of wind took her aslant she came to a pause, like as if she shivered, and went off before it helplessly, bumping and grazing the ice, first on this side, then on that. There was no steering in it, and I cried out – 'I don't believe there's a soul on board.'

After the ghost ship without, Capt. Warrens believed, 'a soul on board' grounded on 'a bank of low ice', he got into a boat with six of his crew and stood up 'and shouted – "Ahoy there! *Gloriana* ahoy!" For I had read the name in tall faded letters on her blistered stern. Not a soul answered.'

So: the ship had a name – *Gloriana*! He stepped on board and espied, through 'an open port-hole near the main chains', a man seated at a table 'covered with papers, charts, and inkpot'. When he entered the cabin he stared into the face of the man:

It was a corpse. Over his cheeks and forehead a green damp mould had spread. It coated his eyeballs, which were wide open, half veiling his horrible stare. In the hand that hung over the arm of the chair was a pen, frozen to the fingers. A log-book lay before him, open, on the table. I bent over it and in the dim light read the last entry –

> '*November 11th, 1762. We have now been seventeen days in the ice. The fire went out yesterday, and our master has been trying ever since to kindle it again, without success. His wife died this –*'

In the 'Awful Incident' in the *Ariel*, the ghost ship, by the log-book, had been in the ice seventy days; the *Gloriana*, seventeen. But in the 'principal cabin' of *Gloriana* there was, again, the body of a woman ('her face [as] fresh as life') and another of a man with 'a steel in one hand and a flint in the other': frozen corpses. In the rest of the ship nothing but more deep-frozen crew-corpses. At the bottom of the gangway stairs, though, not the *Ariel*'s 'dog ... crouched' there but 'a small figure, a cabin-boy, huddled up into a ball for warmth'.

Capt. Warrens and his men re-boarded the *Try Again*.

> We had seen enough to last us in bad dreams for a life-time; and I drew not a clear breath again till, steering southward, we left the canal for open sea, and behind us the dead ship lay hidden by the icebergs. Of course you disbelieve me; I said how it would be. But the owners believed me, right enough, when they saw the log-book of the *Gloriana* there, and read the story of the brig that for thirteen years had been lost to them.

The Frozen Fate of Erik the Red

Erik Thorvaldsson, also known as Erik Raude (*Eirik Rauð* in Old Norse), or Erik Rufus ('Erik the Red'), was born in Norway around the year 950, the son of a Norwegian man, Thorvald Asvaldsson, who was later exiled to Iceland 'because of some killings', according to the Icelandic *Grænlandiga Saga*.

In around 982, a few years after his father's death, Erik, having settled in north-west Iceland, was likewise sent into exile for three years by the Icelandic proto-parliamentary assembly, the *Thing*, for killings *he* committed. He sailed to what he later called 'Greenland' ('Because', said he, 'men will desire much the more to go there if the land has a good name', according to his eponymous Saga), where he spent his outlaw years.

Returning to Iceland, his public relations moniker of 'Greenland', for that ostensibly emerald green and pleasant land to the west, attracted a band of colonist adventurers to voyage back to Greenland with him in a fleet of twenty-five ships, in 985, to establish settlements there. Only fourteen of the vessels arrived; eleven were lost at sea or turned back.

Pause here for another ice-ship story of a frozen crew. In March and April of 1845 a story went round the press in the United States and Canada about a certain 'Erick Raude' who commanded a fleet of twenty-five 'gallies' (probably Viking longships), in 998, crewed by Icelandic 'colonists' and headed towards a land of 'more congenial climate'. True to the sagas about our man Eirik Rauð, so far at least – but with a familiar twist at the end.

A Frozen Crew

In 998, Erick Raude, an Icelandic chieftain, fitted out an expedition of twenty-five gallies, at *Snefell [Snæfellsjökull]*, and having manned them with sufficient crews of colonists, set forth from Iceland, bound to what appeared to them a more congenial climate. They sailed upon the ocean fifteen days, and they saw no land. The next day brought with it a storm, and many a gallant vessel sunk in the deep. Mountains of ice covered the waters as far as the eye could reach, and but a few gallies of the fleet escaped destruction.

The morning of the seventeenth day was clear and cloudless. The sea was calm, and far away to the north could be seen the glare of the icefields reflecting on the sky. The remains of the shattered fleet gathered together to pursue their voyage. But the galley of Erick was not with them. The crew of a galley which was driven farther down than the rest, reported that as the morning broke, the huge fields of ice that had covered the ocean were driven by the current past them, and that they beheld the galley of Erick Raude, borne by a resistless force, and with the speed of the wind, before a tremendous flake of ice. Her crew had lost all control over her – they were tossing their arms in wild agony.

Scarcely a moment elapsed ere it was walled in by a hundred ice hills, and the whole was moved forward and was soon beyond the horizon. That the galley of the narrators escaped was wonderful. It remained, however, uncontradicted, and the vessel of Erick Raude was never more seen.

Half a century after this, a Danish colony was established upon the western coast of Greenland. The crew of the vessel that carried the colonists thither, in their excursions into the interior, crossed a range of hills that stretched to the northward; they had approached, perhaps, nearer to the pole than any succeeding adventurers. Upon looking down from the summit of the hills, they beheld a vast interminable field of ice, undulating in various places, and formed into a thousand grotesque shapes.

They saw not far from the shore a figure in an ice vessel with a glittering icicle in place of a mast, rising from it. Curiosity prompted them to approach, when they beheld a dismal sight. Figures of men, in every attitude of woe, were upon the deck, but they were icy things. One figure alone stood erect, and with folded arms leaning against the mast. A hatchet was procured and the ice split away, and the features of a chieftain disclosed – palid and deathly, but free from decay.

This was, doubtless, the vessel, and that figure the form of Erick Raude. Benumbed with cold, and in the agony of despair, his crew had fallen around him. He alone had stood erect while the chill of death passed over him. The spray of the ocean, and the fallen sleet had frozen as it alighted upon them and covered each figure with an icy robe which the short lived glance of a Greenland sun had not time to remove.

The Danes gazed upon the spectacle with trembling. They knew not but the same might be their fate. They knelt down upon the deck and muttered a prayer in their native tongue, for the souls of the frozen crew, then hastily left the place, for the night was fast approaching. (*The American Penny Magazine and Family Newspaper* [New York], Saturday, 5 March 1845; also in other US and Canadian newspapers on other dates)

Actually, Eirik did arrive at Greenland (though it seems he and the colonists set out from Iceland in 986, a few years earlier than in the story). There on the south-west coast he established the first permanent European settlements. He became a respected and wealthy man with the status of the first 'paramount chieftain' or 'first settler' of Greenland. And when new Icelandic immigrants brought disease and an epidemic that killed many, around the turn of the first millennium, Eirik, too, *might have* succumbed then – or he might have died a few years later from injuries caused by falling off a horse; the date and cause of his death are uncertain. His son, Leif Eriksson, would become the first Viking to reach and explore the North American coast, at the place called Vinland somewhere around Newfoundland.

Death by some imported disease that felled so many others amongst his Greenland colonists, or by a fall from a horse, would have been a prosaic end for Eirik Rauð.

An heroic death by fortitude against the Arctic sleet and cold and ice, as Eirik's faithful but frozen crew fell around him – well, that was epic. Not an actual *saga*, in the sense of the Old Norse genre, to be sure. But an heroic story of stout-hearted, indomitable courage befitting the legacy of an 'Icelandic chieftain' and 'paramount chieftain' of his adopted country. It is precisely in the macabre mould, if not so lowly status, of other frozen ice crews in other ghostly ice ships of those grimly ice-littered polar seas. Yet another, indeed, *chilling* tale of the sea.

2

MYSTERY BOTTLE MESSAGES

Before the introduction of telecommunications on ships around the turn of the twentieth century, there was only one way a person on a sinking ship on the desolate wastes of the high seas could communicate their fate: by scribbling a hurried message, pressing it into an empty bottle, corking it, and casting it to the waves in the hope it might someday be found and the tragedy of their demise known. One such message conjured more mystery than it solved. And another solved the mystery, but only hurriedly and in part.

The Loss of SS *Pacific*

The *Pacific* was a 2,700-ton American paddle-wheel steamship, wooden-built and launched in February 1849 for the Collins Line, to be run on its North Atlantic route between New York and Liverpool. She had capacity for 280 passengers and a complement of 141 crew. Her maiden voyage was from New York to Liverpool on 25 May 1850.

On 23 January 1856 she left Liverpool for New York with 45 passengers and 141 crew (typically light on passengers for a winter crossing of the Atlantic), commanded by Capt. Asa Eldridge. After that, nothing was heard of her – until, that is, five years later in 1861, a bottle message was picked up on the shore of the Scottish Hebridean island of Uist. Rather than clarify the fate of the vessel and her passengers and crew, however, the message only heightened speculation as to the mystery of her loss.

Reminiscences of the Lost Steamship Pacific: Interesting Statement

Our readers may have observed recently, amongst our maritime extracts, the copy of the contents of a slip of paper, found in a bottle some weeks ago, on the western coast of Uist, in the Hebrides [west coast Scotland], and forwarded to us by our agent at Stornoway. The paper in question, apparently the leaf of a pocketbook, used in the hurry of a moment, was covered on both sides with pencil marks, from which the following was with difficulty deciphered:

On board the Pacific, from L'pool to N. York, Ship going down. (Great) confusion on board. Icebergs around us on every side. I know I cannot escape. I write the cause of our loss, that friends may not live in suspense. The finder of this will please get it published.

Wm. Graham

If we are right in our conjecture, the ship here named is the *Pacific*, one of the Collins line of steamers, which vessel left Liverpool on Jan. 23, 1856, three days before the *Persia*, and has not since been heard of; and this slip of paper, three inches by two, is probably the only record of the fate of that missing ship.

Provenance

We have not come to this conclusion hastily. On receiving the frail record from Stornoway, we at once published it, as the best and most expeditious mode of placing it before those who might possibly be interested in the fate of the vessel named. The *Pacific* is by no means an uncommon appellation, more especially among the shipping of the United States, and we did not despair that some light would be thrown upon the 'message from the sea,' which had so singularly been preserved and placed in our hands.

After waiting for some time, we received a communication from Messrs. ZEREGA of New-York, stating that their ship *Pacific*, being in port at the time, of course the record had no reference thereto, but they much feared it might, notwithstanding the difference in the names, apply to their ship *Baltic*, which had left Liverpool in January last, and has not since been heard of; and we were requested at the same time to communicate with Messrs' ZEREGA's Agent's in Liverpool. This we have been careful to do, and at the same time we directed a search to be made amongst the list of passengers and crews both of the *Baltic* and of the *Pacific* of the Collins line.

Discrepancy of Grahams

We have ascertained that no person of the name of GRAHAM was on board the *Baltic* when that vessel left Liverpool last on her passage to New-York, but it appears that a man of that name did ship as helmsman in the *Pacific* in January, 1856. It is true, he shipped by the name of ROBERT GRAHAM, whereas the slip of paper is signed WILLIAM GRAHAM. This, however, is a discrepancy which will not count for much with those who are acquainted with the careless manner in which seafaring people frequently give their names, and the facility for such a mistake presented by the ordinary mode of entering the names of a ship's company.

Conclusive Observations

From the facts elicited so far, we come to the conclusion that the vessel lost, and to which the frail memorandum before us refers, was a ship named the *Pacific*. The writer was evidently some person accustomed to the perils of the sea, for it is difficult to understand how any person whose nerves had not been hardened by the presence of frequent and appalling dangers, could have written with such manifest coolness in the immediate presence of death. This self-possession at once negates the idea that the person who could exhibit it in a moment of such supreme peril, could possibly have mistaken the name of the vessel whose loss he has recorded.

Then, again, we find from the records of the lost *Pacific*, that a person named GRAHAM sailed in her from Liverpool on her ill-fated voyage, and in all human probability was on board at the time she was lost with all hands. This is the strongest point in the entire chain of evidence, for it connects the writer of the memorandum directly with the lost ship, and the ship with the writer. Lastly, since the memorandum has been given to the world, – now some weeks, – we have had no intimation that any ship named the *Pacific*, sailing from Liverpool recently, has been lost, or is even missing. The ship in question must have left that port so long ago that all hope of her recovery has been abandoned.

Fate of the Pacific

Some interests might possibly, even at this distance of time, have been felt in the fate of the *Pacific*, but the company to which that steamer belonged [Collins Line] no longer exists. The remaining ships of the Collins line have been some time since disposed of, and are employed, we believe, or were recently employed, on the line from New-York to Panama.

To sum up – we have the fact that a man of the same surname as he who signed the slip of paper found in a bottle on the shore of the Hebrides, shipped as steersman in the *Pacific* in January, 1856, and the presumption is every way strong against his having mistaken the name of the ship in which he sailed, and was apparently lost. We also know that the *Persia*, which sailed three days after the *Pacific*, narrowly escaped destruction from icebergs on her passage out.

Logical Conclusion

The announcement of the finding of the memorandum and its contents has been now some weeks in our columns, but, with the exception of the communication already referred to, it has produced no response, which is utterly unaccountable except on the supposition either that no vessel named the *Pacific* has been lost, or that she belonged to parties who have ceased to have any interest in her fate. The first hypothesis is contrary to the fact; the second is quite reconcilable with the fact that the vessel referred to in the memorandum is the steamer *Pacific*, of the late Collins line, and no other.

We leave the extraordinary voyage of the bottle which contained GRAHAM's memorandum, to the consideration of those who, like Captain MAURY [Matthew F. Maury (1806–73), famous American Navy oceanographer] and others, have made the phenomena of winds and currents in the ocean their peculiar study.

The Course of Drift

When this bottle was thrown overboard from the *Pacific*, that vessel was surrounded by mountains of ice. This tiny receptacle of the only record of a magnificent ship, escaped the crash which obliterated all traces of the vessel from which it was thrown, was carried, in all probability, thousands of miles on the ice, and was only released when the ice melted in the tropical sun. Thence, the presumption is not a violent one – this fragile messenger was swept by the Gulf Stream, and carried along the course nearly to the extreme verge to which, as we are told, the Gulf Stream is propagated. This bottle was found on the western shore of the Hebrides, where it arrived under the mysterious guidance of those influences which have of late years so earnestly engrossed the attention of scientific geographers. (*The New York Times*, 7 August 1861)

The *Pacific* was generally assumed to have struck an iceberg and sunk, with the loss of all 186 souls on board. No trace of her was ever discovered – until William Graham's message was picked up five years later on the remote Hebridean island of Uist, the only clue to support, if not altogether confirm, the prevailing supposition of her likely fate.

The *Caller Ou* – George Dawson's 'Sad Message from the Sea'

At the end of November 1891 the 674-ton barque *Caller Ou* left Hull on the north-east coast of England with a cargo of just over 1,000 tons of coal bound for Port Elizabeth, South Africa. On board was a 14-year-old lad, George William Dawson, signed on by the vessel's master, Capt. Souter, for a four-year apprenticeship. After the *Caller Ou* sailed, nothing more was heard of her; she was posted missing by Lloyd's in April 1892, her disappearance yet another, and otherwise commonplace, sea mystery.

Almost a year later, in January 1893, a piece of wood was picked up on the beach near Hull. It bore a pencilled message written by the youngster that revealed the tragic fate of the *Caller Ou* – and of little George Dawson – to solve the riddle of the barque's demise.

Sad Message from the Sea

Very sad is the latest message from the sea which has just reached Hull. It consists of a deal batten [plank] picked up the other day on the Yorkshire coast, and inscribed with these words roughly written in pencil: '*Whoever picks this up shall know that* Caller Ou *was run down by an unknown steamer.*' This was on one side – probably as the beginning of a longer message. On the other side were the words 'Caller Ou *run down by unknown steamer (Dawson). No more time. Sinking. May the Lord comfort my mother.*'

The handwriting was identified as that of a lad named Dawson, belonging to Hull, who had sailed in the *Caller Ou* as an apprentice to the trade of the sea. Fourteen months ago the barque went out with coal to the Cape [of Good Hope]. She was driven back by rough weather to Grimsby, where she remained for a few days. Then she resumed her voyage, but she never reached her port. A bucket bearing her name was picked up on the coast of Holland nearly a twelvemonth ago; but, until this last rude missive came to hand, the ocean and the agencies were silent as to her fate. The sea brought it to the very coast of Yorkshire from which she sailed.

All hands must have perished, with the little apprentice boy, and probably no one will ever know where or when she went down. 'Full fathoms five,' etc. – or five hundred. What a picture for the mind's eye! The boy scribbling his message, the ship going down, and the 'unknown steamer' disappearing, perhaps to a like doom. That were almost to be wished. If her skipper survives, he must feel the torments of the murderer. (*The New Zealand Herald*, 4 March 1893)

Mr Zebedee Scaping (1833–1909) was 'for over fifty years Headmaster of the Hull Trinity House Navigation School', according to a plaque in his honour at Zebedee's Yard on the site of the old Trinity House School. In 1898 Mr Scaping wrote an article about Dawson's message concerning the *Caller Ou*, published in one of the first issues of *The Wide World Magazine*, a British monthly published from April 1898 till December 1965 that featured true-life stories of travel and adventure.

From a] THE ILL-FATED BARQUE "CALLER OU." *[Photo.*

Little Dawson's Message.

BY ZEBEDEE SCAPING, HEAD MASTER OF TRINITY HOUSE NAVIGATION SCHOOL, HULL.

A beautiful and pathetic narrative of real life, telling how many months after the lad sailed his fatal message reached his sorrowing mother.

N the month of November, 1891, the smart little barque *Caller Ou* was lying in the Alexandra Dock, at Hull. She was waiting to take in a cargo of coal for Port Elizabeth. There were many larger and finer vessels in the same dock, and a casual observer would not have singled her out from amongst these others, and yet the *Caller Ou* was a doomed ship. A boy, with that kind of craze for the sea which so often takes possession of England's sons, having heard that Captain Souter wanted an apprentice, might be seen clambering up the side to ask for the berth. He was a smart boy, and dressed in the uniform of

GEORGE WILLIAM DAWSON.
From a Photo. by A. T. Osborne, Hull.

a well-known local navigation school.

Although his age was only fourteen and a half years, he was well grown and strongly built, and had a bright and pleasant countenance. The captain was a kindly man, and, liking the appearance of the boy, offered to take him as an apprentice for four years if his parents would give their consent. This was good news, so the boy thought, and with a light heart he reached home, and pleaded with his parents for their permission to join the *Caller Ou*. His mother considered he was too young, and that it would be better he should remain at school until he was fifteen years old; it would be time enough then. But the boy

'Little Dawson's Message', by Zebedee Scaping, Headmaster of Trinity House Navigation School, Hull – 'A beautiful and pathetic narrative of real life, telling how many months after the lad sailed his fatal message reached his sorrowing mother.' (*The Wide World Magazine*, 1898)

3

SEA MONSTERS AND THE OCEANIC REALM

In mari multo latent ('In the sea many things are hidden'),
Oppian, second/third-century Greco-Roman poet

In ancient times little was known of the sea and its inhabitants. A wide field was thus presented for the play of
the imagination, and so the waste of waters came to be
peopled with a host of fanciful monsters. The better
knowledge of modern times, while it has swept the most
of this away, and reduced the remainder to truthful proportions, has at the same time made known the existence
in the sea of animals much more truly wonderful than any
the ancients ever imagined. (*Monsters of the Sea, Legendary
and Authentic*, by John Gibson, 1887)

When we remember how few fish or other inhabitants
of the sea are ever seen compared with the countless
millions which exist, that not one specimen of some
tribes will be seen for many years in succession, and
that some tribes are only known to exist because a

single specimen or even a single skeleton has been obtained, we may well believe that in the sea, as in heaven and earth, 'there are more things than are known in our philosophy.' ('Strange Sea Monsters', *The Inquirer and Commercial News* [Perth, Western Australia], 18 April 1877)

Those that go down to the sea in ships, do see wonders in deep waters. (*Round Cape Horn In Sail*, by Capt. Fred W. Ellis, The Blue Book Company, 1949)

One of the advantages of old-time sailing ships, but which also condemned them to obsolescence by steamships, was their slow speed that allowed their crews a closer connection with phenomena they observed and experienced at sea. Sailing ships averaged speeds of just 5 to 8 knots. At that leisurely pace they could, for instance, feel the disturbance to their hulls of undersea earthquakes (seaquakes), which crew members often described as a deep rumbling or grating or trembling of the vessel as if crunching over a coral reef. Seafarers under sail also saw things in the sea that steamships, running at twice the speed or more of sailing ships, would miss – such as 'sea monsters' or 'sea serpents' or other odd or, to their eyes, monstrous denizens of the deep that they chanced upon.

There have been thousands of recorded sightings (and many more imagined conceptions) of sea monsters and sea serpents through the ages. Sightings were particularly numerous in times when boats and ships were propelled by oars or sails which made virtually no noise to disturb such marine creatures as might have existed beneath their keels and which occasionally came to the surface unaware of silent human voyagers in their midst.

Engines on ships, which proliferated most generally from the end of the nineteenth century and are now, of course, universal, make a lot of noise and vibration through the undersea realm – a noisome disturbance which possibly deters sensitive deep-sea 'monsters' from revealing themselves as frequently now as in the more peaceful but sea monster-ridden past.

The Oceanic Realm

Land takes up about 30 per cent of the Earth's 510m square km surface area. Water – fresh water, including ice, and saltwater – takes up the other 70 per cent or so, about 361m square km. Saltwater (the oceans and seas) accounts for around 97.5 per cent of all the Earth's water, or some 352m square km – just under 70 per cent of the Earth's *surface* area.

Land is only the *surface* area where all land animal species live – and we know that we *don't* know many, if not most, of all the species we live amongst, even though the land is a relatively accessible and well-explored environment compared with the sea.

But the seas and oceans include much more than just their *surface* area. Seawater has immense *depths* (an average of 4km for all the blue planet's saltsea-blueness). The estimated *volume* of the seas and oceans is 1.3bn cubic km. Which is a volume of oceanic living space for salt water organisms to live in far, far in excess of the superficial land area of 150m square km for terrestrial organisms – and a bit more for the avian population – to inhabit.

We landlubbery humans have explored, at a conservative estimate, only around 5 per cent of the underwater world of the ocean. This leaves rather a lot of unexplored undersea biosphere for an unknown number of unknown sea creatures to be discovered, from microscopic bacteria and forms of plankton to macro-organisms of possibly enormous, even monstrous size. Our direct knowledge and discovery of what lives in the depths of the seas and oceans is, to put it mildly, rudimentary. It isn't that we don't know or haven't discovered much; we do, and we have – but 5 per cent *known about* still leaves 95 per cent *unknown about*.

Scepticism about what monsters *might* be lurking in the planet's saltwater abyss was one of the currents running counter to the flood of reported sightings of such mega-creatures well into the twentieth century.

When a certain Colonel T.H. Perkins, of Boston, U.S.A., was asked by Sir Charles Lyell [the most eminent Scottish geologist of the nineteenth century], whether he had heard of the sea-serpent – the one no doubt that was seen many times by hundreds of people off that coast about 1817 – he replied, 'Unfortunately I have seen it.' And that first word tells a tale. Owing to the stupid ridicule with which reports of the appearance of what are generally known as 'Sea-Serpents' are almost always received, even by so-called scientific people, observers are afraid to record unusual appearances at sea.

A favourite device of the sceptics is to label all the various monsters seen as *The* Sea-Serpent or The Great Sea-Serpent, as if there were or could be only one, a mythical monster, like the *Flying Dutchman*, ranging the seas and occasionally sighted by credulous or imbecile persons, who do not know 'a hawk from a handsaw.' ...

When we consider the enormous depths and vast extent of the great seas of our planet, and that the element in which marine creatures live has never suffered the vicissitudes of temperature and catastrophic cataclysms such as have affected the land, we can well believe that Nature has there had a freer hand to originate and perpetuate monsters. The true scientific attitude to take up is that there is nothing impossible per se in these recorded observances; that we have no right to doubt the evidence of such and so many qualified witnesses, because we ourselves have not seen anything of the kind.

Several sceptics have been converted by themselves seeing what they had ridiculed as impossible when seen by others. But what is the intellectual credit of believing only what you see yourself? How does that in itself make the fact more certain? (from 'Sea Monsters', by C.R. Haines, in *The Quarterly Review*, Vol. 256, 1931)

4

THE SEA SERPENT

'That much fable and exaggeration have been mixed up with the history of the Great Sea-Serpent, cannot be doubted; still, however, the inquiry recurs, what portion of truth is involved amidst this error?' (from 'The Great Sea-Serpent', in *The Naturalist's Library*, Vol. VIII; edited by Sir William Jardine; W.H. Lizars, Edinburgh, 1839)

The lore and legend of sea serpents stretches back to antiquity. Nineteenth-century writers often cited the biblical 'Leviathan' of the Old Testament, amongst other biblical references, to show that the creature was 'as old as the oldest record'. But 'the fullest accounts of the monster' only took shape and character when, from the Middle Ages, a resurgent interest in natural history put it four-square into the realms of human experience. The most prominent exponents of the sea serpent story were, at first, medieval Scandinavian (Norse) mythographers and exegetes:

The twin-brother of the kraken, recently described in this paper [and later in this book], both in its marvellous size and in the incredulity which all descriptions have excited, is the famous sea-serpent. Its history is as old as the oldest record. No age and no seafaring nation has been without some account concerning its appearance, and yet to this day serious doubts are entertained as to its existence. It is clearly referred to in the Old Testament, where the prophet Isaiah sings:

In that day the Lord with his sore and great and strong sword – Shall punish leviathan, the piercing serpent, – Even leviathan, that crooked serpent, – And he shall slay the dragon that is in the sea.

Again, when Job pleads his uprightness, and the Lord answered unto Job out of the whirlwind, he mentions behemoth and leviathan, and says concerning that monster:

Canst though draw out leviathan with a hook? – Or his tongue with a cord which thou lettest down? – Canst though put a hook into his nose, or bore his jaw through with a thorn? … – Who can open the doors of his face? His teeth are terrible round about. – His scales are his pride, shut up together as with a close seal. – One is so near to another, that no air can come between them. – By his neesings [sneezing] *a light doth shine, and his eyes are like the eyelids of the morning. – Out of his mouth go burning lamps, and sparks of fire leap out. – Out of his nostrils goeth smoke, as out of a seething pot. – His breath kindleth coals, and a flame goeth out of his mouth … – When he raiseth up himself, the mighty are afraid:*

The sword of him that layeth at him can not hold: the spear, the dart, nor the habergeon [mail- or scale-armoured jacket]. *– He maketh the deep to boil like a pot; he maketh the sea like a pot of ointment. – He maketh a path to shine after him; one would think the deep to be hoary. – Upon earth there is not his like.*

... It is, however, in the Middle Ages that we have the fullest accounts of the monster. Pontoppidan [Erik Pontoppidan, 1698–1764], one of the most learned Scandinavians, who was long Bishop of Bergen, in Norway, and died as Chancellor of Denmark, in Copenhagen, in 1764, states, in his interesting contribution to national history, that in his country every body believed firmly in the great sea-serpent; and if he or any of his guests ventured to speak doubtingly of the huge monster, all smiled, as if he had been uncertain whether eels or herrings really existed. ('The Sea-Serpent', *Harper's Weekly*, Supplement, 29 April 1871)

Amphibious Serpents?

There was spirited debate in certain quarters about some sea serpents' predilection for getting on to dry land and wreaking havoc there.

The good people of those northern regions were so familiar with these wonderful creatures that they spoke of two distinct kinds of sea-serpents – one living in the sea only, the other amphibious, which preferred the land generally, but retired periodically to the great deep. Nicolaus Gramius, minister of the Gospel at Londen [Norway], tells us that, during a destructive inundation, an immense serpent was seen to make its way toward the ocean, overthrowing every thing in its path – animals, trees, and houses – and uttering fearful roarings. The fishermen of Odal were so frightened by the terrible sight that they did not dare go out in their boats for several days. ('The Sea-Serpent', *Harper's Weekly*, Supplement, 29 April 1871)

The seventeenth-century German geographer, historian and writer Everard Werner Happel, known as Happelius (1647–90), included Nicolaus Gramius' account of the land-sea serpent in his 1689 work *Mundus Mirabilis Tripartitus*:

It appears, from several passages in the works of Scandinavian writers, that there is a current belief in the existence of a great serpent of an amphibious nature, which, like that mentioned by the ancient historians, does not confine its depredations to the water ... According to Pontoppidan, it is said, by the people who inhabit the Norwegian coast, that the latter [amphibious] species is not generated in the sea, but on the land; and that when they become so large that they cannot easily move upon the ground, they go into the sea and attain their full growth.

In favour of this tradition, we may quote the following passage from the *Mundus Mirabilis* of Happelius:

'Nicolaus Gramius, minister at Londen in Norway, gives, 16th Jan. anno 1656, of such a serpent, the following account, from the report of Gulbrandi Hougsrud and Olaus Anderson, that they had seen, in the last autumnal inundation, a large water serpent, or worm, in the Spæriler Sea; and it is believed that it had been seen before in Mios, and had been hitherto hid in the River Bang. As soon as it reached the shore of this river, it proceeded, on the dry land, to the Spæriler Sea; it appeared like a mighty mast, and whatever stood in its way was thrown down – even the very trees and huts; the people were terrified with its hissing and frightful roaring, and almost all the fish, in the aforesaid sea, were devoured or drove away by it.

'The inhabitants of Odale were so terrified at this monster, that none would venture to go to the sea to follow their customary fishing and wood-trade, nor would any body walk along the shore. At the end of the autumn, before the waters were frozen, this monster was seen at a distance, and, by its enormous size, surprised every body; its head was as big as an hogs-head, and the thickness of its body, as far as the same appeared above water, was like a tun; the length of the whole body was vast; it reached, as far as the spectators could judge, the length of three Norway dannen-trees, and rather exceeded.' ('On the History of the Great Sea Serpent', *Blackwood's Edinburgh Magazine*, April 1818)

Bishop Erik Pontoppidan's *Natural History of Norway*

The famed and learned cleric Erik Pontoppidan was born in Åarhus, Denmark, in 1698, and appointed Bishop of Bergen, Sweden, in 1747. He included Gramius's account in the work for which he has earned a prime position in the sea monsters annals of fame, *A Natural History of Norway*, published originally in Danish, in two volumes in 1752–53, and in English translation in 1755.

Pontoppidan began Section VI of his *Natural History* with his consideration of the 'sea-monster', directly after his previous commentary on 'Mer-maids' and the like, and particularly, at first, in the context of his ecclesiastic acknowledgement of 'the extraordinary works of the great Creator':

The Söe Ormen, or Sea-snake, serpens marinus magnus, called by some in this country [i.e. Norway] Aale-Tust, is a wonderful and terrible sea-monster, which extremely deserves to be taken notice of by those who are curious to look into the extraordinary works of the great Creator. But here I must again, as I did of the mer-man, give the reader proper authorities for the real existence of this creature, before I come to treat of its nature and properties.

This creature, particularly in the North Sea, continually keeps himself in the bottom of the sea, excepting in the months of July and August, which is their spawning time; and then they come to the surface in calm weather, but plunge into the water again so soon as the wind raises the least wave. If it were not for this regulation, thus ordained by the wise Creator for the safety of mankind, the reality of this snake's existence would be less questioned than it is at present, even here in Norway; though our coast is the only place in Europe visited by this terrible creature ...

I have questioned its existence myself, till that suspicion was removed by full and sufficient evidence from creditable and experienced fishermen and sailors in Norway; of which there are hundreds who can testify that they have annually seen them ... In all my enquiry about these affairs, I have hardly spoken with any intelligent person born in the manor of Nordland, who was not able to give a pertinent answer, and strong assurances of the existence of this fish: and some of our North traders, that come here every year with their merchandise, think it a very strange question, when they are seriously asked, whether there be any such creature; they think it as ridiculous as if the question was put to them, whether there be such fish as the eel or cod.

Capt. de Ferry's Letter

Pontoppidan went on to remark on a 'conversation on this subject', of the existence of the sea serpent, that he had had with a certain Captain Lawrence de Ferry, and of a letter written by de Ferry to corroborate his first-hand encounter with the beast 'by ocular demonstration':

> Last winter I fell by chance in a conversation on this subject with Captain Lawrence de Ferry, now commander in this place, who said, that he had doubted a great while, whether there was any such creature, till he had an opportunity of being fully convinced by ocular demonstration, in the year 1746.

On 22 February 1751 luminaries of the city of Bergen were presented with a letter from Capt. de Ferry, dated the day before and delivered by the city's procurator, John Reutz, to be read before them and two other men, Nicholas Petersen Kopper and Nicholas Nicholson Anglewigen, who were 'admitted to make oath, that every particular set forth in the aforesaid letter is true'. The letter ran thus:

'Mr. John Reutz –

'The latter end of August, in the year 1746, as I was on a voyage, on my return from Trundhiem [Trondheim], on a very calm and hot day, having a mind to put in at Molde, it happened that when we were arrived with my vessel within six English miles of the aforesaid Molde, being at a place called Jukle-Næss, as I was reading in a book, I heard a kind of a murmuring voice from amongst the men at the oars, who were eight in number, and observed that the man at the helm kept off from the land. Upon this I inquired what was the matter, and was informed that there was a sea-snake before us.

'I then ordered the man at the helm to keep to the land again, and to come up with this creature of which I had heard so many stories. Though the fellows were under some apprehension, they were obliged to obey my orders. In the meantime the sea-snake passed by us, and we were obliged to tack the vessel about in order to get nearer to it. As the snake swam faster than we could row, I took my gun, that was ready charged, and fired it; on this he immediately plunged under the water.

'We rowed to the place where it sunk down (which in the calm might be easily observed) and lay upon our oars, thinking it would come up again to the surface; however it did not. Where the snake plunged down, the water appeared thick and red; perhaps some of the shot might wound it, the distance being very little.

'The head of this snake, which it held more than two feet above the surface of the water, resembled that of a horse. It was of a greyish colour, and the mouth was quite

'The Great Sea Serpent [*according to Pontoppidon*]' – engraving by William Home Lizars (1788–1859) for *The Naturalist's Library*, 40 vols (1833–43), edited by Sir William Jardine (1800–74).

black, and very large. It had black eyes, and a long white mane, that hung down from the neck to the surface of the water. Besides the head and neck, we saw seven or eight folds, or coils, of this snake, which were very thick, and as far as we could guess there was about a fathom distance between each fold.

'I related this affair in a certain company, where there was a person of distinction present who desired that I would communicate to him an authentic detail of all that happened; and for this reason two of my sailors, who were present at the same time and place where I saw this monster, namely, Nicholas Pedersen Kopper, and Nicholas Nicholsen Anglewigen, shall appear in court, to declare on oath the truth of every particular herein set forth; and I desire the favour of an attested copy of the said descriptions.

'I remain, Sir, your obliged servant, L. de Ferry

'Bergen, 21st February, 1751.'

And the 'before-named witnesses' – Kopper and Anglewigen – duly 'gave their corporal oaths' to Capt. de Ferry's account, confirming that 'every particular set forth therein [was] strictly true'.

Olaus Magnus and *Carta Marina*

The famous Archbishop of Upsala, Olaus Magnus, who bears testimony to the kraken, also speaks more than once of the amphibious serpents. He states that they leave the shelter of the cliffs near Bergen at night. They have a mane, their bodies are covered with scales, and their eyes send forth a bright light. Out at sea they rear themselves against the ship they encounter, and seize whatever they can obtain on deck. An animal of this kind, he continues, was actually seen, in 1522, near the island of Moos, which measured over fifty feet in length, and was continually turning round. ('The Sea-Serpent', *Harper's Weekly*, Supplement, 29 April 1871)

The Swedish-Scandinavian historian, geographer and Roman Catholic cleric Olaus Magnus (1490–1557) was born at Linköping in southern Sweden, in October 1490. Between 1510 and 1517 he studied in Germany, after which he 'was taken into the higher ecclesiastical service' in still Catholic Sweden. In 1523 Gustav Vasa, the newly elected King Gustave I of Sweden, sent Magnus to Rome to request the Medici pope Clement VII to confirm Magnus's brother Johannes's appointment as Archbishop of Uppsala, the highest ecclesiastical position in Sweden.

Olaus stayed abroad, 'dealing with foreign affairs'. He never again set foot in Sweden: his Catholicism was by then contrary to the turn of the religious tide.

The Protestant Reformation in Sweden started in the late 1520s. Olaus (and Johannes) retained an unflinching commitment to Catholicism. Around 1530 King Gustave invited Olaus and Johannes to return to by then Protestant Lutheran Sweden. Both refused on the grounds of their staunch Catholic principles. Their income was cut off, their property confiscated, and Johannes's archbishopric annulled by Gustave. So they were both effectively self-exiled from Sweden. After a decade living in Gdanzk, Poland (from 1526), they settled in Rome in 1537. (Johannes had been consecrated Archbishop of Uppsala in July 1533.)

When Johannes died in 1544, Pope Paul authorised the consecration of Olaus to succeed his brother as Archbishop of Uppsala, 'but [he] never entered into office, spending the rest of his life in Italy'. Olaus died on 1 August 1557 and was buried in Rome alongside his brother in St Peter's church.

There are two things for which Olaus Magnus is renowned in sea monster chronicles: his *Carta Marina*, of 1539, a 'marine map' which included in its full Latin title 'and Description of the Northern Lands and of their Marvels' (Magnus began work on it in 1527; its publication was funded by the then patriarch of Venice, Gerolamo Querini, who had taken the Magnus brothers under his wing from September 1538 to the end of 1540); and a companion work to the *Carta Marina*, titled *Historia de Gentibus Septentrionalibus* (*History of the Northern Peoples*), published in Latin, in Rome, in 1555. The first English version, published in 1658, was titled *A Compendious History of the Goths, Swedes, & Vandals and Other Northern Nations*.

The *Carta Marina* itself covers the extended Scandinavian geo-political realm of the time, from mainland Scandinavia, down to the Baltic, up and over to the 'Oceanus Britanicus' bordering northern Scotland, the Orkney and Shetland Islands, the Faeroe Islands and Iceland. Its most prominent characteristic, however, is the lustrous seascape of medieval sea creatures portrayed in the waters to the west of mainland 'Scandia', including: the 'balena' (whale); a 'ziphius' (swordfish) devouring a seal; a sea serpent engulfing a sailing ship; diverse tusked, clawed and otherwise fearsome-faced sea monsters per se; and a 'vacca marina' (sea cow); amongst other cartographically illustrative details.

Joseph Nigg's *Sea Monsters: The Lore and Legacy of Olaus Magnus's Marine Map* (Ivy Press, 2013) explains each of the figures in the *Carta Marina* and the significance and legacy of the map for other cartographers of the age. 'Through his map and its voluminous commentary [the *Compendious History*], Olaus became the age's principal chronicler of the

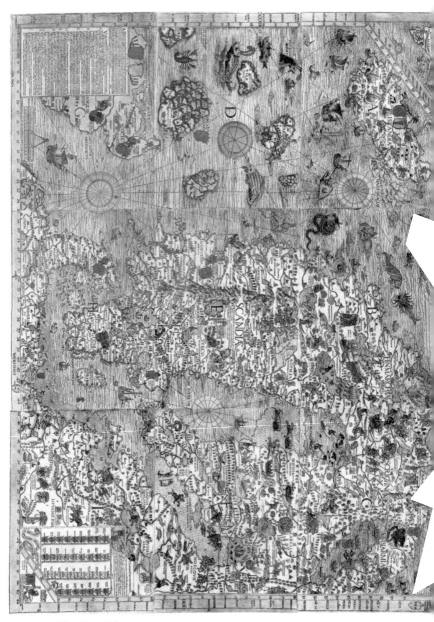

The *Carta Marina*.

sea serpent, the great squid [successor to the kraken], and sea monsters in general.'

The *Compendious History* includes voluminous descriptions of Scandinavia's 'Acts of their famous heroes, the strange Eccentrick customs, Fashions, Attire, Sports, Battels, Feasts, Marriages, Religion ...', et al, arranged in twenty-two books, each with a number of chapters titled by subjects.

Magnus filled Book 8 of the *Compendious History* with accounts of the ancient history of the Danes, mainly abstracted from the Danish historian and theologian Saxo Grammaticus's (*c.*1160–*c.*1220) 'first full history of Denmark', the *Gesta Danorum*, a combination of oral history, myths and legends to glorify Denmark's past from pre-Christian times to about AD 1187. In Chapter 15 of Book 8, he related of an early Danish king, Jarmericus (AD 300–367):

> ... Saxo very largely prosecutes [narrates] the monstrous cruelty of King Jarmericus, which was fiercely continued from his Childhood, unto his old age; which as it exceeds all rage of Beasts, so cannot it be read or heard of by any sensible man, but with great horrour. For by unheard of Tyranny, he often killed with exquisite torments afflicted men. For, by high ingratitude, he slew their King and Queen with fire privately, by whom he was taken captive in war, and set at liberty, and taken into the number of their familiar friends, and made the chief of them, and exalted. Then, when he took fourty Germans, he joyned so many Wolves to them, and strangled them; yet this would not satisfy his bloody mind. For he destroyed their Nobility, thrusting Thongs through their Legs, and then he bound them to the hoofs of huge Bulls, & set Dogs to tear them, and drew them into the Mud and Bogs, a most miserable spectacle.

A 'most miserable spectacle' it might well have been, but Magnus was just getting started. In his own time, in Chapter 17 of Book 8, he offered his own contemporary experience of the king known then as Christiernus II and now as Christian II (1481–1559): the Danish-born king of Denmark and Norway from 1513 till 1523 according to the so-called Kalmar Union of the two countries (and Sweden) from 1397, under a single monarch. (Christian was the *hereditary*, rather than legally *elective*, king of Sweden for a brief time, 1520–21. In 1523 Sweden became an independent nation under the elected King Gustave I.)

Of the Severity of King Christiernus the Second
Christiernus the second, King of Denmark, at sundry times, and divers wayes, obtaining passage into the foresaid Kingdomes [of Sweden], by some Lords of the Danish faction, in the Kingdomes of Swethland and Gothland, that were kindred and of the Danish blood … became so cruell and severe, that taking no respect to his oath, or Letters sealed, or of the sacrament of the Lords body, that was to be trembled at, or of any pity to commiserate any man, he one day commanded, namely November the 8, 1520, the Princes of divers orders, the Lords and Consults and Citizens, to the number of 94, to be beheaded, most wickedly, to which he was egged on by the ill counsell of wicked men: this I saw and trembled at it; and he commanded that their dead bodies should remain unburied 3 dayes, before the City house [City Hall] of the City Stochholme [Stockholm], until they were carried forth of the City to be burned. Truly it was a miserable sight, that questionlesse would afterwards trouble Christiernus himself who was vexed with a thousand miseries.

Not content with that villainy, Christiernus:

> ... hastened to the Gallows, one Magnus who was one
> of Johannes his Peers [i.e. a friend of Magnus's brother
> Johannes], and a most valiant defender of his Country;
> who was fastened to a plank on the ground, and first his
> privities, then his heart was cut out, and they were cast
> into his fathers face, with many insulting opprobrious
> words given to him, that he might shew the greater rage
> and perpetuall horror in doing it ... A long and terrible
> History should be writ by me, who saw all this lamenta-
> ble practice, if I would relate every part of this calamity,
> namely how all things both divine and humane were
> in confusion.

Magnus included more instances of similar, and worse,
atrocities throughout Book 8. But in the interests of objec-
tivity and the sparing of his delicate readers from the most
extreme atrocities of his own age, which he personally witnessed, he set out his store in Chapter 18 thus:

> *More of the Cruelty of the Same King*
> Nor let good men think that I have said what I have
> said, for hate or malice against the Danish Nation,
> and their former actions, or against the severity of
> King Christiernus, but I have purposely left out far more
> terrible things, which cannot be read without groans and
> horrors, much lesse be set down in Books ... But why I
> do write more bitterly than others yet more truly and
> sparingly, he is bold to testify, because with my great
> danger and sorrow, I was present and beheld all these
> Tragedies grieving to see the miseries of my Nation,
> which now seem to be increased a thousand times, and

without remedy, made worse by the wicked constitutions
of Laws, and oppressions of the Subjects.

The *History* wasn't all blood and guts and dismemberments
by cruel tyrants, though Magnus did serve up, as the title
of his book suggested, a compendious banquet of such fare
within Book 8. Most of the *History*'s twenty-two books
narrated a journey through the *natural* rather than the
unnatural history of 'Scandia' lands and 'Kingdomes'.
(The last, Book 22, covered: 'Northern Gnats [midges]',
'A remedy to prevent them', 'Of bees', 'Of honey', 'Of ants',
and 'Of Pearls and the Generation of them'.) The over-
arching characteristic of the *History* was Magnus's curiosity
about and fulsome portrayal of all the creatures of 'Scandia'
lands and 'Kingdomes' and the environment, people and
customs thereabouts.

But then there were monsters – though even in the sea
monsters sections of Book 21 Magnus had a keen eye and
descriptive talent for quite ordinary creatures, with, it
seemed, a particular interest in, even fondness for, whales
to which he dedicated several chapters. He titled Book
21 *De Piscibus Monstrosis* (*Of Monstrous Fishes*), in which
he described the bizarre creatures in his *Carta Marina*.
Chapter 5 began proceedings thus:

Of the Horrible Monsters of the Coast of Norway
There are monstrous fish on the Coasts or Sea of
Norway, of unusual Names, though they are reputed
a kind of Whales, who shew their cruelty at first sight,
and make men afraid to see them; and if men look long
on them, they will fright and amaze them. Their Forms
are horrible, their Heads square, all set with prickles,
and they have sharp and long Horns round about, like

a Tree rooted up by the Roots. They are ten or twelve
Cubits long, very black, and with huge eyes: the compass
[circumference] whereof is above eight or ten cubits: the
Apple [pupil] of the Eye is of one Cubit, and is red and
fiery coloured, which in the dark night appears to fishermen afar off under Waters, as a burning fire, having hairs
like Goose-Feathers, thick and long, like a Beard hanging down; the rest of the body, for the greatness of the
head, which is square, is very small, not being above 14 or
15 Cubits long; one of the Sea-Monsters will drown easily
many ships provided with many Mariners.

The long and famous Epistle of Ericus Falchendorf,
Arch-Bishop of the Church of Nidrosus [Erik
Walkendorf, Archbishop at the Cathedral of Trondheim],
which is the Metropolis [metropolitan – the highest
church authority] of the whole Kingdom of Norway,
and it was sent to [Pope] Leo the Tenth, about the Year
of Grace, 1520, and this confirms this strange Novelty;
and, to this Epistle, was [attached] the head of another
Monster, seasoned [preserved] with Salt.

Magnus reserved Chapter 27 specifically for sea serpents,
whose appearance, he says, 'hapneth not' without auguring
'some wonderful change of the Kingdom' soon after.

Of the Greatness of the Norway Serpent and of Others
They who in Works of Navigation, on the Coasts of
Norway, employ themselves in fishing or Merchandise,
do all agree in this strange story, that there is a Serpent
there which is of a vast magnitude, namely 200 foot long,
and moreover 20 foot thick; and is wont to live in Rocks
and Caves toward the Sea-coast about Berge [Bergen]:
which will go alone from his holes in a clear night, in

Summer, and devour Calves, Lambs, and Hogs, or else he goes into the Sea to feed on Polypus [octopus or squid], Locusts, and all sorts of Sea-Crabs. He hath commonly hair hanging from his neck a Cubit long, and sharp scales, and is black, and he hath flaming shining eyes. This Snake disquiets the Shippers, and he puts up his head on high like a pillar, and catcheth away men, and he devours them; and this hapneth not but it signifies some wonderful change of the Kingdom near at hand; namely that the Princes shall die, or be banished; or some Tumultuous Wars shall presently follow.

There is also another Serpent of an incredible Magnitude in a Town, called Moos, of the Diocess of Hammer, which, as a Comet portends change in all the World, so, that portends a change in the Kingdom of Norway, as it was seen, Anno 1522, that lifts himself high above the Waters, and rouls [rolls] himself round like a sphere. This Serpent was thought to be fifty Cubits long by conjecture, by sight afar off: there followed this the banishment of King Christiernus, and 2 great persecutions of the Bishops; and it shew'd also the destruction of the Countrey.

Pontoppidan, who had quite a lot to say about the 'Sea-snake' himself in his *Natural History of Norway*, wrote somewhat sceptically of Magnus's serpents. Of the first one in the *Historia* – Chapter 24: 'Of very long worms' – Pontoppidan wrote: 'I have never heard of this sort from any other person, and should hardly believe the good Olaus, if he did not say that he affirmed this from his own experience' – which he did.

Of the second, in Chapter 27, cleric Erik wrote wryly, but in a spirit of 'enlighten'd' generosity:

Of the other Sea-snake the same author writes after-wards, chap. xxvii. but he mixes truth and fable together, according to the relations of others; but this was excusable in that dark age, when that author wrote. Notwithstanding all this, we in the present *more enlighten'd age* are much obliged to him, for his industry and judicious observations.

So, Magnus's sea serpent was an omen for disasters – like 'a Comet portends a change in all the World'. (Halley's comet had, in fact, made one of its regular visits to within sight of Earthlings in the year 1531 – just as Lutheranism was uprooting Roman Catholicism in Sweden.)

What Magnus referred to as the 'banishment of King *Christiernus*' was about Christian II. In 1523 (the year after Magnus's serpent 'lifts himself high above the Waters') Christian was deposed by his uncle, who assumed the throne as Frederick I. Christian went into exile in the Netherlands (the 'banishment') where he spent most of the rest of his life (from 1532 till 1559) imprisoned by Uncle Frederick in two castles.

As for Magnus's portent of 'the destruction of the Countrey' (literally Sweden, but really the entire Scandinavian region and particularly Denmark) by the augury-serpent: not only was the Kalmar Union disbanded in 1523, but also with all the other political and social turmoil at that time, Lutheranism was being adopted in both Norway and Sweden in the late 1520s, as part of the Protestant Reformation to overthrow the age-long hegemony of Roman Catholicism. Magnus, a high officer of the Roman Catholic Church, would have reviled such a heretical state of affairs.

The 'Monstrous Hog'

One of the sea creatures in the *Carta Marina* was a 'monstrous Hog' or 'Sea-Pig', which headed Chapter 18 as 'De Porco monstroso Oceani Germanici' ('Of the monstrous Hog of the German Ocean [i.e. North Sea]'), perhaps the most copied illustration of all the map's monstrous creatures. He had earlier, in Chapter 13 of the original Latin text, described a 'monstrous Fish found on the North shore of England, Anno 1532':

> I Spake before of a monstrous Fish found on the shores of England, with a clear description of his whole body, and every member thereof, which was seen there in the year 1532, and the Inhabitants made a prey of it [caught it as a prize]. Now I shall revive the memory of that monstrous Hog that was found afterwards, Anno 1537, in the same German Ocean, and it was a Monster in every part of it. For it had a Hogs head, and a quarter of a Circle, like the Moon, in the hinder part of its head, four feet like a Dragons, two eyes on both sides in his Loyns, and a third in his belly, inclining towards his navel; behind he had a Forked-Tail, like no other Fish commonly.

And there, in the 1658 English version of the *History*, the description of Magnus's 'monstrous hog' ended. In the original Latin version, however, Magnus had considerably more to say about the significance of the creature. The seventeenth-century English translators glossed over – banished, indeed – the rest of that text, probably because of its Roman Catholic perspective at a time when Europe was fractured by the schism of nascent Protestantism. English Puritans were trying as much as possible to cleanse vestigial

Catholic traditions and practices from the relatively new Protestant Church of England. What Catholic Magnus had to say in Latin in the mid-sixteenth century ran, by the mid-seventeenth century, rather against Protestant proclivities – which, no doubt, English translators would have been chary of bucking.

The late-twentieth-century translators of the *Historia*, Peter Fisher and Humphrey Higgens, were free of such restraint in their three-volume *A Description of the Northern Peoples, Olaus Magnus (1555)*, edited by P.G. Foote and published for the Hakluyt Society in 1998. Their English continuation of the original Latin text in Chapter 27 concerning the 'monstrous Hog' ran thus:

> ... In the city of Rome at that time an interpretation was printed and published, explaining the significance of the beast's individual parts, which showed how heretics generally pursue a swinish existence. By the *moon behind the head* is meant distortions of the truth, since it grows not on the pig's forehead but at the nape of its neck. The *eyes in its loins and belly* are full of temptation, and for this reason they must be cut out. Lastly, the *four dragon's feet* signify the grossly evil desires and acts of mankind, bursting in viciously from the four corners of the earth, and appearing in the fish very much as though it were some prying ruffian.
>
> Whatever the import of this strange pig may be, then, it can properly be displayed as a symbol to the unclean men of this wretched age, urging them to recoil from monstrous habits and to embrace goodness and benevolence.

The 'interpretation' that Magnus referred to, 'explaining the significance of the beast's individual parts', was a pamphlet published by a printer then in Rome, Antonio

Blado (1490–1567), titled *Monstrum in Oceano Germanico a piscatoribus nuper captum, & eius partium subtilis, ac Theologica Interpretatio* (*Monster in the North Sea Recently Caught by Fishermen: A Subtle and Theological Interpretation of Its Parts* – English translation by Alexander Boxer, June, 2014). The pamphlet began:

> What was recently reported to me from Germany, good reader, be it monster or freak of nature, whatever it is I wanted not only to offer you an illustration but also to interpret it according to the authority of our sacred teachers [the four doctors of the Roman church: Saints Andrew, Augustine, Jerome and Gregory]. They say it was found in the German Sea [i.e. the North Sea], along which shore there also roam very many monsters which have devised for themselves new laws of the Christian faith and religion and, if it please the Gods, new Gods as well. (Translation from the Latin text by Alexander Boxer; the full Latin text and Alexander Boxer's English translation is at his website: idolsofthecave.com)

The Germanic reference seemed to be a fairly pointed finger at the theologian who kindled and then fanned the flames of the Protestant Reformation that was so inimical to the Catholic arch-prelate Olaus Magnus: Martin Luther (1483–1546), whom one Catholic called, at the Diet of Worms (1521) convened to contest Luther's ninety-five anti-Catholic 'theses', 'a demon in the appearance of a man'.

So the 'new Gods' of Protestantism would have galled Magnus as they did Blado. And the 'monstrous Hog' of the 'German Ocean' was nothing less than a symbol of the 'swinish existence' of heretic followers of Luther's 'new laws of the Christian faith and religion'.

And so *might*, by analogy, the whole monster-scape of the *Carta Marina* be nothing less than an extended allegory on the tumult of those times, from the villainies and 'far more terrible things, which cannot be read without groans and horrors, much lesse be set down in Books' which Magnus described of earlier rulers, to the arch-villain of his own time, the anti-Catholic 'demon' Luther, whose 'heresy' Magnus most vilified, perhaps, most illustratively with his demon-scape of sea monsters?

Might that allegory, then, be a reflection of Magnus's own troubled mind, of the evil of 'the unclean men' that his mind's eye perceived to have infected the *zeitgeist* of what he called 'this wretched age', and of his despair about such monstrosity that assailed his Catholic calling to 'embrace goodness and benevolence'?

There was an established tradition, in medieval bestiaries and the like, of attributing moral significance to specific creatures of the animal kingdom. An ostensible moral suffusion of the entire *Carta Marina* monster-scape would not have been without precedent – as the uber-moral Magnus knew all too well. And as he *might* have wanted us to understand, too.

The 'Stronsay Beast' of Orkney

One of the earliest modern forensic examinations of an actual sea monster happened in the Orkney Islands, in 1808, when a 'gigantic serpent', as it was first termed, washed ashore there. Examination of it 'by competent persons' revealed, apparently though not conclusively, a rather more mundane reality:

... Nor were they seen only out at sea, when mistakes would be natural, and fright or intense curiosity might lead to unconscious exaggeration; but the body itself has been found, and examined by competent persons. Thus, to mention but one instance, in 1808, the body of a gigantic serpent was washed on shore at Stronsay, one of the Orkneys. A Dr. Barclay was summoned at once, and in the presence of several justices of the peace and some men of learning an affidavit was drawn up, which stated that the monster measured over fifty feet in length and nine feet in circumference; that it had a kind of mane running from behind the head nearly to the tail, which was brilliantly phosphorescent at night; and that its gills, nearly five feet long, were not unlike the plucked wings of a goose.

Sir Everard Home, it is true, believed it to be a basking shark of uncommon size. ('The Sea-Serpent', *Harper's Weekly*, Supplement, 29 April 1871)

The examination of the remains of the so-called 'Stronsay Beast' concluded almost unanimously that it was actually the rotting carcass of a dead basking shark, a common inhabitant of the waters around Scotland's Western Isles, especially in summer.

Sir Everard Home, in the 99th volume of the *Philosophical Transactions*, considers it to have been a *squalus maximus* (i.e. a basking shark); but as he only gained his information at second-hand, his conclusions may not be incontrovertible, especially as the *subject* separated before any absolutely correct drawing, or detailed description could be obtained. The effigies given with Sir Everard's paper, makes the animal a long-necked, six-legged, fringy-backed, long-tailed, queer-looking fellow.

It was dubbed *Halsydrus* (meaning 'sea-water snake') *Pontoppidani*. ('Marvels in Marine Natural History, Part II', *United Service Magazine*, Vol. 51, 1846).

The sketch of the 'Beast' by the artist Sir Alexander Gibson – the 'effigies given with Sir Everard's paper' – in fact bore no resemblance to a basking shark except in length. But any detritus of a dead and well-decomposed sea creature of that size would appear, indeed, like a 'queer-looking fellow', if it actually appeared like anything other than an amorphous gelatinous mass.

Not all luminaries agreed that the 'Stronsay Beast' was of the basking shark clan. The Orkney-born polymath (zoologist, chemist, meteorologist) Dr Thomas Stewart Traill (1781–1862), a Fellow of the Royal Society of Edinburgh from 1819, presented a 'Communication' to the society, read at a meeting on 3 January 1854: 'On the supposed Sea-Snake, cast on shore in the Orkneys in 1808, and the animal seen from H.M.S. *Daedalus*, in 1848.'

Dr Traill characterised the sketch of the animal as 'a very absurd suppositious drawing of the animal'. Based on his examination of 'the skull and several vertebrae' sent to 'the museum of our university [i.e. Edinburgh]', and on the notes of 'those who had seen and measured' what was left of the creature, Traill concluded: 'Both McQuhae's [captain of HMS *Daedalus*] and the Orkney animal would appear to be cartilaginous fish, totally different from any genus known to naturalists.'

In short, still a mystery. And there remained questions about the authenticity of sea serpents more generally:

... Does the sea-serpent belong only to the realm of fancy, or is it really one of the great wonders of the deep?

The question has never yet been finally decided. That there must be in existence animals of serpent-like form and of gigantic proportions seems to be well established by the concurrent testimony of English, American, and Norwegian eye-witnesses; and the mere fact that no specimen exists in the museums, and that no such monster has been encountered of late years, does not by any means disprove the experience of so many ages.

On the other hand, great allowance must no doubt be made for the effect of fear, which enlarges all objects; the desire to excite wonder, which leads men to embellish their accounts; and the natural tendency to add to original accounts, which results often unconsciously in exaggeration, and has in all probability furnished us with such wonderful creatures as the kraken, the roc, and the phenix.

Nothing in these descriptions is, besides, incompatible with the laws of nature; and the study of fossil remains establishes beyond doubt the fact, that in former ages gigantic reptiles have peopled the sea which were far more surprising in size and shape than the much-doubted sea-serpent. There is no necessity, therefore, to ascribe all such encounters to simple mistakes. Now and then, perhaps, a long string of algæ [seaweed], moving slowly under the impulse received by gentle winds or unknown currents, or masses of phosphorescent infusoria [minute sea creatures like plankton], floating for miles and miles on the calm surface of the sea, may have led superstitious sailors to fancy they saw giant serpents.

But it is, on the other hand, by no means improbable that the vast deep, of which so little is as yet known to man, may still hold some of the giants of olden days, and that of the many well-trained, intelligent people who nowadays 'go down to the sea in ships, and do business in great waters,' some may yet see these 'works of the Lord, and his wonders in the deep.'

Fortunately, there is no doubt any longer surrounding the true king of the seas – the whale – and yet he is of truly monstrous proportions. It is a perplexed chapter, to be sure, in natural history, to say how many species of whales there are; for Jack Tar comes home with confused accounts of Sulphur-bottoms, Broad-noses, Razor-backs, and Tall-spouts, and a host of other names by which he learns to distinguish unprofitable whales, not worth the toils and perils of capture.

But, after all, this only shows that the family is very fully known; and well might this be so, if we remember that already in the ninth century a Norwegian Ohthere [Ohthere of Hålogaland, ninth-century Norwegian Viking seafarer], whose wonderful adventures were taken down by no less a man than King Alfred himself, speaks of having slain sixty such monsters in two days. This is, of course, impossible; but we must bear in mind that there is nothing in nature so wonderful that the human mind does not love to add a finishing touch of its own, and make it yet a little more monstrous. ('The Sea Serpent', *Harper's Weekly*, Supplement, 29 April 1871)

Sceptics, of whom there were many, smirked at the existence of a monster serpent – a 'wonder in the deep' – that they considered 'a gigantic fraud'. And yet many others, eminent naturalists amongst them, considered it wholly plausible that, in the vast unknown depths of the oceans, there could well be unknown species of animals that grew to an enormous size. And which sometimes surfaced into the light of seafarers' sights. Like sea serpents.

Strange Sea Monsters

Mr. Richard A. Proctor, writing on the subject of the sea-serpent, says that it has long been regarded by most persons as simply a gigantic fraud, and he gives reasons. Either the object which appeared like a sea-serpent was something altogether different – a floating tree entangled in seaweed, the serpentine outline of distant hills half lost under a scudding haze, or, if a single living creature at all, then one of a known species seen under unusual and deceptive conditions – or else the circumstantial accounts which could not be thus explained away were concoctions of falsehood.

Yet, as the naturalist Goose [*sic* – Gosse: the English naturalist and marine biologist Phillip Henry Gosse (1810–88)] has long since pointed out, in his curious essay on 'The Great Unknown,' it is altogether unlikely that men know all the forms of animals which exist in the ocean, and the antecedent probability against the theory of the existence of creatures such as the great sea-serpent has been described to be is not sufficient to outweigh the evidence which has been given respecting such creatures.

No one who has read the account given by the officers and men of the [ship] *Daedalus*, for instance, can for a moment suppose that they were deceived in any one of the ways ingeniously imagined; we must assume that they all told untruths before we can reject the belief that some as yet unknown sea creature was seen by them.

Travellers are sometimes said to tell marvellous stories; but it is a noteworthy fact that, in nine cases out of ten, the marvellous stories of men have been confirmed. Men ridicule the tale, brought back by those who had sailed far to the South, that the sun there moves from right to

Similarity of the Latest Seen Sea-Serpent to its Predecessors.
(*The Illustrated London News*, 30 June 1906)

left, instead of from left to right, as you face his mid-way place; but we know that those travellers told the truth.

The first account of the giraffe was laughed to scorn, and it was satisfactorily proved that no such creature could possibly exist. The gorilla would have been jeered out of existence but for the fortunate arrival of a skeleton of his at an early stage of our acquaintance with that prepossessing cousin of ours. Monstrous cuttlefish were thought to be monstrous lies, till the [French warship] *Alecton*, in 1861, came upon one and captured its tail, whose weight of 40 lbs. led naturalists to estimate the entire weight of the creature at 4,000 lbs., or nearly a couple of tons …

… As for stories of sea-serpents, naturalists have been far less disposed to be incredulous than the general public. Dr. Andrew Wilson, for instance, after speaking of the recorded observations in such terms as I have used above, says:- 'We may, then, affirm safely that there are many verified pieces of evidence on record of strange marine forms having been met with, which evidences, judged according to ordinary and common sense rules, go to prove that certain undescribed marine organisms do certainly exist in the sea depths.'

As to the support which natural history can give to the above proposition, 'zoologists can but admit,' he proceeds, 'the correctness of the observations. Certain organisms, and especially those of marine kind (e.g. certain whales), are known to be of exceedingly rare occurrence. Our knowledge of marine reptilia is confessedly very small; and best of all, there is no counter-objection or feasible argument which the naturalist can offer by way of denying the above proposition. If, therefore, we admit the possibility that gigantic members of these water snakes may occasionally be developed, we should state a powerful case for the assumed and probable existence of a natural 'sea-serpent.'

We confess we do not well see how such a chain of probabilities can be readily set aside supported as they are in the possibility of their occurrence by zoological science, and in the actual details of the case by evidence as trustworthy in many cases as that received in our courts of law.'

When we remember how few fish or other inhabitants of the sea are ever seen compared with the countless millions which exist, that not one specimen of some tribes will be seen for many years in succession, and that some tribes are only known to exist because a single specimen or even a single skeleton has been obtained, we may well believe that in the sea, as in heaven and earth, there are more things 'than are known in our philosophy.' (*The Inquirer and Commercial News* [Perth, Western Australia], 18 April 1877)

Natural History, *The Zoologist* and Sea Monsters

Explorers, adventurers and missionaries, as well as all stripes of dilettante and science-seasoned natural historians, have poked their questing minds into the world of animals, plants and the planet's other natural marvels since ancient times. *Blackwood's Edinburgh Magazine*'s 'On the history of the great sea serpent', from April 1818 observed: 'According to the old histories, it is a strange and terrible sea monster, which greatly deserves to be taken notice of by those who are curious to look into the extraordinary works of nature.'

Amongst which, in the previous number of the magazine, was included the kraken. In the eighteenth century sea monsters, but principally the sea serpent, became a great focus of interest in publications that were 'curious to look into the extraordinary works of nature'. By the beginning of the Victorian age, from, say, the 1840s, forensic inquiry into the nature, and even existence, of sea monsters was already a well-established field of endeavour (and sceptical cynicism), increasingly for popular consumption by the educated classes.

One of the many journals and magazines that emerged to publish both learned and popular articles and news about the natural world was *The Zoologist* – 'A Popular Miscellany of Natural History'. It was founded in 1843 by Edward Newman (1801–76), an entomologist, botanist, writer and quite illustrious editor of the journal for over thirty years until shortly before, as his fulsome *Zoologist* obituary phrased it, he was 'at length called away to his eternal rest' on 12 June 1876.

Newman's *Zoologist* included, numerously, accounts of sea serpents. His own view on the creature's acceptability within the pages of his 'popular miscellany' was unequivocal: it (and he) would be a 'public advocate' for the factual evidence of its existence, for which he was very happy to publish accounts of its appearances recorded as *'fact'*.

The Great Sea Serpent

It has been the fashion for so many years to deride all records of this very celebrated monster, that it is not without hesitation I venture to quote the following paragraphs in his defence ... Naturalists, or rather those who choose thus to designate themselves, set up an authority above that of fact and observation, the gist of their enquiries is whether such things ought to be, and whether such things ought not to be; now fact-naturalists take a different road to knowledge, they inquire whether such things are, and, whether such things are not. The 'Zoologist,' if not in itself the fountain-head of this fact movement, may at least claim to be the only public advocate of that movement; and it is therefore most desirable, that it should call the attention of its readers to the following remarkable paragraphs. (*The Zoologist*, 1847)

Thus began a long and varied career of sea serpent appearances on the stage of *The Zoologist*, always to the tune of Newman's *'fact'* and in the public interest that he advocated. In the 1848 journal alone – a year of most intense sea serpent accounts – Newman dedicated eighteen consecutive pages (pp. 2306–24) to the subject, much of it centred around HMS *Daedalus*'s encounter (more of which soon).

After Newman *The Zoologist* became increasingly less obliging to utterances on sea serpents and monstrous claims of their kith or kin. Under the guidance of William Lucas Distant (1845–1922), who was editor from 1897 till 1916 when the journal was amalgamated with *British Birds*, the *'fact'* of the sea serpent had assumed a more ambiguous notation. In a book review of Surgeon-General Sir Joseph Fayrer's *Recollections of my Life*, in the July 1900 issue of the journal, the reviewer noted:

The myth [*sic*] of the great Sea-serpent is again before us. The author had corresponded with Lieutenant Forsyth, of H.M.S. *Osborne*, relative to 'a marine creature seen by the officers of the ship not far from Sicily.' Sir Joseph is of opinion that 'it can hardly be doubted that the numerous reports that we have had from time to time, though many of them perhaps are not very well authenticated, are sufficient to show that some undescribed gigantic ophidian or sea creature still remains to be identified.'

Notwithstanding the reviewer's scepticism, Sir Joseph certainly seemed convinced that a sea serpent – 'some undescribed gigantic ophidian [i.e. snake-like] or sea creature' – was a legitimate subject for inquiring minds to ponder. It most certainly had a long and diverse run with *The Zoologist*'s readers. '*Fact.*'

Long before *The Zoologist*'s (and Newman's mission) to present the 'fact' of mysterious 'sea monsters' akin to 'undescribed gigantic ophidians', an occurrence off

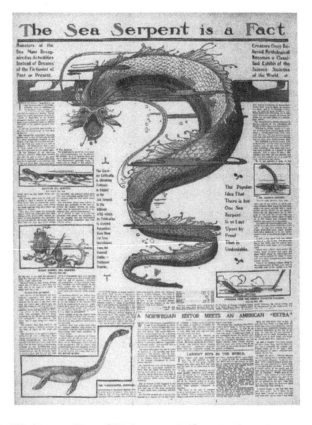

(The Washington Times [Washington, DC], 24 April 1904)

Greenland in the eighteenth century protagonised virtually all sea monster narratives.

Hans Egede's Greenland 'Sea Monster'

Born in Denmark, Hans Egede (1686–1758) 'was educated for the Christian ministry, and became pastor to a congregation at Vogen, in Norway'. Early in his pastoral vocation he became interested in the fate of old Norse settlers in Greenland, led by Erik Rufus ('Erik the Red', our frozen-heroic *Eirik Rauð* from earlier) in the late tenth century, of whom 'no intelligence had been received for several centuries'. He conceived of a Christian mission to Greenland 'to discover the old Norwegian settlements [there], or to form a new one, and to devote his life to the instruction of the barbarous and uncivilized Greenlanders in the salutary truths of the Christian doctrine'.

Egede eventually persuaded 'some merchants and others' to finance the cost of a ship to take him and his family to Greenland for Egede 'to lay the foundation of the meditated establishment' – namely, a Lutheran Christian mission. Egede himself established the Bergen Greenland Company with the capital he raised, to set up a colony on the west Greenland coast, with broad administrative and juridical powers. In the spring of 1721 King Frederick IV of Denmark appointed Egede 'to be pastor of the new colony, and missionary to the Heathen' there.

On 12 May 1721 he and his wife Gertrude, thirteen years older than Hans (whom he had married in 1707), and their four children embarked on the ship *Haabet* ('Hope') to make the voyage to Greenland along with two other vessels with forty other colonisers. On 3 July they arrived on the west Greenland coast at Ball's River, 'in the 64th degree of North latitude', where he established the new colony (Haabets Colonie – 'Hope Colony') and 'gradually introduced some additional rays of intellectual light' into the minds of the 'natives'.

In 1735 Egede's wife died from an epidemic of smallpox that had ravaged the local Inuit population. In 1736 he returned to Copenhagen with his wife's body, to bury her, having left the Greenland mission-colony in the care of his son Paul. He died at the age of 72 at Falster, Denmark, on 5 November 1758.

Hans Egede earned virtual sainthood in Greenland, and later honours in his native Denmark. In the sea serpent pantheon of patriarchs, though, he has been remembered uniquely for his description and the related illustration of the sea monster he espied 'On the 6th of July, 1734, when off the south coast of Greenland ... whose head, when raised, was on a level with our main-top.'

Hans Egede's Sea Serpent Sighting. (*Illustrated London News*, 28 October 1848)

... Long before the great Sea-Serpent was suspected of being a visitor of the British Isles, or of the New World, it was regarded as a well-known member of the Fauna of Scandinavia. Thus, Hans (afterwards Bishop) Egede, in 'A Full and Particular Relation (Narrative) of his Voyage to Greenland, as a Missionary, in the year 1734,' published in Danish, at Copenhagen, 1740, records:-

'On the 6th of July, 1734, when off the south coast of Greenland, a sea monster appeared to us, whose head, when raised, was on a level with our main-top. Its snout was long and sharp, and it blew water almost like a whale; it had large broad paws (the Danish word is *'laller,'* which signifies something between paws and fins; a seal's flappers are called *'lallen.'*); its body was covered with shell-fish, or scales (the Danish word used here signifies either); its skin was rough and uneven; in other respects it was as a serpent; and when it dived, its tail, which was raised in the air, appeared to be a whole ship's length from its body.' (*The Illustrated London News*, 28 October 1848)

Norwegian 'Convolutions'

Back to latter-day Norway and another attestation to the credibility of sea serpents thereabouts. A letter dated 25 October 1848, 'from a gentleman long resident in Norway', J.D. Morries Stirling, noted that his friend 'the late Dr. Newmann, Bishop of Bergen – a man much and justly respected for his learning, research, and energy – made it [i.e. the existence of sea serpents] the subject of enquiry within the last twenty or twenty-five years among his clergy and those of the adjoining dioceses'. The 'testimony of known and respectable persons in various walks of life', most particularly by local fishermen, was strong evidence for the beast's probable existence.

Mr Morris included a 'hurried statement' of his own testimony 'as to the existence of a large fish or reptile of cylindrical form (I will not say Sea-Serpent)':

Three years ago, while becalmed in a yacht between Bergen and Sogn, in Norway, I saw (at about a quarter of a mile astern) what appeared to be a large fish ruffling the otherwise smooth surface of the Fjord, and, on looking attentively, I observed what looked like the convolutions of a snake. I immediately got my glass, and distinctly made out three convolutions, which drew themselves slowly through the water; the greatest diameter was about ten or twelve inches. No head was visible, and from the size of each convolution I supposed the length to be about thirty feet. The master of my yacht (who, as navigator, seaman, and fisherman, had known the Norwegian coast and North Sea for many years), as well as a friend who was with me, an experienced Norwegian sportsman and porpoise shooter, saw the same appearance at the same time, and formed the same opinion as to form and size. I mention the fact of my friend being a porpoise shooter, as many have believed that a shoal of porpoises following each other has given rise to the fable, as they called it, of the Sea-Serpent.

I remain, my dear sir, faithfully yours, J.D. Morries Stirling (*The Illustrated London News*, 28 October 1848)

Minister Maclean's Encounter in the Western Isles of Scotland

In June of 1808 Donald Maclean, the minister of a parish on the island of Eigg, in the Hebridean Western Isles off the Scottish mainland, chanced upon, as *The Illustrated London News* of 28 October 1848 called it, 'a great animal which excited considerable astonishment and alarm among the Western Isles of Scotland'. His 'unvarnished account' is memorialised in a letter he wrote to the Wernerian Natural History Society, an offshoot of the Royal Society of Edinburgh. The society was established in January 1808 to present and hear lectures and readings by learned individuals on diverse subjects of natural history. Mr Maclean 'dates his letter from the Hebrides; and it is truly amusing to see how the simple pastor allows his terror to appear in every sentence'. (From *The Monsters of the Deep: And Curiosities of Ocean Life* (1875), by French anthropologist Armand Landrin (1844–1912))

Letter from the Reverend Mr. Maclean of Small Isles [group of islands of the Inner Hebrides]

To the Secretary of the Wernerian Natural History Society Eigg Island, 24th April 1809

Sir: ... According to my best recollection, I saw it in June 1808, not on the coast of Eigg, but on that of Coll [a nearby island]. Rowing along that coast, I observed, at about the distance of half a mile, an object to windward, which gradually excited astonishment. At first view, it appeared like a small rock. Knowing there was no rock in that situation, I fixed my eyes on it close. Then I saw it elevated considerably above the level of the sea, and after a slow movement, distinctly perceived one of its eyes.

Alarmed at the unusual appearance and magnitude of the animal, I steered so as to be at no great distance from the shore. When nearly in a line betwixt it and the shore, the monster directing its head (which still continued above water) towards us, plunged violently under water. Certain that he was in chace of us, we plied hard to get ashore. Just as we leaped out on a rock, taking a station as high as we conveniently could, we saw it coming rapidly under water towards the stern of our boat. When within a few yards of the boat, finding the water shallow, it raised its monstrous head above water, and, by a winding course, got, with apparent difficulty, clear of the creek where our boat lay, and where the monster seemed in danger of being imbayed. It continued to move off, with its head above water, and with the wind, for about half a mile, before we lost sight of it.

Its head was rather broad, of a form somewhat oval. Its neck somewhat smaller. Its shoulders, if I can so term them, considerably broader, and thence it tapered towards the tail, which last it kept pretty low in the water, so that a view of it could not be taken so distinctly as I wished. It had no fin that I could perceive, and seemed to me to move progressively by undulation up and down. Its length I believed to be from 70 to 80 feet.

When nearest to me, it did not raise its head wholly above water, so that the neck being under water, I could perceive no shining filaments thereon, if it had any. Its progressive motion under water I took to be rapid, from the shortness of the time it took to come up to the boat. When the head was above water, its motion was not near so quick; and when the head was most elevated, it appeared evidently to take a view of distant objects.

About the time I saw it, it was seen about the island of Canna. The crews of thirteen fishing-boats, I am told, were so much terrified at its appearance, that they in a body fled from it to the nearest creek for safety. On the passage from Rum to Canna, the crew of one boat saw it coming towards them, with the wind, and its head high above water. One of the crew pronounced its head as large as a little boat, and each of its eyes as large as a plate. The men were much terrified, but the monster offered them no molestation. From those who saw it, I could get no interesting particulars additional to those above mentioned.

I remain, Sir, &c. – Donald Maclean. (*Memoirs of the Wernerian Natural History Society*, Vol. I, *For the years 1808,–9,–10*; Edinburgh, 1811)

The Dutch zoologist Antoon Cornelis Oudemans (1858-1943), in his encyclopedic compendium and critique of sea serpent sightings, *The Great Sea Serpent* (1892), suggested a reproductive impulse that might have driven the Maclean monster's dash for the reverend's boat: it confirmed Oudemans's 'supposition ... that the animal is sometimes very inquisitive. Pontoppidan would say "it thought to see the other sex, for it was pairing time!"' A sort of Siren sea serpent, then.

An Aberdonian Sea Monster

On the other side of Scotland, off Aberdeen, a 'terrible story' in January 1901 narrated the incident of a steam trawler apparently pursued by 'a very large animal of a dark colour' – a 'monster' – which caused 'utmost consternation amongst the crew'.

Chased by a Sea Serpent

A terrible story is told by the captain and crew of the steam trawler *Craig-Gowan*, of Aberdeen, which arrived in Fraserburgh lately, storm-bound. Having heard that the crew of the *Craig-Gowan* had seen some strange animal when a mile or so north of Rattray Head [just south-east of Fraserburgh], a correspondent of the *Aberdeen Journal* waited upon them and had an interview with the skipper, Captain J. Ballard.

'We left Aberdeen at 12 noon, and all went well, until off Rattray Head, when the wind freshened almost into a gale, and the sea rose very rapidly. We were steaming 10 knots when the gale burst. At this time we noticed a smack some distance off seaward. She had the smallest bit of sail set, and was heading southward. I went below for something, and had been down but a few minutes when J. Watt, chief engineer, called me up, saying that a whale or some extraordinarily large animal had been following in our wake.

'On reaching the deck I found several of the crew looking over the weather rail. On joining them I saw, greatly to my surprise, a very large animal of a dark colour, which seemed racing with us, but which was about 50 ft. to windward. I had often seen whales, but at once saw the animal was not a whale, but some sea monster, the like of which I had never seen in my life.

'As it rose several portions of its body were visible at one time. It seemed to make its way through the water, showing repeated portions of a dark brown body. The men seemed to be very much struck by its strange appearance, and I suggested to try some plan to get rid of it, but no one seemed to grasp any plan likely to affect so huge an animal. We had left our deck hose at Aberdeen, but

I asked Mr. Watt and his assistant, Dallas, to bring up a furnace rake. The animal was now uncomfortably near. We could even see that the skin was covered by some substance like a rough coating of hair.

'Securing the furnace rake to a stout line, I threw it at the animal, but it fell short. I again tried; this time the rake landed across the animal's back, and we suddenly drew the line.

'Judge of our surprise and alarm when the monster raised its body (the fore part) clean out of the water, and made direct for the *Craig-Gowan*. Everybody rushed aft, some down the companion way, and some down the engine room stairs. I stood almost petrified with the sudden development of affairs. I plainly saw the monster rise up until its head was over our gaff peak, when it lowered itself with a motion as sudden as lightning, carrying away the peak halyards, and sending the gaff, sail and all, down on deck.

'The utmost consternation amongst the crew now ensued, and it was a time before we got matters squared up. The animal had then entirely disappeared, and we did not see it again. We held on for Fraserburgh, where we arrived at 6 p.m., and, being afraid that our story would be discredited, we said nothing of it: at least, as little as possible, until this account, which is a true one, was given as stated.'

Captain Ballard describes this experience as being one of the strangest in his lifetime, and says he would not again like to undergo another quarter of an hour's terror like that gone through for any money. The animal's head, he added, was long and flat, and he distinctly saw its eyes, and also saw its mouth open.

'Its body was long, and of a round shape on back, and flat below. Several large fin-like flippers played about rapidly, the sound of their flapping against the body being quite audible as it rose up out of the sea. It must have been of a great length; how long I cannot hazard an opinion.' (*Otago Daily Times* [New Zealand], 19 January 1901)

A Loch-Monster (... but not 'Nessie')

In September 1893 a certain Dr Farquhar Matheson, 'of London', was 'spending some time at his home in the north-west of Scotland'. One day he and his wife were 'enjoying a sail ... on Loch Alsh, [a sea inlet] which separates the Island of Skye from the mainland'. In the early afternoon they saw a 'sea-monster' that Dr Matheson 'described shortly afterwards to several gentlemen' who 'laughed at him at first, because it is so usual to laugh at sea-serpent stories'. The ridicule 'made him decide to say very little about the matter' for two years. He then, however, in 1895, consented to *The Strand Magazine* recording publicly 'for the first time' the circumstances and nature of what he and his wife saw on the loch that fine and clear late summer Scottish Highlands day (a fairly unusual circumstance in itself!). It published Dr Matheson's narrative in its August 1895 issue.

> Dr. Matheson is a trained observer, and one of the men least likely to be the subject of an illusion. What he saw he described shortly afterwards to two gentlemen ... [and] his interesting experience is here for the first time put on record. The occurrence took place in September, 1893, while Dr. Matheson was spending some time at his home in the north-west of Scotland. He was at the time enjoying a sail with his wife on Loch Alsh ...
>
> 'It was a beautiful day,' said Dr. Matheson, 'clear as possible, the sun shining brightly, and without clouds. The

time was between one and two. Our sail was up and we were going gaily along, when suddenly I saw something rise out of the Loch in front of us – a long, straight, neck-like thing as tall as my mast. I could not think what it was at first. I fancied it might be something on land, and directed my wife's attention to it. I said, "Do you see that?" She said she did, and asked what it could be, and was rather scared. It was then 200yds. away and was moving towards us.

'Then it began to draw its neck down, and I saw clearly that it was a large sea-monster – of the saurian [i.e. lizard-like] type, I should think. It was brown in colour, shining, and with a sort of ruffle at the junction of the head and neck. I can think of nothing to which to compare it so well as the head and neck of the giraffe, only the neck was much longer, and the head was not set upon the neck like that of a giraffe; that is, it was not so much at right angles to it as a continuation of it in the same line. It moved its head from side to side, and I saw the reflection of the light from its wet skin.'

Asked if the creature appeared to have scales, Dr. Matheson said he should judge not. It showed a perfectly smooth surface. He went on to say that it was in sight about two minutes and then disappeared. Then it rose again three different times, at intervals of two or three minutes. It stood perpendicularly out of the water, and seemed to look round.

'When it appeared the second time,' said Dr. Matheson, 'it was going from us, and was travelling at a great rate. It was going in the direction of the northern outlet of the Loch, and we were sailing in its wake; I was interested, and followed it. From its first to its last appearance we travelled a mile, and the last time we saw it it was about a mile away.'

As to the body of the monster, Dr. Matheson said, 'I saw no body – only a ripple of the water where the line of the body should be. I should judge, however, that there must have been a large base of body to support such a neck. It was not a sea-serpent, but a much larger and more substantial beast – something of the nature of a gigantic lizard, I should think. An eel could not lift up its body like that, nor could a snake.'

As to the possibility of his being the subject of an optical illusion, Dr. Matheson said, 'This is a common theory. But what I saw precludes all possibility of such an explanation. In the case of an optical illusion, what the eye sees becomes attenuated, and thus gradually disappears. But in the case of the creature I saw, it slowly descended into the water; it reappeared the same way, gradually ascending. I saw it move its head from side to side, and I noticed the glistening of the light on its smooth, wet skin.'

The doctor added, 'In the evening at dinner I described to some gentlemen who were present, Sir James Farrar amongst the number, what I had seen. As I said, they laughed at the story at first, and suggested various ways in which I might have been deceived; but when I showed them that none of their theories would fit the case, they admitted that the sea-serpent, or sea monster, could not be altogether a myth.' ('The Sea-Serpent', by Alfred T. Story, *The Strand Magazine*, August 1895)

Our Scots sea serpent spotter Dr Farquhar Matheson was born in 1840 in the small village of Dornie, just to the east of Loch Alsh. Having studied medicine at Glasgow and Aberdeen universities, 'he moved to London, specialising in ear, nose and throat diseases and rising to eminence in this field', becoming 'one of the best known and most influential Scots in London in the late 1890s'. By 1896 (the year after the *Strand* article), Dr Matheson was president of the Gaelic Society of London, as well as being 'a Fellow of several scientific societies'.

So, a man of science and reason, weaned on the enlightened empiricism of Hume and Locke, not a man to be pish-poshed about claims of spurious observational skills for the 'saurian' serpent he saw that September afternoon on the waters near his Highlands home. Dr Matheson died in London on 23 August 1905 and was buried at Kirkton graveyard, near Balmacara on the shores of Loch Alsh.

An Irish Visitor: The Kilkee 'Sea Monster'

In October 1871 the sea serpent made a singular visit to the Emerald Isle, turning up near the small coastal village of Kilkee, Co. Clare, on the west coast of Ireland. A group of 'several ladies and some gentlemen', including a 'well-known clergyman' from the north of Ireland (well before the division

Startling appearance of a monster sea-serpent off Kilkee on the Irish coast (From a Sketch by an Eye-witness). (*The Days' Doings*, 21 October 1871)

of the island into Northern Ireland and the Republic in the south), were admiring the Atlantic ground-swell crashing onto the rocks when, suddenly, 'their attention was arrested by the appearance of an extraordinary monster'. The incident was reported in a tabloid-style newspaper of the day, *The Days' Doings*, complete with a fairly sensational illustration of the 'monster' and the ladies' and gentlemen's alarm at it.

A Monster Sea-Serpent Off the Irish Coast

There has been some excitement in Kilkee at the appearance, the other day, of an extraordinary marine visitor, who, from all accounts, seems to belong to the genus of the 'great unknown,' whose existence has been for the last two hundred years a point of dispute among the most learned naturalists in every country. A party of strangers staying at Kilkee, composed of several ladies and some gentlemen – one of whom is a well-known clergyman in the north of Ireland – went down to see, among other points of interest, a place known as the 'Diamond Rocks,' and remained there for some time watching the heavy ground-swell from the Atlantic which came dashing in with tremendous force against the cliffs.

The clergyman aforementioned ... states that, all of a sudden, their attention was arrested by the appearance of an extraordinary monster who rose from the surface of the water about seventy yards from the place where they were standing. It had an enormous head, shaped somewhat like a horse, while behind the head and on the neck was a huge mane of seaweed-looking hair which rose and fell with the motion of the water; the eyes were large and glaring, and, by the appearance of the water behind, a vast body seemed to be beneath the waves.

As the creature was coming towards our informant, he was unable to judge of its length with the same accuracy as if it had been proceeding in a parallel direction; but all agreed that it was the most gigantic creature they had ever seen. One of the ladies nearly fainted at the sight, and all had their nerves considerably upset by the dreadful appearance of this extraordinary creature. Its movements were apparently feeble, and gave the idea of exhaustion as it slowly rose to the top of each succeeding wave, raising its huge head above the surface as it did so, and then as slowly sank into the trough between the waves.

The whole appearance lasted for some minutes, till at length the creature sank, in the sight of all, about a gunshot from the shore, and vanished in the same mysterious way that it had come … This is the first time, we believe, that one of these strange sea-monsters has been seen on the coasts of the British Isles, and much excitement has been caused by its appearance in this particular neighbourhood. (*The Days' Doings*, 21 October 1871)

It certainly wasn't, of course, 'the first time that one of these strange sea-monsters has been seen on the coasts of the British Isles', but it probably was the first time such a *frightful-looking* live sea monster-creature had been portrayed in 'a Sketch by an Eye-witness'.

Transatlantic Apparitions

A number of other sightings recorded by correspondents in the local and scientific press described 'sea monsters' or 'serpents' as far afield as Nova Scotia and the Gulf of

Mexico, and the Atlantic Ocean in between. An open-ocean sighting was logged by a vessel in 1786:

> Lastly, to the *Zoologist* for November, 1847, a correspondent communicated 'an extract from the log-book of a very near relative, dated August 1, 1786, on board the ship *General Coole*, in lat. 42° 44' N., and long. 23° 10' W [just north-east of the Azores]. 'A very large snake passed the ship; it appeared to be about 16 or 18 feet in length, and 3 or four feet in circumference, the back of a light ash colour, and the belly thereof yellow.' According to the log, the ship was becalmed at the time. You may rely on the correctness of this (says the writer); and anyone desirous of satisfying himself may see the original log. – S.H. Saxby, *Banchurch, Isle of Wight*, Sept. 8, 1847.' (*The Illustrated London News*, 28 October 1848)

HMS *Daedalus* (and Others) and 'The Great Sea-Serpent'

One of the watershed events in sea serpent chronicles concerned a British navy vessel's sighting of the creature in the South Atlantic in 1848 that attracted reams of speculation about it and related other encounters. That year, two ships came across a 'great sea-serpent' in the South Atlantic off the coast of Africa, separated in time by six weeks and in distance by about 1,000 miles. The first, and most renowned, was by the British navy's HMS *Daedalus*, about 350 miles off the coast of what is now Namibia, on 6 August. Later, on 20 September, an American brig, the *Daphne*, reported sighting the creature close to the Congolese coast further north. Considering that the two sightings were forty-four days and about 1,000 miles apart, the 'enormous serpent' would have to have covered just about 23 miles a day from the *Daedalus*'s position to the *Daphne*'s – if it was the same beast – a not particularly arduous cruising speed of about 1 knot or so.

The Great Sea-Serpent

'Strange things come up to look at us –
The masters of the deep' – Song, *'The Return of the Admiral'*

A new attestation of the existence of the Great Sea-Serpent has just been placed upon official record, and has very naturally resuscitated the interest attached to this much vexed question. We purpose, therefore, to present to our readers this testimony in the documentary form and order in which it originally appeared; and it will next be shown that the first report has already received some corroboration, and has called forth some unpublished evidence upon the subject.

The first intelligence of this new evidence appeared in the *Times* of the 10th inst., in a communication from Plymouth, dated Oct. 7, as follows:-

'When the *Daedalus* frigate, Captain McQuhae, which arrived here on the 4th inst., was on her passage home from the East Indies, between the Cape of Good Hope and St. Helena, her captain, and most of her officers and crew, at four o'clock one afternoon, saw a Sea-Serpent. The creature was twenty minutes in sight of the frigate, and passed under her quarter. Its head appeared to be about four feet out of the water, and there was about sixty feet of its body in a straight line on the surface. It is calculated that there must have been under water a length of thirty or forty feet more, by which it propelled itself at the rate of fifteen miles per hour.

The diameter of the exposed part of the body was about sixteen inches; and when it extended its jaws, which were full of large jagged teeth, they seemed sufficiently capacious to admit of a tall man standing upright between them. The ship was sailing north at the rate of eight miles an hour. The *Daedalus* left the Cape of Good Hope on the 30th of July, and reached St. Helena on the 16th of August.'

Capt. McQuhae's Corroboration

'Her Majesty's ship *Daedalus*, Hamoaze [estuary by Royal Navy base at Devonport], Oct. 11.

'Sir, – In reply to your letter of this day's date, requiring information as to the truth of a statement published in the *Times* newspaper, of a Sea-Serpent of extraordinary dimensions having been seen from her Majesty's ship *Daedalus*, under my command, on her passage from the East Indies, I have the honour to acquaint you, for the information of my Lords Commissioners of the Admiralty, that at 5 o'clock P.M., on the 6th of August last, in latitude 24° 44'S., and longitude 9° 22'E. [about 350 miles off the Namibian coast], the weather dark and cloudy, wind fresh from the N.W., with a long ocean swell from the S.W., the ship on the port tack heading N.E. by N., something very unusual was seen by Mr. Sartoris, midshipman, rapidly approaching the ship from before the beam. The circumstance was immediately reported by him to the officer of the watch, Lieutenant Edgar Drummond, with whom and Mr. William Barrett, the Master, I was at the time walking the quarter-deck. The ship's company were at supper.

'On our attention being called to the object, it was discovered to be an enormous Serpent, with head and shoulders kept about four feet constantly above the surface of the sea; and as nearly as we could approximate by comparing it with the length of what our maintopsail-yard would show in the water, there was at the very least sixty feet of the animal *à fleur d'eau* [i.e. on the surface], no portion of which was, to our perception, used in propelling it through the water, either by vertical or horizontal undulation. It passed rapidly, but so close under our lee quarter that had it been a man of my acquaintance I should have easily recognised his features with the naked eye; and it did not, either in approaching the ship or after it had passed our wake, deviate in the slightest degree from its course to the S.W., which it held on at the pace of from 12 to 15 miles per hour, apparently on some determined purpose.

'The diameter of the Serpent was about 15 or 16 inches behind the head, which was, without any doubt, that of a snake; and it was never, during the 20 minutes that it continued in the sight of our glasses [binoculars], once below the surface of the water – its colour a dark brown, with yellowish-white about the throat. It had no fins, but something like the mane of a horse, or rather a bunch of seaweed, washed about its back. It was seen by the quartermaster, the boatswain's mate, and the man at the wheel, in addition to myself and officers above mentioned.

'I am having a drawing of the Serpent made from a sketch taken immediately after it was seen, which I hope to have ready for transmission to my Lords Commissioners of the Admiralty by tomorrow's post. – I have, &c.,

'Peter McQuhae, Captain.'

'To Admiral Sir W.H. Gage, G.C.H., Devonport.'
The drawing above-named has been received by the Lords Commissioners of the Admiralty, and, by the courtesy of Captain McQuhae, our Artist has been permitted to copy this pictorial evidence, as well as further

The Sea-Serpent When First Seen from H.M.S. *Daedalus* (*The Illustrated London News*, 28 October 1848)

The Sea-Serpent Passing Under the Stern of the *Daedalus* (*The Illustrated London News*, 28 October 1848)

to illustrate the appearance of the Serpent, under the
supervision of Captain McQuhae, and with his approval
of the authenticity of their details as to position and form.
(*The Illustrated London News*, 28 October 1848)

The report of the *Daedalus* sea serpent was a lodestar against
which numerous other sightings were compared for both
authenticity and corroboration, and by discourse and dis-
sent. One of the most vocal dissenters was Sir Richard
Owen (1804–92), an eminent pioneering paleontologist (he
coined the term 'dinosaur' in 1841), biologist and comparative anatomist in the Victorian era, who weighed in against
McQuhae's sighting in a lengthy letter to *The Times*, dated
9 November 1848 (it ran over four pages, 2312–16, in the
1848 *Zoologist*). Owen knocked out all suggestion that the
Daedalus 'animal', as he insisted on calling it, was a 'sea
serpent'. Having rather looked down his nose (with forensic qualifications) at Capt. McQuhae's insistence on a 'sea
serpent', his conclusion was: 'Guided by the above interpretation of the "mane of a horse, or a bunch of sea-weed," the
animal was not a cetaceous mammal, but rather a great seal.'

And, he specified, most likely 'Anson's sea-lion, or
that known to the southern whalers by the name of "sea-
elephant," ... which attains the length of from 20 to 30 feet'. To
which Capt. McQuhae made an indignant rebuttal in *The Times*
of 21 November 1848 (reproduced in *The Zoologist* of 1848). So
continued the back-and-forth sparring on the great Victorian
debate of the great sea serpent versus other 'sea saurians',
ophidians, plesiosaurs, ichthyosaurs, great seals, great seaweed
and other mysterious and eclectic *objets du mer*, great or otherwise (eighteen consecutive pages in the 1848 *Zoologist* alone).

The next communication is the following letter, addressed,
within the previous ten days, to the editor of the *Globe*:-

'Mary Ann of Glasgow, Glasgow, Oct. 19, 1848

'Sir. – I have just reached this port, on a voyage from Malta to Lisbon; and my attention having been called to a report relative to an animal seen by the master and crew of her Majesty's ship *Daedalus*, I take the liberty of communicating the following circumstance:-

'When clearing out of the port of Lisbon, upon the 30th of September last, we spoke the American brig *Daphne*, of Boston, Mark Trelawny master; she signalled for us to heave to, which we did, and standing close round her counter lay to while the mate boarded us with the jolly-boat, and handed a packet of letters, to be despatched per first steamer for Boston on our arrival in England. The mate told me that when in lat. 4° 11'S., lon. 10° 15'E. [just off the Congo coast], wind dead north, upon the 20th of September, a most extraordinary animal had been seen – from his description, it had the appearance of a huge serpent or snake, with a dragon's head.

'Immediately upon its being seen, one of the deck guns was brought to bear upon it, which, having been charged with spike-nails and whatever other pieces of iron could be got at the moment, was discharged at the animal, then only distant about forty yards from the ship. It immediately reared its head in the air, and plunged violently with its body, showing evidently that the charge had taken effect. The *Daphne* was to leeward at the time, but was put about on the starboard tack, and stood towards the brute, which was seen foaming and lashing the water at a fearful rate.

'Upon the brig nearing, however, it disappeared, and, though evidently wounded, made rapidly off at the rate of fifteen or sixteen knots an hour, as was judged from its appearing several times on the surface. The *Daphne* pursued for some time; but the night coming on, the master was obliged to put about and continue his voyage.

'From the description given by the mate, the brute must have been nearly 100 feet long, and his account of it agrees in every respect with that lately forwarded to the Admiralty by the master of the *Daedalus*. The packet of letters to Boston I have no doubt contains the full particulars, which I suppose will be made public. There are letters from Captain Trelawny to a friend in Liverpool, which will probably contain some further particulars, and I have written to get a copy, for the purpose of getting the full account.

'I have the honour to be, Sir, your most obedient servant,

'James Henderson, Master – Broomielaw [River Clyde, Glasgow], Berth No. 4.' (*The Illustrated London News*, 28 October 1848)

The *Royal Saxon*

The *Daedalus* sighting 'elicited another sea-serpent story which appeared in the *Bombay Bi-monthly Times* for January 1849' (from Charles Gould's *Mythical Monsters*, 1886), in the form of a report by a gentleman named and titled 'R. Davidson, Superintending Surgeon, Nagpore Subsidiary Force', whose correspondence was dated 'Kamptu, [Kamptee, in the Nagpur district of Maharashtra state, India], 3rd January 1849'.

I see, in your paper of the 30th of December [1848], a paragraph in which doubt is expressed of the authenticity of the account given by Captain M'Quhæ of the great 'sea-serpent.' When returning to India, in the year 1829, I was standing on the poop [deck] of the Royal Saxon, in conversation with Captain Petrie, the commander of that ship. We were at a considerable distance south-west of the Cape of Good Hope, in the usual track of vessels to this country, going rapidly along (seven or eight knots) in fine smooth water. It was in the middle of the day, and the other passengers were at luncheon, the man at the wheel, a steerage passenger, and ourselves being the only persons on the poop.

Captain Petrie and myself, at the same instant, were literally fixed in astonishment by the appearance, a short distance ahead, of an animal of which no more generally correct description could be given than that by Captain M'Quhæ. It passed within thirty-five yards of the ship without altering its course in the least; but as it came right abreast of us, it slowly turned its head towards us. Apparently about one-third of the upper part of its body was above water, in nearly its whole length; and we could see the water curling up on its breast as it moved along, but by what means it moved we could not perceive ...

The *Royal Saxon* observers estimated the length of the creature by comparing it, when alongside, with the length of the vessel which was stated in all reports as 'about six hundred feet'. This was wrong: one of the biggest deep-sea sailing ships ever built, the *Great Republic*, launched in 1853, was 4,550 tons and only 334ft long. A Canadian-built *Royal Saxon* around that time was 1,100 tons and 180ft-long. This *Royal Saxon* was just 510 tons; it was therefore probably only around 100–120ft in length. Whatever it was, the observers concluded about the creature they saw that, 'as well as its other dimensions, [it was] greater than the animal described by Captain M'Quhæ' from the deck of the *Daedalus* – which is to say, roughly in line also with the creature seen by the mate of the *Daphne* off the Congo coast earlier in 1848: 'the brute must have been nearly a hundred feet long'.

The *Castilian*'s Sighting Off St. Helena

In the mid-1800s Capt. George Harrington was commander of the 1,064-ton ship *Castilian* which regularly took emigrants from Liverpool to Australia (or 'the Colonies' of that continent as they were, until federated into the Commonwealth of Australia in January 1901). In December 1857, about 10 miles off the South Atlantic island of St. Helena, 'ship sailing about 12 miles per hour', he and other officers of the watch sighted 'a huge marine animal'. Capt. Harrington was confident that it belonged to the serpent tribe, and therefore was 'glad to confirm' the *Daedalus* sighting in 1848 'as to the existence of such an animal as that described by' the *Daedalus*'s commander Capt. McQuhae, and quite near the *Daedalus*'s position at the time.

Another Peep at the Sea-Serpent

I beg to enclose you a copy of an extract from the meteorological journal kept by me on board the ship *Castilian*, on a voyage from Bombay to Liverpool ... I am glad to confirm a statement made by the Commander of Her Majesty's ship *Dædalus*, some years ago, as to the existence of such an animal as that described by him. – *G.H. Harrington; 14 and 14½, South Castle Street, Liverpool, February 2, 1858.*

'Ship Castilian, Dec. 12, 1857, north-east end of St. Helena, bearing north-west, distance 10 miles.

'At 6 30 p.m., strong breezes and cloudy, ship sailing about 12 miles per hour. While myself and officers were standing on the lee side of the poop, looking towards the island, we were startled by the sight of a huge marine animal which reared its head out of the water within 20 yards of the ship, when it suddenly disappeared for about half a minute and then made its appearance in the same manner again, showing us distinctly its neck and head about 10 or 12 feet out of the water.

'Its head was shaped like a long nun buoy [i.e. conical], and I suppose the diameter to have been seven or eight feet in the largest part, with a kind of scroll, or tuft of loose skin, encircling it about two feet from the top; the water was discoloured for several hundred feet from its head, so much so that on its first appearance my impression was that the ship was in broken [i.e. shoal] water, produced, as I supposed, by some volcanic agency since the last time I passed the island, but the second appearance completely dispelled those fears, and assured us that it was a monster of extraordinary length, which appeared to be moving towards the land.

'The ship was going too fast to enable us to reach the mast-head in time to form a correct estimate of its extreme length, but from what we saw from the deck we conclude that it must have been over 200 feet long. The boatswain and several of the crew who observed it from the topgallant forecastle state that it was more than double the length of the ship, in which case it must have been 500 feet; be that as it may, I am convinced that it belonged to the serpent tribe; it was of a dark colour about the head, and was covered with several white spots.

Having a press of canvass on the ship at the time I was unable to round to without risk, and therefore was precluded from getting another sight of this leviathan of the deep.

'George Henry Harrington, Commander; William Davies, Chief Officer; Edward Wheeler, Second Officer.' (*The Zoologist*, 1858)

Not everyone, however, was quite so convinced that it was truly a 'leviathan of the deep'. At least not a living one of 'the serpent tribe'.

The Sea-Serpent. – In your paper [i.e. *The Times*] of the 5th inst. [i.e. February 1858] is a letter from Captain Harrington, of the ship *Castilian*, stating his belief that he had seen the great sea-serpent near St. Helena. His confidence is strengthened from the fact of something similar having been seen by Her Majesty's ship *Dædalus* near the same position. The following circumstance, which occurred on board the ship *Pekin*, then belonging to Messrs. T. and W. Smith, on her passage from Moulmein [Burma/Myanmar], may be of some service respecting this 'queer fish.'

On December 28th, 1848, being then in lat. 26 S., long. 6 E., nearly calm, ship having only steerage way, saw about half a mile on port beam a very extraordinary-looking thing in the water, of considerable length. With the telescope we could plainly discern a huge head and neck, covered with a long shaggy-looking kind of mane, which it kept lifting at intervals out of the water. This was seen by all hands, and declared to be the great sea-serpent.

I determined on knowing something about it, and accordingly lowered a boat, in which my chief officer and four men went, taking with them a long small line in case it should be required. I watched them very anxiously, and the monster seemed not to regard their approach. At length they got close to the head. They seemed to hesitate, and then busy themselves with the line, the monster all the time ducking its head, and showing its great length. Presently the boat began pulling towards the ship, the monster following slowly.

In about half an hour they got alongside; a tackle was got on the main yard and it was hoisted on board. It appeared somewhat supple when hanging, but so completely covered with snaky-looking barnacles about 18 inches long, that we had it some time on board before it was discovered to be a piece of gigantic sea-weed, 20 feet long and 4 inches diameter, the root end of which appeared when in the water like the head of the animal, and the motion given by the sea caused it to seem alive. In a few days it dried up to a hollow tube, and as it had a rather offensive smell was thrown overboard.

I had only been a short time in England when the *Dædalus* arrived and reported having seen the great sea-serpent, – to the best of my recollection near the same locality, and which I have no doubt was a piece of the same weed. So like a huge living monster did this appear, that had circumstances prevented my sending a boat to it I should certainly have believed I had seen the great sea-snake. – *Frederick Smith; Newcastle-on-Tyne, February 19, 1858.* (From *The Times*, 13 February 1858, republished in *The Zoologist*)

A subsequent series of punches and counter-punches in print succeeded the contentious 'gigantic sea-weed' versus 'great sea-serpent' controversy. Oudemans, in his *The Great*

Sea Serpent, nominated it amongst his twenty-three conjectures for mistaken identities of the sea serpent as:

> The seventeenth explanation …: [that] the sea-serpent is nothing else but a gigantic sea-weed detached from the bottom of the sea.

So, a 'leviathan', apparently, 'of the deep'; just not an actual monster.

Sea Serpent Passed by HMS *Plumper*

Another Royal Navy ship, HMS *Plumper*, did not get quite as much attention as the *Daedalus* for its sea serpent sighting at the end of December 1848 – none at all by Mr Newman in his *Zoologist*! But 'A Naval Officer' finally sent a brief report and a 'rough' sketch of the fore-part of the creature he saw, after he was 'requested by several gentlemen' to do so, to *The Illustrated London News*, where it was reproduced in April 1849.

The Great Sea Serpent

To the Editor of the *Illustrated London News*:

H.M.S. *Plumper*, Portsmouth Harbour, April 10, 1849 – Not having seen a sketch of the extraordinary creature we passed between England and Lisbon, and being requested by several gentlemen to send you the rough one I made at the time, I shall feel much obliged by your giving it publicity in your instructive and amusing columns.

On the morning of the 31st December, 1848, in lat. 41° 13' N., and long. 12° 31' W., being nearly due west of Oporto, I saw a long black creature with a sharp head, moving slowly, I should think about two knots, through the water, in the north-westerly direction, there being a fresh breeze at the time, and some sea on. I could not ascertain its exact length, but its back was about twenty feet if not more above water; and its head, as near as I could judge, from six to eight. I had not time to make a closer observation, as the ship was going six knots through the water, her head E. half S., and wind S.S.E.

The creature moved across our wake towards a merchant barque on our lee-quarter, and on the port tack. I was in hopes she would have seen it also. The officers and men who saw it, and who have served in parts of the world adjacent to whale and seal fisheries, and have seen them in the water, declare they have neither seen nor heard of any creature bearing the slightest resemblance to the one we saw. There was something on its back

Supposed Appearance of the Great Sea-Serpent, from H.M.S. *Plumper*, Sketched by an Officer on Board. (*The Illustrated London News*, 14 April 1849)

that appeared like a mane, and, as it moved through the water, kept washing about; but before I could examine it more closely, it was too far astern. – I remain, yours very truly, A Naval Officer. (*The Illustrated London News*, 14 April 1849)

The *Sacramento*'s Encounter near the Azores

The American ship *Sacramento*, commanded by a certain Capt. Nelson, was on a voyage from New York to Melbourne in July 1877 when the vessel passed (or was passed by) a 'sea monster' or 'great snake' south-west of the Azores. The sketch that accompanied the report was cited by a noted cryptozoologist of the time, Charles Gould (in his *Mythical Monsters*, 1886), as bearing a remarkable resemblance to a large alligator (which it indeed does), 'suggesting that possibly such a creature may have been blown by winds or carried by currents to the position where it was seen'. However, that does beg the question, and stretch the credulity of what a very large alligator (a fresh water animal) found mainly in the southern United States might be doing swimming around the salty North Atlantic.

Another Sea Serpent

The great sea snake has again turned up, having been seen quite distinctly by the captain of the ship *Sacramento*, which arrived [at Melbourne] on 20th Oct. from New York. The following is the extract concerning the sea monster from Captain Nelson's log-book:

'30th July, in [latitude] 31.59 north and [longitude] 37 west [about 500 miles southwest of the Azores].

Was called on deck by the man at the wheel [John Hart], who stated that a great snake was passing a short distance from the vessel. On [my] reaching the deck the monster was plainly visible, moving steadily through the water, propelling itself by two large flippers or fins, situated a short distance behind the head. It was about forty feet long and the girth of a beef barrel, the colour being yellow.

'The man at the wheel states that he distinctly saw the eyes of the animal when he first called the captain, who says that he did not hurry up when he was called, as he did not believe in the existence of such a creature; but when he did get on deck, he saw it clearly enough to be certain that it was a living animal.' (*The Illustrated Australian News* [Melbourne], 31 October 1877)

The Sea Serpent, As Sighted By The Ship Sacramento, From A Sketch By The Man At The Wheel. (*Australasian Sketcher* [Melbourne], 24 November 1877)

The helmsman of the *Sacramento* at the time, seaman John Hart, testified to the accuracy of a sketch of the creature (whether he made the sketch himself, which was very good quality, or it was made by an artist according to Hart's description, is not clear) which appeared on the front page of the *Australasian Sketcher* dated Saturday, 24 November 1877, including his statement of what he saw:

> This is a correct sketch of the serpent seen by me while on board the ship *Sacramento*, on her passage from New York to Melbourne, I being at the wheel at the time. It had the body of a very large snake; its length appeared to me to be about 50ft. or 60ft. Its head was like an alligator's, with a pair of flippers about 10ft. from its head. The colour was of a reddish brown. At the time seen it was lying perfectly still, with its head raised about 3ft. above the surface of the sea, and as it got 30ft. or 40ft. astern it dropped its head. – John Hart.

A Nova Scotian 'Denizen of the Deep'

It took quite a few years before a sea serpent encounter by five Army personnel off the east coast of Nova Scotia, in 1833, came to public attention, in *The Zoologist* of 1847. The men had set off from Halifax for Mahone Bay, 40 miles down the coast, on a fishing trip. Around the half-way mark they were 'favoured with a view of the "true and veritable sea serpent,"' which had previously been 'treated as a tale not much entitled to belief'.

The Sea Serpent

On the 15th of May, 1833, a party, consisting of Captain Sullivan, Lieutenants Maclachlan and Malcolm of the Rifle Brigade, Lieutenant Lyster of the Artillery, and Mr. Ince of the Ordnance, started in Halifax in a small yacht for Mahone Bay, some forty miles to the westward on a fishing excursion. The morning was cloudy, and the wind at S.S.E., and apparently rising; by the time we reached Chebucto Head, as we had taken no pilot with us, we deliberated whether we should proceed or put back, but after a consultation we determined on the former, having lots of ports on our lee.

Previously to leaving town, an old man-of-war's-man we had along with us busied himself in inquiries as to our right course: he was told to take his departure from the Bull Rock off Pennant Point, and that a W.N.W. course would bring us direct on Iron Bound Island at the entrance of Mahone or Mecklenburgh Bay; he, however, unfortunately told us to steer W.S.W., nor corrected his error for five or six hours; consequently we had gone a long distance off the coast.

We had run about half the distance, as we supposed, and were enjoying ourselves on deck smoking our cigars, and getting our tackle ready for the approaching campaign against the salmon, when we were surprised by the sight of an immense shoal of grampuses [probably orcas (killer whales), or possibly Risso's dolphins], which appeared in an unusual state of excitement, and which, in their gambols approached so close to our little craft that some of the party amused themselves by firing at them with rifles; at this time we were jogging on at about five miles an hour, and must have been crossing Margaret's

Bay: I merely conjecture where we were, as we had not seen land since a short time after leaving Pennant Point.

Our attention was presently diverted from the whales and 'such small deer' by an exclamation from Dowling, our man-of-war's-man, who was sitting to leeward, of, 'Oh! Sirs, look here!' We were started into a ready compliance, and saw an object which banished all other thoughts save wonder and surprise.

At the distance of from 150 to 200 yards on our starboard bow we saw the head and neck of some denizen of the deep, precisely like those of a common snake, in the act of swimming, the head so far elevated and thrown forward by the curve of the neck as to enable us to see the water under and beyond it. The creature rapidly passed, leaving a regular wake, from the commencement of which to the fore part, which was out of water, we judged its length to be about eighty feet; and this is within rather than beyond the marks.

We were of course all taken aback at the sight, and with staring eyes and in speechless wonder stood gazing at it for full half a minute; there could be no mistake, no delusion, and we were all perfectly satisfied that we had been favoured with a view of the 'true and veritable sea serpent,' which had been generally considered to have existed only in the brain of some Yankee skipper, and treated as a tale not much entitled to belief.

'The Queerest Thing'

Dowling's exclamation is worthy of record, 'Well, I've sailed in all parts of the world, and have seen rum sights too in my time, but this is the queerest thing I ever see,' – and surely Jack Dowling was right. It is most difficult to give correctly the dimensions of any object in the water. The head of the creature we set down at about six feet in length, and that portion of the neck which we saw, at the same; the extreme length, as before stated, at between eighty and one hundred feet. The neck in thickness equalled the bole of a moderate sized tree. The head and neck of a dark brown or nearly black colour, streaked with white in irregular streaks. I do not recollect seeing any part of the body.

Such is the rough account of the sea serpent, and all the party who saw it are still in the land of the living, – Lyster in England, Malcolm in New South Wales with his regiment, and the remainder still vegetating in Halifax.

W. Sullivan, Captain, Rifle Brigade, June 21st, 1831; A. Maclachlan, Lieutenant, Ditto, August 5th, 1824; G.P. Malcolm, Ensign, Ditto, August 13th, 1830; B. O'Neal, Lyster, Lieutenant, Artillery, June 7th, 1816

Henry Ince, Ordnance Store-keeper at Halifax

[The dates (above) are those on which the gentlemen received their respective commissions; I am not aware of their present rank. I am indebted to Mr. W.H. Ince for this interesting communication: this gentleman received it from his brother, Commander J.M.R. Ince, R.N. It is written by their uncle, Mr. Henry Ince, the Ordnance Store-keeper at Halifax, Nova Scotia.] (*The Zoologist*, 1847, pp. 1714–16)

And Another in the Gulf of Mexico …

A bizarre animal 'of at least 100 metres in length' was reported by the commander of the French ship *Ville de Rochefort*, in the Gulf of Mexico, in 1840. (Oudemans in his *The Great Sea Serpent*, commented: 'The length of at least 100 meters (about 320 feet) is at all events exaggerated.')

What Capt. d'Abnour described was more monstrous than most other sea serpents of the time.

The Sea Serpent

Not long since the *Boston Daily Advertiser* announced a new appearance of this marine monster, about whose existence the world is so naturally incredulous. A French captain has just related to us a remarkable circumstance, which he has himself witnessed, and his recital exhibits a degree of cautious reserve, which is well calculated to shake the obstinacy of the most sceptical. We shall preface his narrative by the remark that the sea serpent has been recently alleged to have been seen at different points along the whole line of the American coast.

Captain D'Abnour, commander of the Ville de Rochefort, makes the following statement:-

'On the 21st of April 1840, while we were in 24 deg. 13 min. N. latitude, and 89 deg. 52 min. W. longitude (calculated from the meridian of Paris [NB: France retained its own prime meridian – 0° longitude – through Paris, for navigation, until 1914 when it conceded to the international standard of the Greenwich prime meridian established in 1884]), in the Gulf of Mexico, we were running under a light breeze from E.N.E. with beautiful weather. In a few hours we distinguished something like a long chain of rocks, falling off by a gentle inclination at the two extremities, and elevated at the middle by only a few feet over the level of the sea. Against this object the sea broke gently.

'As we approached, we remarked [observed] that its different parts changed their position, and even their form, and we became perfectly certain that it was not a reef. A little later, we distinguished by the assistance of a telescope a long chain of enormous rings, resembling a number of barrels linked together, and in form very like the back of a silk-worm. It was a three-quarters view of the object which we had first obtained.

'As the ship approached, these appearances became more distinct, and we presently saw the extremity of an enormous tail, longitudinally divided into two sections, white and black. This tail appeared to wind itself up, and repose on a part of the object itself. Then, at the other extremity, we saw a membrane rising to the height of about two metres from the water, and inclining itself at a considerable angle upon the mass (without leaving it, however); and this led me to the conjecture that the monster before us was provided with an apparatus for the purpose of respiration, like the lampreys. At last we perceived something like an antenna rising from the water, terminated by a crescent of at least five metres from one extremity to the other.

'We could not approach sufficiently near to acquire any very positive idea as to what we had seen; but everything led us to believe that it was an enormous serpent of at least 100 metres in length.' (*The Zoologist*, pp. 1715–16, 1847; translated from the French from the *Journal du Havre*, 15 September 1840)

The *Lorraine*'s Mid-Atlantic Encounter

A 'waterspouting monster' made its appearance to the passengers and crew of a French ship off south-west Ireland in 1904, en route from Le Havre to New York. To all who saw it, it was a 'sea serpent'. To anyone now looking at a large sea creature up to 100ft long, spouting water and with the insouciance of a 'well-tempered old thing', it would pretty universally be called ... a whale.

Summer Sea Serpent Tale Comes to Port – Lorraine*'s Passengers Report Horrible Waterspouting Monster – Colors, Brown, Blue, &c. – Must Have Been a Hundred Feet Long, Says Passenger – Liner's Log Noncommittal*

The French liner *La Lorraine*, in from Havre last night, brought the finest sea serpent story of the decade. It was on Sunday last, according to the passengers, when the great ship was plowing through the water at a twenty-two-knot clip, that the monster was sighted about a mile off the starboard bow. The morning was ideal for sighting strange things at sea, and most of the passengers were on deck looking for them.

The French Line ship *La Lorraine*; postcard sent by a passenger from Le Havre on 27 October 1904, four months after the sighting of a 'sea serpent' en route from Le Havre to New York.

The liner was then in latitude 49.50 north and longitude 17.06 west [about 130 miles south-west of Ireland]. The time was 12:20 A.M. Five minutes later the Lorraine had arrived abreast of the great monster, which was then only about 400 yards away.

When the sea serpent came to the surface, say the passengers, it was accompanied by what looked like a big waterspout, but which, it later transpired, was water cast into the air by the gyrations of the monster's gigantic fins. For at least ten minutes, these same passengers say, the sea serpent remained on the surface, after which he disappeared for probably ten minutes, after which once again he came to the surface, this time remaining in plain view for perhaps a quarter of an hour.

'It was the sight of a lifetime,' said one of the passengers, 'and never again do I expect to see his like. His head was as big as a barrel, and from what I imagine must have been his mouth there spouted into the air a stream of water that looked like the stream that issues from the nozzle of one of New York's water towers. In color he was brown and blue and in some places black. We never saw all of him at the same time, but judged by what we did see I imagine he must have been at least eighty or a hundred feet long, while as for his circumference that would be impossible to compute so tremendously proportioned was he.

'Despite the awful ugliness of his head and body, he nevertheless seemed to be a well-tempered old thing, and at no time did he evince the slightest interest in the great ship that was speeding past him.

'I never believed in sea serpents before, but now I know that such monsters do live, and I am firmly convinced that I have looked upon the king of the whole pack.' (*The New York Times*, 2 July 1904)

The *Valhalla*'s Encounter with a 'Large Marine Animal' Off Brazil

In the early years of the 1900s, James Lindsay, 26th Earl of Crawford (1847–1913), owned a 1,700-ton auxiliary steam/sailing yacht, the *Valhalla*, with which he embarked on a series of three voyages for scientific research and discovery. The voyages, starting and ending at Cowes, Isle of Wight, covered some 72,000 miles of all the world's oceans. Each one collected a substantial number of bird specimens in particular.

The naturalist who accompanied Lord Crawford on *Valhalla* was Michael John Nicoll (1880–1925), who had a particular interest in and enthusiasm for birds (which would explain why *Valhalla* returned with predominantly avian specimens). Nicoll later wrote a book about the three expeditions, *Three Voyages of a Naturalist* (1908). The third voyage, from 8 November 1905 to 13 May 1906, was memorable for him: 'It was not until the autumn of 1905 that I again set out in the *Valhalla* on my last and, perhaps, most interesting voyage.' Interesting not only because 'The results obtained during this voyage were more important than those of the preceding two', but also for 'an important incident which occurred on the high seas ... when in latitude 7° 14' S., longitude 34° 25' W., and about fourteen miles from the coast of Brazil near Para, a creature of extraordinary form and proportions was sighted by two of us'.

Nicoll noted: 'A full account of it was given at a meeting of the Zoological Society of London, on 19th June, 1906', with Edmund Gustavus Bloomfield ('E.G.B.') and Meade-Waldo (1855–1934), an English ornithologist and conservationist who sailed on the voyage with Nicoll and Lord Crawford.

Description of an Unknown Animal Seen at Sea Off the Coast of Brazil. By E.G.B., Meade-Waldo, F.Z.S, and Michael J. Nicoll, F.Z.S.

The following are accounts of a large marine animal seen off the coast of Brazil [just east of Recife on the north-east coast], copied from the journals made by us during our cruise in the Earl of Crawford's yacht *The Valhalla*:-

Meade-Waldo's Account

'On Dec. 7th, 1905, at 10.15 A.M., I was on the poop [after deck] of the *Valhalla* with Mr. Nicoll, when he drew my attention to an object in the sea about 100 yards from the yacht; he said: "Is that the fin of a great fish?" I looked and immediately saw a large fin or frill sticking out of the water, dark seaweed-brown in colour, somewhat crinkled at the edge. It was apparently about 6 feet in length and projected from 18 inches to 2 feet from the water. I could see, under the water to the rear of the frill, the shade of a considerable body.

'I got my field glasses on to it (a powerful pair of Gorz Triëder), and almost as soon as I had them on the frill, a great head and neck rose out of the water in front of the frill; the neck did not touch the frill in the water, but came out of the water in *front* of it, at a distance of certainly not less than 18 inches, probably more. The neck appeared about the thickness of a slight man's body, and from 7 to 8 feet was out of the water; head and neck were all about the same thickness. The head had a very turtle-like appearance, as had also the eye. I could see the line of the mouth, but we were sailing pretty fast, and quickly drew away from the object, which was going very slowly.

'It moved its neck from side to side in a peculiar manner: the colour of the head and neck was dark brown above, and whitish below – almost white I think. When first seen it was about level with the poop of the yacht, and on the starboard side. I made it out by the chart to be in about S. lat. 7° 4', long. 34° 20', but I think this is not quite correct. Mr. Nicoll got the correct position from the captain. The depth of the water where we saw it was about 300 fathoms, but quickly went to as much as 1,300 fathoms.

'Since I saw this creature I consider on reflection that it was considerably larger than it appeared at first, as I proved that objects, the size with which I was well acquainted, appear very much smaller than they really are when seen on the ocean at a similar distance with nothing to compare them with.'

Nicoll's Account

'At 10.15 A.M. on Thursday, December 7, 1905, when in lat. 7° 14' S., long. 34° 25' W., in a depth of from 322 to 1340 fathoms, Meade-Waldo and I saw a most extraordinary creature about 100 yards from the ship and moving in the same direction, but very much slower than we were going. At first, all that we could see was a dorsal fin about four feet long sticking up about two feet from the water; this fin was of a brownish-black colour and much resembled a gigantic piece of ribbon seaweed. Below the water we could distinctly see a very large brownish-black patch, but could not make out the shape of the creature. Every now and then the fin entirely disappeared below the water.

'Suddenly an eel-like neck about six feet long and of the thickness of a man's thigh, having a head shaped like that of a turtle, appeared in front of the fin. This head and neck, which were of the same colour above as the fin, but of a silvery-white below, lashed up the water with a curious wriggling movement. After this it was so far astern of us that we could make out nothing else.

'During the next fourteen hours we "went about" twice and at about 2 A.M. the following day (Dec. 8th), in lat. 7° 19' S., long. 34° 04' W., the first and third mates, Mr. Simmonds and Mr. Harley, who were on the bridge at the time, saw a great commotion in the water. At first they thought it was a rock awash about 100–150 yards away on the port side, just aft of the bridge, but they soon made out that it was something moving and going slightly faster than the ship, which at that time was doing about 8½ knots. Mr. Simmonds hailed the deck, and one of the crew who was on the "look-out" saw it too.

'Although there was a bright moon at the time [almost full] they could not make out anything of the creature itself, owing to the amount of wash it was making; but they say that from the commotion in the water it looked as if a submarine was going along just below the surface. They both say most emphatically that it was not a whale, and that it was not blowing, nor have they ever seen anything like it before. After they had watched it for several minutes it "sounded" off the port bow, and they saw no more of it.' (*Proceedings of the General Meetings for Scientific Business of the Zoological Society of London*, May–December 1906)

In *Voyages of a Naturalist*, Nicoll added:

This creature was an example, I consider, of what has been so often reported, for want of a better name, as the 'great sea-serpent.' I feel sure, however, that it was not a reptile that we saw, but a mammal. It is, of course, impossible to be certain of this, but the general appearance of the creature, especially the soft, almost rubber-like fin, gave one this impression. It is often said that, if there were such a monster, remains of it would have been found long ago, but this is not necessarily so. Supposing the 'sea-serpent' lives in deep holes, such as there were in the spot where we saw our 'monster,' then there would be little remains being washed ashore, and the amount of deep-sea dredging that has yet been done is very small, so that it is not surprising that no parts of this creature have been obtained in that way.

That it is not more often reported is not to be wondered at, when one realizes how often it is that a ship may sail for days together without sighting another ship, even in seas where there is considerable traffic. Also it must be remembered that such ridicule is generally bestowed on the reports of sea-monsters that many persons hesitate to describe what they have seen. I know myself of several instances of unknown sea-monsters having been seen by reliable witnesses, who, to avoid the inevitable 'chaff,' would not publicly state their experiences.

Pauline Witness to 'Vicious Monster' vs 'Great Leviathan'

One of the most sensational eye-witness accounts of a monster from the depths seen on the surface of the high seas concerned two such creatures, near the island of Fernando de Noronha off the north-east coast of Brazil. The barque *Pauline*, commanded by Capt. George Drevar, was en route from Shields, north-east England, 'bound with coals for Her Majesty's Naval Stores at Zanzibar' in 1875 when, on 8 July, she came across a sight that a seafarer might witness – well, once in a blue moon would be quite often by comparison.

A Wonderful Story of the Deep – An Immense Sea-Monster Captures and Swallows a Sperm Whale

British sea captains are becoming famous by reason of their discoveries of sea-monsters. Some weeks ago *The World* published an amusing story of a monster marine trog seen by the officers and crew of an English steamer in the Straits of Malacca, and now Captain Drevar, of the bark *Pauline*, of London, who has just arrived at Cork from a long voyage, favors the public with the following account of an ocean marvel:

'Bark *Pauline*, July 8, 1875, latitude 5 degrees 13 minutes north, longitude 35 degrees west, Cape San Roque, northeast coast of Brazil, distance twenty miles, at 11 a.m., the weather fine and clear, wind and sea moderate, observed some black spots on the water, and a whitish pillar some thirty feet high above them. At the first sight I took all to be breakers, as the sea was splashing up fountain-like about them, and the pillar a pinnacle rock, bleached with the sun, but the pillar fell with a splash and a similar one rose. They rose and fell alternately in quick succession, and good glasses [binoculars] showed me it was a monster sea serpent coiled twice round a large sperm whale.

'The head and tail parts, each about thirty feet long, were acting as levers, twisting itself and its victim round with great velocity. They sank out of sight every two minutes, coming to the surface still revolving; and the struggles of the whale and two other whales that were near, frantic with excitement, made the sea in their vicinity like a boiling cauldron, and a loud and confused noise was distinctly heard.

'This strange occurrence lasted some fifteen minutes, and finished with the tail portion of the whale being elevated straight in the air, then waving backward and forward, and lashing the water furiously in the last death struggle, when the whole body disappeared from our view, going down head foremost to the bottom, where, no doubt, it was gorged at the serpent's leisure; and that monster of monsters may have been many months in a state of coma digesting the huge mouthful.

'Then, two of the largest sperm whales that I have ever seen moved slowly thence toward the vessel, their bodies more than usually elevated out of the water, and not spouting or making the least noise, but seeming quite paralyzed with fear; indeed, a cold shiver went through my own frame on beholding the last agonizing struggle of the poor whale that had seemed as helpless in the coils of the vicious monster as a bird in the talons of a hawk.

'Allowing for two coils round the whale, I think the serpent was about 160 or 170 feet long, and 7 or 8 feet in girth. It was in color much like a conger-eel; and the head, from the mouth being always open, appeared the largest part of its body. It is curious that the whale, that lives on the smallest food of any fish in the ocean, should itself be but a meal for another monster; for I think it as feasible that the serpent swallowed the whale as that a boa-constrictor can consume a whole bullock.

'I am aware that few believe in the existence of the great sea serpent. People think that as so many vessels are constantly on the ocean it would be seen oftener. But the northeast coast of Brazil, noted for its monster reptiles, is peculiarly adapted for the growth of sea monsters. The temperature of the air and water is seldom below 81 degrees, the shore for a thousand miles is bordered by a coral wall or reef, and numerous banks and reefs extend for a considerable distance from the land, while there are strong and various currents and no ports; so that ships for business or pleasure seldom go near it.

'It was unexpected circumstances led me to the home of the sea serpent, and I think it may be allowed that the serpent retains some portion of that cunning mentioned in Scripture. At least it has wit enough not to leave a good feeding ground and secure home to go wandering about the ocean like a fish, and be tortured and captured for man's pleasure and profit. I think Cape San Roque is a landmark for whales leaving the South for the North Atlantic. The warm water is also good for its breeding; if the Crystal Palace Company, or some enterprising Barnum, offered a suitable reward for the serpent's capture, I am sure a steam whaler, with suitable hooks baited with some animal and steel wire lines, would effect its capture while following a profitable whaling business.

'I wrote thus far little thinking I would ever see the serpent again; but at 7 a.m. July 13th, in the same latitude and some eighty miles east of San Roque, I was astonished to see the same or a similar monster. It was throwing its head and about forty feet of its body in a horizontal position out of the water as it passed onwards by the stern of our vessel. I began musing why we were so favored with such a strange visitor, and concluded that the band of white paint, two feet wide, above the copper [on the hull of the vessel], might have looked like a fellow-serpent to it, and no doubt attracted its attention ...

'While thus thinking, I was startled by the cry of "There it is again!" and a short distance to leeward, elevated some sixty feet in the air, was the great leviathan, grimly looking toward the vessel. As I was not sure it was only our freeboard it was viewing, we had all our axes ready, and were fully determined, should the brute embrace the *Pauline*, to chop away for its backbone with all our might; and the wretch might have found for once in its life that it had caught a Tartar.

'This statement is strictly true, and the occurrence was witnessed by my officers, half the crew and myself; and we are ready at any time to testify on oath that it is so, and that we are not in the least mistaken.' (*Sacramento Daily Union* [California], 31 March 1877)

This eye-witness account by an experienced sea captain and some of his crew was apparently not good enough for some landlubberly cynics when it was published. 'Much ridicule was cast upon the story by certain journalists ... and Captain Drevar bitterly resented the doubts cast upon his veracity and capabilities for observation' ('The Sea-Serpent', by Alfred T. Story, in *The Strand Magazine*, August 1895). Capt. Drevar bristled in such high dudgeon by the aspersions cast upon him that he:

appeared before Mr. Raffles, stipendiary magistrate at the Dale Street Police Court, Liverpool, accompanied by some of his officers and crew, and made the following declaration:-

'We, the undersigned, captain, officers, and crew of the barque *Pauline*, of London, do solemnly and sincerely declare that on July 8th, 1875, in latitude 5° 13' S., longitude 35° W., we observed three large sperm whales, and one of them was gripped round the body with two turns of what appeared to be a large sea serpent. The head and tail appeared to have a length beyond the coils of about 30ft., and its girth 8ft. or 9ft. The serpent whirled its victim round and round for about fifteen minutes, and then suddenly dragged the whole to the bottom, head first. – George Drevar, Master; Horatio Thompson; Henderson Landells; Owen Baker; William Lewarn.'

Whether it really was a sea serpent that 'whirled its victim round and round for about fifteen minutes, and then suddenly dragged the whole to the bottom, head first', presumably Capt. Drevar would have had had no reason to make up such a salty, much less fishy yarn. But was it, actually, more likely to have been a giant squid, which are known to attack sperm whales? In which case it would have been an equally spectacular, and even rarer sight to human witness of two monsters of the deep embattled *on the surface* of the high seas than the numerous narratives of sea serpent sightings.

Edward Newman in *The Zoologist*'s report of the incident in February 1876, was in no doubt (though the likelihood that the whale was later 'gorged at the serpent's leisure', as Capt. Drevar described it and Newman thought it, rather than the other way around, was probably somewhat fanciful!):

> There can be no hesitation in explaining this narrative, if true, to have reference to a gigantic cephalopod; it would be a marvellous instance of just retribution, for the whales feed on cephalopods, if the cephalopods every now and then devour a whale by way of retaliation. – *E. Newman*

The 'Sea Serpent' and Sperm Whale as Seen from the *Pauline*. (*Sea Monsters Unmasked*, by Henry Lee, 1883)

Frank Bullen in his *The Cruise of the 'Cachalot'* (1893), a semi-autobiographical account of a nineteenth century whaling voyage, also witnessed a gargantuan tussle between a giant squid and a sperm whale. Bullen wrote that, as they headed towards the Malacca Straits between the Malayan peninsula and the island of Sumatra, he was 'leaning over the lee rail' of the *Cachalot* 'at about eleven p.m.' one night, when:

> ... suddenly I started to my feet with an exclamation, and stared with all my might at the strangest sight I ever saw. There was a violent commotion in the sea right where the moon's rays were concentrated ... A very large sperm whale was locked in deadly conflict with a cuttle-fish, or squid, almost as large as himself, whose interminable tentacles seemed to enlace the whole of his great body ... The occasions upon which these gigantic cuttle-fish appear at the sea surface must, I think, be very rare ... The imagination can hardly picture a more terrible object than one of these huge monsters brooding in the ocean depths ... The very thought of it makes one's flesh crawl.

The *Oakhurst* and a 'Strange Monster'

Sometime in the mid-1890s – the date isn't mentioned – a young apprentice, Fred Ellis, was sailing on the ship *Oakhurst* through the south-east trades of the South Atlantic, 'in warmer conditions and glad to discard our boots', having come round Cape Horn from Callao, Peru. Perfect conditions for the appearance of a 'strange monster'.

It was warm but not unpleasantly hot. It was the second dog-watch [6–8 p.m.], and I with my fellow apprentices had finished our tea of dandyfunk, washed down with stewed, milkless, unsweetened tea, and had repaired to the deck, in anticipation of one of old Mick's [the oldest seaman on the ship] yarns, when we were startled by an excited yell from the forecastle-head:

'Hell's bells! look over there to port. What the hell can it be?'

All hands made a rush for'ard and gazed over the port rail, towards the point indicated. We saw a strange sight. I have remarked it was practically calm, with scarcely enough wind to fill our sails, visibility was excellent, and the majority of the crew were on deck, it being the dog-watch. Slightly on our port bow, we observed the strange sight that had evoked the excited exclamation from Yorky. And no wonder he was excited, for before our astonished eyes was the most remarkable sight that any of my shipmates had ever seen, and there were some with forty or more years of sea travel to look back on. And I, with thirty-five years at sea behind me, have never again seen anything like it. Those that go down to the sea in ships, do see wonders in deep waters.

This is what we saw: a long column-like neck or body, thicker than a man's body, crowned by a head, which appeared to us altogether too small for such a massive body; fascinated, we watched it rise out of the sea, until there was visible at least fifteen feet and as straight as a pole; it then remained stationary for a considerable time, its head turning, as though taking observation within its range of vision round the horizon; then it slowly submerged and was seen no more.

We had been little more than half a mile distant from the strange monster, so we had a close-up view. It was of a dull colour, which I should classify as greeny-slate. How much of it was beneath the surface, of course, I do not know. Everyone on deck saw it, but no one had ever seen its like before, so none could give it a name. Its head, both in shape and appearance, resembled the head of a giraffe more than anything else I could imagine. Naturally, it supplied a topic for yarning that was not missed, although Mick's yarn on the main hatch that dog-watch was missing. (From *Round Cape Horn In Sail*, by Capt. Fred W. Ellis, The Blue Book Company, 1949)

A 'Sea-Serpent' Stranded at Bermuda

In January 1860 a strange, elongated, dorsal-spiny-finned creature washed up on the shoreline of Bermuda in a bay along the south shore of that island that contemporary reports named as 'Hungary' Bay (actually, *Hungry* Bay). A local man, George Trimingham, was walking along the shore there when he 'heard a strange splashing in the water, and almost directly afterward saw "a huge sea-monster" stranded on the shore, and rapidly dying from exhaustion'.

Mr Trimingham's report of the 'monster' aroused considerable interest within Bermuda as well as with amateur and scientific sea-serpentologists around the world. A layman's description of the Hungry Bay 'sea-serpent' was communicated by a correspondent from Bermuda, in *The New York Times*, shortly after the discovery of the creature.

Remarkable Discovery in Marine Zoology – The Question of a
Great Sea-Serpent Settled – Capture of One at the Bermudas

Bermuda, Monday, Jan. 30, 1860

I have, on this occasion, to communicate to the readers of the *Times* a most interesting circumstance, which
cannot fail to arrest the attention of scientific men in
general, but especially such as take a deep interest in
marine zoology. It is no less a matter than the solution
of the question, whether a sea-serpent actually lives in
the great waters of the ocean? A most singular fish, of
the Gymnetrus genus, answering in a very remarkable
degree to the accounts of a 'Sea-Serpent' frequently given
to the world by nautical men, was captured at Hungary
Bay, on the south side of these islands, on the 22d inst.
[i.e. 22 January 1860].

Without further preface, I append the following
description, which I cut from the editorial columns of
The Bermudian of the 25th, all the facts of which, I have
reason to know were supplied to the editor of that paper
by one of the gentlemen who discovered and secured this
great ichthyological specimen:

Its color was bright and shining silver. This brilliant
covering of the skin was, from the struggling of the
animal, scattered in great profusion about the place. The
skin had a rough, warty feeling to the touch, but was
destitute of any scales. There was a dorsal fin running
nearly the whole length of the creature, composed of
short slender rays united by a transparent membrane, and
separated at intervals of less than an inch; in other words
the slight back fin had a number of regular gaps in it.

It had a curiously shaped head, the like of which we
have not seen in any of the numerous illustrations of

ichthyology we have examined. From a drawing which is now before us (for we had not the good fortune to see the creature itself) the conformation of the head, in profile, is not unlike that of a dog. There is a distinctly defined forehead, with a projecting mouth. The eye, large, flat, and exceedingly brilliant. It had very small pectoral fins, and minute ventral fins proceeding from the thorax. It had large gills, but was, we are told, destitute of teeth.

But its most remarkable feature was a beautiful crestal appendage, consisting of eight long spines, of a rich red color, which sprang from the top of the head, commencing at the frontal edge of the forehead and following each other singly about an inch apart, the three first of these spines being connected halfway upwards from the cranial covering by a gauzy filament, but all the rest were wholly destitute of any membraneous appendage. These delicate crestal spines, which the creature had the power to raise or depress at pleasure, were of irregular lengths – the longest, growing from about the centre of the top of the head, being three feet in length, and the rest ranging from eighteen inches to two and-a-half feet. The larger number of these appendages were flattened at the extreme end, somewhat like the tip of a spear.

The length of this singular inhabitant of the briny world was sixteen feet seven inches from the front edge of the lips to the end of the tail. It was eleven inches deep, measuring through from the top of the back, at about one-third of its length from the head, and its thickness, laterally, was from five to six inches, at the same distance from the head. Thence the body tapered gradually until it terminated in a bluntish point of about half an inch in diameter – the tail having no finny or any other append-age. (*The New York Times*, 11 February 1860)

Looking at a drawing of the Hungry Bay 'great sea-serpent' which appeared in *Harper's Weekly*, two things are apparent: first, that the sketcher of the fish took considerable liberties with the background landscape of 'Hungary Bay' that in no way resembles the actual shoreline there; and second, that, though surely serpentine, the fish so depicted was, just as surely, an oarfish (sometimes called ribband – or 'riband' – fish, scabbard fish, or tape-fish), a rarely seen fish which could easily be identified as that 'singular inhabitant of the briny world', namely, the sea serpent, reports of which were by then coming thick and fast. (Oarfish were first described almost a hundred years beforehand, in 1772.)

A member of the Linnaean Society of London, 'Mr. J. Mathew Jones, Esq.' who was by coincidence visiting Bermuda at the time, examined the fish. Mr. Jones's forensic report appeared in *The Zoologist* of 1860 (pages 6986–89), shortly after the original account appeared in that same journal (pages 6934–35).

An Account of the Bermudian Riband Fish,
by J. Mathew Jones, Esq.

Order, Acanthopterygu; Family, Cepoladae; Genus, Gymnetrus; Species.

Body attenuate, compressed, naked, tuberculate; cuticle, a silvery covering of metallic lustre. Length, from facial to caudal extremities, sixteen feet seven inches. Depth, at fourteen inches from facial extremity, nine inches, and increasing gradually to near the ventral extremity of the stomach, when it attained its greatest depth of eleven inches, and then decreased by degrees to the caudal termination. Width, at the same distance and through the spinal column, two and a half to three inches. These dimensions are in the extreme ...

The Great Sea-Serpent, Found in Hungary [*sic* – Hungry] Bay, Bermuda, on January 22, 1860. (*Harper's Weekly*, 3 March 1860)

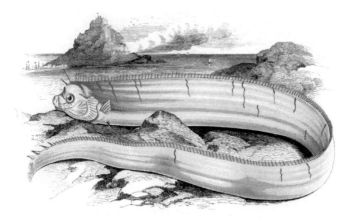

Banks's Oarfish. (*A History of the Fishes of the British Islands*, in four volumes (1862–65), by Cornish naturalist/ichthyologist Jonathan Couch (1789–1870))

Thereafter followed a lengthy inventory of jargon-rich physiological description that zoologically inclined readers might find terribly interesting (and so can peruse in the original) but which to us lesser mortals ... well, is not terribly so. Mr. Jones concluded that the animal he

The tape fish. (*Earth, Sea and Sky*, by Henry Davenport Northrop, 1887)

described as '*the Bermudian Riband Fish*' was indeed a kind of lesser 'Great Sea Serpent'.

> The most notable fact, in connection with the capture of the present specimen, will doubtless be the interest and attraction it will produce in the scientific world, for most assuredly we have in the specimen now before us many of the peculiarities, save size, with which the appearance of that hitherto apocryphal monster, the 'great sea serpent,' as detailed by navigators, is invested.
>
> The lengthened filaments crowning the caput, joined anteriorly by the connecting membrane, and extending to the shoulders, would, viewed from a vessel's deck, present to the spectator the mane so accurately described as a singular feature in the gigantic specimen

seen by Captain McQuhae, R.N., and officers, of
H.M.S. *Daedalus* ...

Here, then, we have a partial elucidation of the various
statements which have at intervals appeared in the
columns of the united presses of England and America,
emanating from the pens of travellers, and usually headed
'Occurrence of the Great Sea-Serpent'.

In *The Zoologist* of 1856, a certain A.G. More submitted that
an explanation for the 'reality [of the sea serpent], in some
at least of the many instances of his reported appearance'
could be attributed to ribband fish. Our old friend Edward
Newman, editor of *The Zoologist*, had certain reservations
about the identity of the Hungry Bay *faux*-serpent at the
end of the original report of the incident, articulated before
Mr Jones's forensic analysis appeared in a later number:

> I place implicit reliance on the narrative, except as to
> the animal being identical with that seen by Captain
> McQuhae [of HMS *Daedalus*], of which I think there is
> no evidence. Mr. J.M. Jones is an old subscriber to the
> *Zoologist*, and a most intelligent naturalist; but the query
> occurs to me, 'Is not this sea serpent a ribband fish?'

To which the member from the Linnaean Society of
London responded, unequivocally: 'Yes.' And, moreover, that it was probably the same fish that was seen by
Capt. McQuhae in 1848. But the intrepid scepticism of
editor Newman reflected rather more circumspection and
reserved judgement:

> In reference to the last question mooted by Mr. Jones,
> the similarity of ['*the Bermudian riband fish*'] to Captain

McQuhæ's sea serpent, I do not consider myself competent to express an opinion. I am quite willing for the present to allow every sea serpent to hold on its own course …

In other words: whether or not the Hungry Bay specimen was the same as the *Daedalus* creature, let each of the multitude of *other* sea serpents from hither and yon 'hold on its own course' and be identified according to its merits, 'riband' or otherwise.

Small Boat Encounters – The Andrews Brothers

One of the interesting things about the latter half of the nineteenth and early years of the twentieth centuries was that it became a fancied notion of certain well-brined mariners and some other less salty and rather more reckless adventurers to attempt to sail small boats from the American East Coast across the North Atlantic to Britain and Europe. Sometimes their intentions were simply to achieve the feat and survive. Some did it to make the fastest passage by the smallest vessel. Some just never made it. Occasionally some of them engaged with marine creatures that were, to put it mildly, surprising – monstrous, even.

On 7 June 1878 two intrepid New England Yankee brothers, Capt. William A. and Asa Walter Andrews, sailed out of Boston, Massachusetts, on their 19ft single-masted dory, the *Nautilus*, to try to navigate 'the smallest boat that ever started to cross the Atlantic Ocean', which eventually they accomplished. Roughly two-thirds of the way across they sighted 'what appeared to be a part of a huge monster in the shape of a snake'. Capt. William Andrews recorded the incident in the ship's log:

The Log of the Nautilus, Sea Serpent Story

'Wednesday, July 17th [1878]. – Wind S.S.W.; course E. by S. half S.; sea smooth. These good weather spells kind of knock spots out of our ideas of making a quick passage. Just thirty-four days out. I never took much stock about sea serpents, but I have good reason to believe, after what I saw last evening, before dark, that there are denizens of the deep that have never been thoroughly explained or illustrated by our zoological societies.

'It was during a moment of intense calm, and I had been watching some whales sporting and spouting at a short distance behind me, when, on turning and looking in the opposite direction, I was startled to see what appeared to be a part of a huge monster in the shape of a snake; it was about two hundred feet off. I saw twelve or fifteen feet of what appeared to be the tail of a huge black snake from five to fifteen inches in diameter, the end being stubby, or round, and white. It was in the air in a corrugated shape in motion, and in the act of descending. I also saw a dark shadowy form in the water corresponding with the tail; also the wake on the water as if more had just gone down, the whole being in motion after the manner of a snake; also heard the noise of the descending part, and saw the splash on the water.

'Walter being just at that moment at the cuddy, where I kept the hatchet, getting some tea for supper, I told him to pass me the hatchet quick, which he did. He heard the splash and saw the form in the water. I wanted the hatchet, not because I thought I should have to use it, but because I thought it would be a good thing to have it handy, in case I should want to use it. Walter had a swim an hour before near the boat, and the thought of sea serpents being around kind of took away his relish for that kind of sport for the present.' (from *A Daring Voyage Across the Atlantic Ocean by Two Americans, the Brothers Andrews*, by Capt. William A Andrews, 1880)

The Andrews brothers' mid-Atlantic sighting of the 'huge monster' in 1878 was interesting enough. But even more intriguing was that Capt. William *seemed* to have witnessed another similar beast ten years later during his unsuccessful solo attempt to cross the Atlantic in an even smaller dory-style boat, the 14ft *Dark Secret*. He set off, alone, from Boston again, on 18 June 1888, but was picked up by Capt. Bjonness, of the Norwegian barque *Nor*, 'in latitude 46° [north] and west longitude 39° 50' [approximately half-way across] in rather an exhausted condition'.

But the reason for Capt. Andrews's decision to abandon the attempt on the Atlantic crossing by what would, at the time, have been the smallest ever craft to do so, was less exhaustion than fear. Jans Carlsen, a Norwegian seaman on the *Nor*, explained to a *New York Times* reporter when the vessel (and Andrews) arrived at New York on 11 September 1888:

'Cjaptain Andjrews,' said he, 'cjame willingjly onj boarjd, because hej wasj frightjened byj the seaj serpjent.'

The rest of his tale, with the redundancy of Norwegian orthography eliminated, is to this effect:

'Captain Andrews told me that at 10 o'clock in the morn-ing of Wednesday, Aug. 15, four days before we sighted him, as he was in latitude 45° 10' and west longitude 41° 20', merely drifting along, he saw less than a hundred yards to leeward the head and neck of an enormous brown sea serpent, projected at an angle of 10 degrees above the water and going at the rate of three knots an hour. The sea was perfectly smooth, and through it the monster swished, leaving a long wake of tumbling foam behind.

'The portion of him visible was about six feet, but it was impossible to estimate his entire length. The snake kept his eyes straight ahead of him and the little boat and its trembling occupant escaped his notice, but the 15 minutes during which his snakeship kept in sight were by long odds the worst in Capt. Andrew's experience, and he made up his mind that, come what would, he would board the next vessel he met, and he accordingly came back with us.' ('Picked Up in Midocean – The Dark Secret and her Captain Home Again', *The New York Times*, 12 September 1888)

Was it the same 'monster' Capt. Andrews and his brother had encountered ten years earlier on their *Nautilus*? Or was it, rather astonishingly, and coincidentally, yet another beast entirely? Or did Capt. Andrews simply repeat the incident from his *Nautilus* crossing? (The circumstances and description were very similar.) In the summer of 1901 Capt. Andrews attempted another transatlantic voyage, from Atlantic City, New Jersey, to Spain, with his recently wed wife, in another small dory, the 20ft long *Flying Dutchman*. A week into the voyage he encountered and spoke the steamship *Durango*; after that, silence, presumed lost at sea – taking the mystery of whether he had experienced a single-but-repeated, or second-and-brand-new sea serpent sighting to his presumably watery grave.

Howard Blackburn and the *Great Republic*

Originally from Nova Scotia, Howard Blackburn (born 17 February 1879) was a burly 6ft 2in, 200lb character, and unarguably one of the most famous fishermen and small boat sailors, as well as intrepid entrepreneur, out of Gloucester, Massachusetts. The incident that enshrined Blackburn as a heroic Gloucester-man happened in the winter of 1883. Aged 23 or 24 years old, he and a shipmate, the Newfoundlander Tom Welch, became separated in their small fishing dory from their mother ship, the *Grace L. Fears*, during a fierce winter storm on the fishing ground of the Burgeo Bank, just to the south of the island of St Pierre and Miquelon off Newfoundland. Although Blackburn survived the ordeal (Tom Welch did not), he later had all his fingers (and other bits of his anatomy) amputated because of frostbite and gangrene.

Digitally deprived but otherwise undaunted, Blackburn made a successful solo trans-Atlantic voyage in the summer of 1899, in his 34ft Gloucester fishing sloop *Great Western*. Two years later, on Sunday 9 June 1901, the Gloucester-man-hero set off again to conquer the Atlantic on his own in his new boat, the 25ft long sloop *Great Republic*. Reaching Lisbon thirty-nine days later, on 18 July, he had made 'the fastest non-stop singlehanded passage across the Atlantic ever sailed'. Half way across, however, Blackburn witnessed a phenomenon that recalled Capt. Andrews's encounter (or possibly encounters) beforehand – a curious but not altogether, it would appear, singular sighting.

July 1, 4 P.M. While sitting on the wheelbox steering, boat making about three miles an hour, suddenly I saw something just abaft the starboard beam lashing the water into foam. I stood up and saw what looked like a coil of very large rope. I hove the wheel down and trimmed the sheets in sharp by the wind. The boat would not fetch it on that tack, but passed within 35 or 40 feet to the leeward of it. As I drew near I could see that it looked like a large snake, but had a tail more like an eel. It was fully 12 to 15 feet in length. It was holding in its mouth either a small turtle or a good-sized fish, with which it was lashing the water into foam. Its head moved so rapidly from side to side that I could not tell its shape, but am inclined to think it resembled that of a serpent. The tail and parts of the body that I could see plainly appeared to be smooth and of a light lead color … It must have been a baby sea-serpent. (From *Lone Voyager*, Joseph Garland's biography of Howard Blackburn)

John Ridgway's 'Sea Serpent'

In the summer of 1966 two intrepid Englishmen, now renowned for their maritime exploits, Sergeant Chay Blyth and Captain John Ridgway, rowed across the Atlantic from Cape Cod to Ireland in their 20ft wooden Yorkshire dory *English Rose III*. Both men were experienced seamen, of a highly pragmatic mien, and neither given to undue exaggeration or imaginative embellishment. On the night of 25 July, 'just before midnight', when they were midway across the Atlantic, at approximately 43° 30' N latitude, 37° 30' west longitude, Ridgway was at the oars as Blyth slept.

I was shocked to full wakefulness by a swishing noise to starboard. I looked out into the water and suddenly saw the writhing, twisting shape of a great creature. It was outlined by the phosphorescence in the sea as if a string of neon lights were hanging from it.

It was an enormous size, some thirty-five or more feet long, and it came towards me quite fast. I must have watched it for some ten seconds. It headed straight at me and disappeared right beneath me.

I stopped rowing. I was frozen with terror at this apparition. I forced myself to turn my head to look over the port side. I saw nothing, but after a brief pause I heard a monstrous splash.

I thought that this might be the head of the monster crashing into the sea after coming up for a brief look at us. I did not see the surfacing – just heard it.

I am not an imaginative man, and I searched for a rational explanation for this incredible occurrence in the night as I picked up the oars and started rowing again. Chay and I had seen whales and sharks, dolphins and porpoises, flying fish – all sorts of sea creatures but this monster in the night was none of these. I reluctantly had to believe that there was only one thing it could have been – a sea serpent. (from *A Fighting Chance*, by John Ridgway and Chay Blyth, 1966)

The Great American Sea-Serpent

In the early 1800s there was a spate of sightings of sea serpents off the New England coasts of Massachusetts and Maine. Because of its proximity to Yankee shores, the animal was dubbed:

The Great American Sea-Serpent

The Sea-Serpent, seen by Captain McQuhae [of *Daedalus* fame] on the 6th of August [1848], seems to confirm the accounts of a similar animal seen at different periods off the north-eastern coast of the United States, between Cape Cod and Penobscot Bay [Maine].

In consequence of the reports of a great Sea-Serpent having been frequently seen during the month of August, 1817, both in the harbour of Gloucester, Massachusetts, and at a short distance out at sea, off the same coast, the Linnaean Society of Boston appointed a committee to collect evidence with regard to the existence and appearance of such animal ... (*The Illustrated London News*, 28 October 1848)

In 1817 a committee was established by the Linnaean Society of New England, in Boston, to 'examine upon oath some respectable men of that place [i.e. Plymouth, on the Massachusetts coast], with regard to the appearance of the animal in 1815' and 'for the purpose of collecting any evidence which may exist respecting a remarkable animal, denominated a *Sea Serpent*, reported to have been recently seen in and near the Harbour of Gloucester'. One of the dozen or so eyewitness depositions received by the committee was from Capt. Elkanah Finney ('Mariner'), of Plymouth, describing 'an unusual animal, which was seen by him in the outer harbour of Plymouth, in June 1815':

'I, Elkanah Finney of Plymouth, in the county of Plymouth, Mariner, testify and say: That about the twentieth of June, A.D. 1815, being at work near my house, which is situated near the sea-shore in Plymouth, at a place called Warren's cove, where the beach joins the main land; my son, a boy, came from the shore and informed me of an unusual appearance on the surface of the sea in the cove. I paid little attention to his story at first; but as he persisted in saying that he had seen something very remarkable, I looked towards the cove, where I saw something which appeared to the naked eye to be a drift sea-weed. I then viewed it through a perspective glass, and was in a moment satisfied that it was some aquatic animal, with the form, motion, and appearance of which I had hitherto been unacquainted.

'It was about a quarter of a mile from the shore, and was moving with great rapidity to the northward. It then appeared to be about thirty feet in length; the animal went about half a mile to the northward; then turned about, and while turning, displayed a greater length than I had before seen; I supposed at least a hundred feet. It then came towards me, in a southerly direction, very rapidly, until he was in a line with me, when he stopped, and lay entirely still on the surface of the water. I then had a good view of him through my glass, at the distance of a quarter of a mile.

'His appearance in this situation was like a string of buoys. I saw perhaps thirty or forty of these protuberances or bunches, which were about the size of a barrel. The head appeared to be about six or eight feet long, and where it was connected with the body was a little larger than the body. His head tapered off to the size of a horse's head. I could not discern any mouth. But what I supposed to be his under jaw had a white stripe extending the whole length of the head, just above the water. While he lay in this situation, he appeared to be about a hundred or a hundred and twenty feet long. The body appeared to be of a uniform size. I saw no part of the animal which I supposed to be a tail. I therefore thought he did not discover to me his whole length.

'His colour was a deep brown or black. I could not discover any eyes, mane, gills, or breathing holes. I did not see any fins or legs. The animal did not utter any sound, and it did not appear to notice any thing. It remained still and motionless for five minutes or more. The wind was light with a clear sky, and the water quite smooth. He then moved to the southward; but not with so rapid a motion as I had observed before. He was soon out of my sight.

'The next morning I rose very early to discover him. There was a fresh breeze from the south, which subsided about eight o'clock. It then became quite calm, when I again saw the animal about a mile to the northward of my house, down the beach. He did not display so great a length as the night before, perhaps not more than twenty or thirty feet. He often disappeared, and was gone five or ten minutes under water. I thought he was diving or fishing for his food. He remained in nearly the same situation, and thus employed for two hours.

'I then saw him moving off, in a north-east direction, towards the light house. I could not determine whether its motion was up and down, or to the right and left. His quickest motion was very rapid; I should suppose at the rate of fifteen or twenty miles an hour. Mackerel, manhaden, herring, and other bait fish abound in the cove where the animal was seen. Elkanah Finney' (*Report of a Committee of the Linnaean Society of New England, Relative to a Large Marine Mammal*, 1817)

A number of other men (and a youth, 'John Johnston, jun … of the age of seventeen years'), some of whom were mariners and several shipmasters, also declared in writing, under oath, that they saw the sea serpent at least once, and some on various occasions, around the coast north and south of Boston, in August 1817.

It was seen on the 10th of August, 1817, in the harbour of Gloucester, at a distance of about 130 yards. The head, which was about a foot above the water, appeared much like the head of a sea-turtle, and the colour of the body was a dark brown. The animal was then moving rapidly through the water, at the rate of from 20 to 25 miles an hour. It was seen a second time by the same person, on the 23rd of August; it was then lying perfectly still, and the deponent judged that the portion which he saw was at least 50 feet long. The body appeared to be about as thick as that of a man.

Solomon Allen, ship-master, also saw the animal in the harbour of Gloucester, on the 12th, 13th, and 14th of August, and estimated it to be between 80 and 90 feet in length, and the body to be about the thickness of a half-barrel. The head was something like a rattlesnake's, but was nearly as large as the head of a horse, and was sometimes carried about two feet above the water. It appeared to have bunches of protuberances on the back. Mr. Nash, however, who took the depositions, and had also seen the animal, considers that those apparent bunches were merely caused by the animal's vertical motion.

Matthew Gaffney ('ship carpenter') saw it a distance of about 30 feet, and *fired* at it. 'I aimed at his head,' says the deponent, 'and I think I must have hit him. He turned towards us immediately after I had fired, and

I thought he was coming at us; but he sank down and went directly under our boat, and made his appearance at about 100 yards from where he sank. He did not turn down like a fish, but appeared to settle down like a rock. He did not, however, appear more shy after being fired at, but continued playing as before.'

John Johnson, who saw it on the 17th of August, within two oars' length, judged it to be at least 50 feet long. W.B. Pearson, merchant, when in a sailing-boat, on the 18th of August, off Webber's Cove, saw a strange marine animal, which he believed to be the same that had been seen several times in the harbour of Gloucester. It passed under the stern of the boat, and afterwards (turning) crossed the bow at about 30 yards' distance. From what he saw of the animal, he should say that it was nothing short of 70 feet in length. It turned very short, and appeared as limber and as active as an eel, considering its comparative size.

Robert Bragg, mariner, saw the animal from the deck of the schooner *Laura*, about a mile and a half from Cape Ann. It passed very swiftly by the vessel, at a distance of about 30 feet; and about 14 feet of the body was above the level of the water to the height of six inches. The head was like a serpent's, rather blunt, and larger than the body. When about 30 feet astern of the vessel it threw out its tongue, which appeared to be about two feet long, and something like a fisherman's harpoon. The Serpent was in sight about ten minutes, and seemed to move at the rate of about fourteen miles an hour. (*The Illustrated London News*, 28 October 1848)

Three depositions of that sighting from the schooner *Laura* were made: by 'Sewell Toppan, Master of the schooner Laura', and by both crew members, Robert Bragg and another man, William Somerby, helmsman at the time. Capt. Toppan concluded: 'I have been to sea many years, and never saw any fish that had the least resemblance to this animal.'

Penobscot Bay Sightings

Besides the depositions of eleven persons who had seen the animal in August, 1817, the Committee received several communications relative to a similar animal which had previously been seen on the coast of Maine, several years before. The Rev. Abraham Cummings says that, in Penobscot Bay, within the thirty years preceding 1809, a Sea-Serpent, supposed to be about 60 feet long, and as thick as a sloop's mast, had been several times seen. Mr. Cummings saw it himself, at a distance of about 80 yards, and judged it to be about 70 feet long. It was also seen by the British in their expedition to Bagaduse [*sic* – Bagaduce, near Penobscot Bay] during the first American war [the American Revolutionary War of 1775–83], and they supposed it to be at least 300 feet long; but this Mr. Cummings considers to be an exaggeration.

It was again seen in 1809 and 1811. The Committee were also informed that, about 1780, as a schooner was lying at the mouth of the river Penobscot, or in the bay, one of these enormous creatures leaped over it between the masts; that the men ran into the hold for fright, and that the weight of the serpent sank the vessel one *streak* or plank. The schooner was about eighteen tons burthen ... (*The Illustrated London News*, 28 October 1848)

In case of any understandable scepticism that 'one of these enormous creatures' might actually have leapt over a schooner between its masts in about 1780, and thereby tainted the evidence that such creatures existed:

Another way to account for it – Summer-Hotel Proprietor (*to the Sea-Serpent*). 'Say, look-a-here! Boarders is all-fired scarce at my place this Summer. What will you charge for four or five first-class "Appearances" off my beach?' (*Harper's Weekly*, 25 August 1883)

'No wonder the sea serpent frequents our coast', drawn by Charles Dana Gibson. (*Colliers Weekly*, 1906)

... the following declaration, which was drawn up and attested in the proper form, at Hingham [Massachusetts], on the 12th of May, 1818, must carry conviction even to the most incredulous:-

'I, the undersigned, Joseph Woodward, Captain of the *Adamant* schooner, of Hingham, being on my route from Penobscot to Hingham, steering W.N.W, and being about ten leagues from the coast, perceived, last Sunday, at two P.M., something on the surface of the water, which seemed to me to be of the size of a large boat. Supposing that it might be part of the wreck of a ship, I approached it; but when I was within a few fathoms of it it appeared, to my great surprise, and that of my whole crew, that it was a monstrous serpent. When I approached nearer it coiled itself up, instantly uncoiling itself again, and withdrew with extreme rapidity. On my approaching again it coiled itself up a second time, and placed itself at the distance of sixty feet at most from the bow of the ship.

'I had one of my guns loaded with a cannon-ball and musket-bullets. I fired at the head of the monster; my crew and myself distinctly heard the ball and bullets strike against his body, from which they rebounded, as if they had struck against a rock. The serpent shook his head and tail in an extraordinary manner, and advanced towards the ship with open jaws. I had caused the cannon to be reloaded, and pointed it at his throat; but he had come so near that all the crew were seized with terror, and we thought only of getting out of his way; he almost touched the vessel; and had not I tacked as I did, he would certainly have come on board.

'He dived; but in a moment we saw him appear again, with his head on one side of the vessel and his tail on the other, as if he was going to lift us up and upset us. However, we did not feel any shock. He remained five hours near us, only going backward and forward.

... 'The fears with which he had first inspired us having subsided, we were able to examine him attentively. I estimate that his length is at least twice that of my schooner, that is to say, 130 feet; his head is full 12 or 14; the diameter of the body below the neck is not less than 6 feet; the size of the head is in proportion to that of the body. He is of a blackish colour; his ear-holes (*ouies*) are about 12 feet from the extremity of his head. In short, the whole has a terrible look.

... 'When he coils himself up, he places his tail in such a manner that it aids him in darting forward with great force; he moves in all directions with the greatest facility, and astonishing rapidity.' ('Marvels in Marine Natural History, Part II', *United Service Magazine*, Vol. 51, 1846)

The 'Great American Sea Serpent' has made many more appearances in New England and adjacent waters than were chronicled by the Linnaean Society of New England in August 1817. As June (J.P.) O'Neill has written in the Introduction to her meticulous work *The Great New England Sea Serpent* (Down East Books, 1999): '... that August remains singular in that it was the first time that men of scholarship and means had an opportunity to conduct a scientific study of a creature thought to exist only in myth'.

It was, indeed, the precursor to our *Zoologist* editor Edward Newman's insistence on '*Fact*'. And by 'fact' it was meant the actual observations of the creature over the centuries, and the first-hand (or as nearly so as possible) narratives of such encounters.

The creatures, regular sightings of which off the US Eastern Seaboard continued into the nineteenth and twentieth centuries, often (but not always) appeared in the summer months, which gave newspaper cartoonists plenty of material for their humorous artwork.

An American Monster – The 'Wonderful Fish' of Eastport

'Down-Easters', as folks from the north-east coast of Maine are called, were astonished in early August 1868 to find that a 'monster' of a fish had been captured along their shore at Eastport. It was 'a monster of such marvellous peculiarities, and *unknown to science*' that it was 'destined to make a popular sensation wherever exhibited … at Portland during the forthcoming State Fair, and … thence bound for Boston, New York, and other principal cities'. In its issue of 24 October 1868, *Harper's Weekly* ran an account of the incident, with a description of it taken from a Bangor newspaper, the *Daily Whig*, accompanied by a 'representation' of 'the wonderful fish' drawn by the then notable New England artist Charles A. Barry (1830–92).

A Wonderful Fish

This curiosity of natural history, caught 'Down East,' near Eastport, Maine, a few weeks ago [on 3 August], has attracted so much attention and excited so much wonder, even among naturalists, that we give a representation of it in the accompanying illustration. The Bangor *Daily Whig* gives the following detailed description of this fish:

'The strange animal recently captured near Eastport, meagre reports of which had reached us, arrived in this city [i.e. Bangor] a few days ago, and has been on exhibition, during which it has been visited by our citizens, all of whom have expressed their wonder as well at the remarkable size of the monster as at its anomalous character. This animal, part beast and part fish, is over thirty feet in length, and girths twenty-one feet. It has one enormous dorsal fin, two side belly fins, and a broad shark-like tail.

'About one-third of its length from its tail, in connection with small fins, it has two huge legs, *terminating in web feet*. Its mouth makes a line five or six feet in length, the whole extent of which is set with innumerable small teeth, very much resembling in size and shape the kernel of a species of sharp pointed popcorn. It has a series of gills which overlap each other like the flounces once the style in ladies' dresses. Its immense body, which was estimated to have weighed when captured about eleven tons, had no frame work of bones, its most solid portions consisting of cartilage, incapable of preservation. Its skin is dark and tough, like that of the elephant and rhinoceros.

'*There is no record of his species*, and to none is it a greater wonder than to naturalists, whose attention is being drawn to it ... Professor Baird, of the Smithsonian Institution at Washington, ... is as yet unable to place it in the known lists of the animal kingdom. It is indeed a veritable wonder calculated to excite popular curiosity, and to invite the researches of the scientific ...

'On Sunday, August 3, the monster was discovered near the shore on the west side of Eastport Island, where Passamaquoddy Bay is connected with Lake Utopia by a marsh a quarter of a mile long. Being attacked by musketry, it struck for the marsh, and probably for the lake, which was undoubtedly its home, and before being rendered incapable of locomotion, it had worked its way with its fins and legs a number of rods [1 rod = 5 metres]. The report of its presence at once spread to the town, attracting a large number to the spot to aid in its destruction. It received some seventy musket balls, and although attacked in the forenoon, it exhibited signs of life the following day ...' (*Harper's Weekly*, 24 October 1868)

It has long since been generally accepted that 'the wonderful fish' of Eastport, Maine described in the *Daily Whig* as a 'monster' that was 'part beast and part fish' was, like the 'Stronsay Beast' in the Orkneys, most likely a basking shark. Charles A. Barry, who drew the 'representation' of the fish for *Harper's*, was particularly known for a portrait of Abraham Lincoln drawn 'from life', in 1860 (though not particularly for much else). His drawing included some details that he was not likely to have reproduced 'from life' by having seen the animal himself, but rather by its description in the press. He certainly reinforced its monstrous characteristics by the fish's malevolent mouth and eyes, and its curiously fringed fins, in accordance with the press's sensationally awe-struck wonder at it. The fish's 'web-feet' only added to the monstrousness of it. (Basking sharks do have quite pronounced fins protruding from their after-belly. These could easily be morphed by the imagination into 'web-feet', to enhance the animal's strangeness.)

But, contrary to those reports, in 1868 the fish was not 'unknown to science' – far from it. The Norwegian bishop and naturalist Johan Ernst Gummerus (1718–73) first described and classified the animal as *Cetorhinus* (from the Greek 'ketos', meaning marine monster, or whale, and 'rhinos', meaning

'The wonderful fish, caught near Eastport, Maine, Aug. 3, 1868', drawn by Charles A. Barry. (*Harper's Weekly*, 24 October 1868)

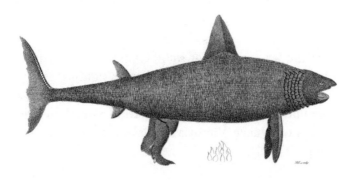

Basking Shark – *male*; Hill, *sculp.* (1 June 1804, G. Kearsley, Fleet Street)

nose: so, marine-monster-nose …) *maximus*, long before the locals massacred the Eastport beast with their musketry.

Basking sharks do indeed have small teeth, about ¼in long – like 'sharp pointed pop-corn' – and can indeed run to 30 or 40ft long. But they are benign filter-feeders that live on plankton, not malign 'monsters' that Barry's drawing of a glowering 'part beast and part fish' suggests. But monsters from the sea being all the rage in those days, and thereabouts, so 'monstrous' did 'the wonderful fish' become.

Barry's wasn't the only, or even the first, drawing of a basking shark depicted as some bipedal marine monster straight out of the Ordovician. A copperplate engraving of a 'Basking shark – male', made by 'Hill *sculp*' (possibly Samuel Hill (*c*.1765–*c*.1809), a well-known American engraver from Boston, Massachusetts), and published in London by G. Kearsley of Fleet Street, in 1804, showed the animal poised with hind legs and scaly skin akin to a predatory giant lizard. Another 'monstrous' representation of what is, in fact, a gentle giant of the sea.

Royal Sighting of a 'Gigantic Sea Monster' in the Mediterranean

In 1877 the sea serpent – or some kindred 'sea monster' – received a royal warrant, of sorts, from a sighting of what can only be described from the accompanying sketches as a large but otherwise ambiguous marine animal, by crew members on Queen Victoria's royal yacht *Osborne*, then cruising off Sicily.

The 'Sea Serpent'

We are indebted to Lieut. W.P. Haynes, of H.M.S. *Osborne*, for the sketch of the sea monster seen by the officers and crew of that vessel off the north coast of Sicily on the 2nd inst. In a letter accompanying the sketch he says:

'My attention was first called by seeing a long row of fins appearing above the surface of the water at a distance of about 200 yards from the ship, and "away on our beam." They were of irregular heights, and extending about 30 or 40 feet in line (the former number is the length I gave, the latter the other officers), in a few seconds they disappeared, giving place to the fore part of the monster. By this time it had passed astern, swimming in an opposite direction to that we were steering, and as we were passing through the water at 10½ knots, I could only get a view of it, "end on," which I have shown in the sketch.

'The head was bullet-shaped, and quite 6 feet thick, the neck narrow, and its head was occasionally thrown back out of the water, remaining there for a few seconds at a time. It was very broad across the back or shoulders, about 15 or 20 feet, and the flappers appeared to have a semi-revolving motion, which seemed to paddle the monster along. They were about 15 feet in length. From the top of the head to the part of the back where it became immersed, I should consider 50 feet, and that seemed about a third of the whole length. All this part

The Sea Serpent in the Mediterranean – A Sketch from HM Yacht *Osborne* Off the North Coast of Sicily on the Second of June. (*The Graphic*, 30 June 1877)

was smooth, resembling a seal. I cannot account for the fins unless they were on the back below where it was immersed.' (*The Graphic*, 30 June 1877)

'Marine Monster!' in the Gulf of Suez

In 1879 another very fish-like sea monster made an appearance in the Gulf of Suez between the Red Sea and the Suez Canal, off the coast of Egypt. HMS *Philomel*, a British auxiliary (sail and steam) warship, was steaming off Cape Zaafarana, about three-quarters of the way up the Gulf, on the afternoon of 14 October that year (just ten years after the opening of the Suez Canal), when the officers and crew watched in wonder at the caperings of the beast 'rather more than a mile distant on the port bow'. Mr W.J. Andrews, the assistant paymaster of the vessel, described the encounter to accompany a sketch ('Another Marine Monster!') made at the time to illustrate the sighting:

Another Marine Monster! – A sketch in the Gulf of Suez from H.M.S. *Philomel*, Oct. 14, 1879. (*The Graphic*, 29 November 1879)

'This strange monster was seen by the officers and ship's company of the ship at about 5.30 P.M. on October 14, when in the Gulf of Suez, Cape Zafarana bearing at the time N.W. seventeen miles, lat. 28° 56' N., long. 32° 54' E. When first observed it was rather more than a mile distant on the port bow, its snout projecting from the surface of the water, and strongly marked ripples showing the position of the body. It then opened its jaws, as shown in the sketch, and shut them again several times, forcing the water from between them as it did so in all directions in large jets. From time to time a portion of the back and dorsal fin appeared at some distance from the head.

'After remaining some little time in the above-described position, it disappeared, and on coming to the surface again it repeated the action of elevating the head and opening the jaws several times, turning slowly from side to side as it did so. On the approach of the ship the monster swam swiftly away, leaving a broad track like the wake of a ship, and disappeared beneath the waves.

'The colour of that portion of the body that was seen was black, as was also the upper jaw. The lower jaw was grey round the mouth, but of a bright salmon colour underneath, like the belly of some kind of lizard, becoming redder as it approached the throat. The inside of the mouth appeared to be grey with white stripes, parallel to the edges of the jaw, very distinctly marked. These might have been rows of teeth or some substance resembling whalebone. The height the snout was elevated above the surface of the water was at least fifteen feet, and the spread of the jaws quite twenty-five feet.' (*The Graphic*, 29 November 1879)

To anyone with a passing knowledge of the feeding habits of humpback whales, where, from below, they corral a school of fish and then, enormous jaws agape, surge upwards from the depths to swallow as many as they can through their great baleen ('whalebone')-curtained maw, the *Philomel* sketch is very nearly as accurate a depiction of the behaviour as you might want from an amateur observer.

City of Baltimore's Sighting in the Gulf of Aden

Not far from the *Philomel* sighting, a British steamship, the *City of Baltimore*, came across a much more seriously serpentine creature in the Gulf of Aden, between the coasts of Yemen and what is now Djibouti, earlier in the same year, 1879. As with the *Philomel*'s account, a sketch of the incident accompanied a narrative written by a witness on the steamship which was recorded in *The Graphic* magazine for 19 April 1879:

> The following is an abstract of the account given by our correspondent, Major H.W.I. Senior, of the Bengal Staff Corps, to whom we are indebted for the sketch from

The Sea Serpent – Marine monster seen from the S.S. *City of Baltimore* in the Gulf of Aden, Jan. 28. (*The Graphic*, 19 April 1879)

which our engraving is taken: 'On the 28th January 1879, at about 10 A.M., I was on the poop deck of the steamship *City of Baltimore*, in latitude 12° 28' N., longitude 43° 52' E. I observed a long black object a-beam of the ship's stern on the starboard side, at a distance of about three-quarters of a mile, darting rapidly out of the water and splashing in again with a noise distinctly audible, and advancing nearer at a rapid pace. In a minute it had advanced to within half-a-mile, and was distinctly recognisable as the "veritable sea-serpent."

'I shouted out "Sea-serpent! sea-serpent! Call the captain!" Dr. C. Hall, the ship's surgeon [doctor], who was reading on deck, jumped up in time to see the monster, as did also Miss Greenfield, one of the passengers on board. By this time it was only about five hundred yards off, and a little in the rear, owing to the vessel then steaming at the rate of about ten knots an hour in a westerly direction. On approaching the wake of the ship, the serpent turned its course a little way, and was soon lost to view in the blaze of sunlight reflected on the waves of the sea. So rapid were its movements, that when it approached the ship's wake, I seized a telescope, but could not catch a view, as it darted rapidly out of the field of the glass before I could see it. I was thus prevented from ascertaining whether it had scales or not; but the best view of the monster obtainable, when it was about three cables' length, that is, about five hundred yards, distant, seemed to show that it was without scales. I cannot, however, speak with certainty.

'The head and neck, about two feet in diameter, rose out of the water to a height of about twenty or thirty feet, and the monster opened its jaws wide as it rose, and closed them again as it lowered its head and darted forward for a dive, reappearing almost immediately some hundred yards ahead. The body was not visible at all, and must have been some depth under water, as the disturbance on the surface was too slight to attract notice, although occasionally a splash was seen at some distance behind the head. The shape of the head was not unlike pictures of the dragon I have often seen, with a bull-dog appearance of the forehead and eye-brow. When the monster had drawn its head sufficiently out of the water, it let itself drop, as it were, like a huge log of wood, prior to darting forward under the water.' (*The Graphic*, 19 April 1879)

Major Senior's account was also attested to and signed by his two other witnesses, Dr Hall and Miss Greenfield.

'The Vagabond's' View

Doubters of the existence of sea serpents were, and probably still are, plentiful. Decidedly not amongst that sceptical crowd was a colourful character of the late nineteenth century in Australia who styled himself 'The Vagabond'. He was in fact an Englishman named John Stanley James, born in 1843 in Walsall, Staffordshire, who arrived in Sydney in 1875. From then he re-monikered himself as Julian Thomas and 'cultivated an air of mystery about his past as part of his "Vagabond" public persona'. From 1876 he began to write a series of articles for the Melbourne daily newspaper *The Age*, and its weekly publication *The Australasian*, mainly about his travels around the Pacific, under the sobriquet of 'The Vagabond'. In September 1881 he wrote a piece in *The Australasian* that testified to his belief that sea serpents were either real or, at the very least, potentially a real 'marine monster' of magnitude comparable to the whale:

I fully believe in this great marine monster. I have as much evidence as to its existence as of anything not seen. Some years ago, Captain Austin Cooper and the officers and crew of the *Carlisle Castle*, on a voyage to Melbourne, saw the 'varmint.' A description and sketch of it were published in the *Argus*. This, when it arrived in London, it being the 'silly season' in journalism, was seized and torn to pieces by one of the young lions of the *Daily Telegraph*, in a leading article, in which much fun was poked at the gallant sailor.

'I don't see any more sea-serpents,' said my Irish friend to me. 'It is too much to be told that one of Green's commanders can't tell the difference between a piece of sea-weed and a live body in the water [R & H Green were the shipowners of the *Carlisle Castle*]. If twenty serpents come on the starboard, all hands shall be ordered to look to port. No London penny-a-liner [i.e. hack journalist] shall say again that Austin Cooper is a liar and a fool.' After this we softened down over some Coleraine whiskey.

Again, some three years ago, the monster was plainly seen off the great reef of New Caledonia by Commandant Villeneuve, and the officers of the French man-of-war, the *Seudre*. Chassepots [a type of gun] were procured to shoot it, but before it came within easy range it disappeared. During my late visit to Fiji, Major James Harding, who was an officer in Cakoban's army when that chief, 'by the grace of God' was king of Fiji, described exactly the same creature as passing within a few yards of his canoe on a clear moonlight night in the Bay of Suva. It swam towards a small island outside the reef, which is known amongst Fijians as the 'Cave of the Big Snake.'

Major Harding is a cool, brave soldier, who saw much hot work with Cakoban's men against the hill tribes of Vonua Levu. He was once riddled by bullets, and left for dead. Accustomed for years to travel about the reefs in canoes, every phase of the aspect of the waters was known to him, and he was not likely to be frightened with false fire. The extraordinary thing is, that the English sailor, the French commander, and the Fijian soldier, all gave the same account of this monster. It is something with a head slightly raised out of the water, and with a sort of mane streaming behind it, whilst the back of a long body is seen underneath the water.

So, from these instances, in which I know the witnesses, I fully believe in the sea-serpent. What is there very wonderful in it, after all? The whale is the largest living thing. Why shouldn't the waters produce snakes of gigantic size? ('The Vagabond', in Supplement to the *Australasian*, 10 September 1881)

The English author John Ashton (1834–1911) gave *his* verdict on the credibility of the sea serpent in his 1890 work *Curious Creatures in Zoology*, which looked at a myriad gallery of strange creatures of fact and fable, including the venerable sea serpent and a brief review of sightings or encounters with it: 'I think the verdict may be given that its existence, although belonging to "Curious Zoology," is not impossible, and can hardly be branded as a falsehood.'

5

THE KRAKEN

In the early days, when as yet the sea had not become the highway of the nations, little was known of the denizens of the deep. The element in which they lived, with its dangers and its depths, forbade too close a scrutiny; but it gave free play to the glowing imaginations of the dwellers by the sea, who thus manufactured monsters of their own out of the living wonders of the deep. Such a monster was the kraken, famous in the traditions of the Scandinavian coasts. ('The Legendary Kraken', *Monsters of the Sea, Legendary and Authentic*, by John Gibson, 1887)

According to the ancient legend, the kraken is a foul, colossal beast, of shapeless body, with arms as long as the longest serpent's, and covered with innumerable suckers. He does not content himself with attacking the other denizens of Ocean; he lusts after the flesh and blood of man. It is especially at night, and in the fury of the tempests, that he rises from the bottom of the abyss to assail the unhappy voyagers overtaken by the whirlwind. It then embraces the masts and rigging with its gigantic arms, and endeavours to drag down under the seething waters the ship and all on board. The sole means of escape is by severing its tentacles with blows of an axe; yet it is by no means certain that they will not grow again immediately, like the heads of the hydra.

It is easy to understand the terror with which the recital of the frightful exploits of such an enemy must formerly have inspired ignorant minds prone to super-stitious fancies. (*The Mysteries of the Ocean*, by Arthur Mangin, translated from the French by W.H. Davenport Adams, 1870)

The kraken is a good example of a creature combining the doppelganger characteristics of sea *monster* as myth which 'inspired ignorant minds prone to superstitious fancies', and sea *creature* as real, palpable, pulpy, tentacular flesh. The mythical monster of folklore – acres (sometimes *miles*) in size, monstrous in appearance, devilish by nature – almost certainly owes at least part, if not most, of its monstrousness to one of the greatest and still most mysterious of real sea monsters: *Architeuthis*, the giant squid – or, as the sea monster sleuth Henry Lee has called it, the 'gigantic calamary', 'gigantic cuttle' and 'great cephalopod', amongst other monikers.

The Kraken

In the whole range of fabulous monsters there is not one that has met with greater incredulity, and yet main-tained its hold on the wonder of man with more constant tenacity, than the kraken. From time immemorial it has appeared again and again on the pages of travelers, and

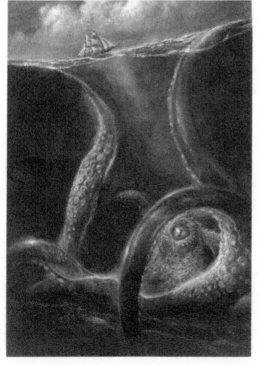

The kraken, as seen by the eye of imagination. (*The Mysteries of the Ocean*, by Arthur Mangin, 1870)

The kraken.

from the oldest philosopher to the days of Lacépède [French naturalist Bernard-Germain-Étienne de La Ville-sur-Illon, compte de Lacépède (1756–1825)] and Buckstone [possibly Francis (Frank) Trevelyan Buckland (1826–80)] these faint traces of its true character and gigantic proportions have been carefully examined, and when stripped of the usual exaggerations, been found to agree with the actual dimensions of a genuine and formidable monster.

Aristotle, whose history has so often been the laughing-stock of the half informed, and whom the skeptics of all ages have been delighted to use as a type of unreliable naturalists, has of late recovered, step by step, the veneration which he enjoyed in the Middle Ages. It would be an interesting task to gather the great facts constantly represented, in scientific works even, as new discoveries, of which a correct sketch is already in the work of the ancient savant. Thus he seems to have known, better than any naturalist down to our own day, the nature of the polypus, who, in all probability, has filled the imagination of men for so many centuries under the name of the kraken.

Trebius [second century BC Roman statesman and author of a natural history] tells us a story, on the other hand, in which undoubted facts are already half hidden under a mass of exaggerations, of which Aristotle never became guilty, however common they were in the writings of the ancients. A polypus, he says, came every night from the great deep on shore at Carteja, in order to feed upon salt meat. These robberies incensed the people, who in vain tried to discover the intruder, although they surrounded their drying-places with high palisades.

The polypus took advantage of a large tree which stood near them, and, by means of an overhanging branch that could support his weight, he slipped in night after night. At last, however, his hour came; the dogs discovered him one morning, as he tried to make his way back to the sea, and soon hosts of men surrounded the monster – at a distance only, for the novelty of the sight, the hideousness of the monster all covered with brine, his enormous size, and the horrible odor which he diffused on all sides nearly petrified the poor fishermen.

In the mean time he was fighting the dogs bravely, now striking them to the ground with his two larger arms, and now beating them painfully with his whip-like tentacles. At last the men gained courage, and with their tridents they overcame and dispatched the monster. We must add, for the honor of Pliny, who quotes the account of Trebius, that he looks upon it as a prodigy, and in his quiet, quaint way gives the reader to understand his reluctance to vouch for the statement.

The head and the arms of the giant were, however, brought to Lucullus [a wealthy Roman gourmand (110–57 BC)] and carefully measured. The former was of the size of a cask, capable of holding fifteen amphoræ, with a beak in proportion; the arms were thirty feet long, and so large that a man could hardly span them; what remained of the flesh weighed still over seven hundred pounds. Whether Lucullus had it dressed for his table is not stated; we know, however, that the Romans were as fond of the flesh of these hideous creatures as the fishermen of the coasts of Normandy are in our day; it is firm, but savory, and assumes, when cooked, a white and pink color, which looks most appetizing ...

Pliny adds the crowning piece of wonder: A polypus, he says, exists in the great ocean, called Arbas, whose feet are of such enormous size that they prevent it from coming into the Mediterranean, as the Straits of Gibraltar are too shallow for such a giant! ...

The Norwegians, especially, loved to tell wondrous tales; how their bold seamen landed on a deserted island which showed no trace of life, not a shrub nor a blade of grass; and while they still wandered about, marveling at the utter desolation, the island began to heave and to move, and behold! they found themselves on the back of the monster! Great authorities came to confirm the stories; saints and bishops lent the weight of their sacred character to the accounts given by laymen and heretics.

Erik Falkendorf [Walkendorf], a bishop of Nidros, wrote, in 1520, a long letter on the subject to Pope Leo X. He was sailing, on a Sunday, in a Norwegian vessel along the distant coast, and bewailed his inability to celebrate holy mass on firm land. As he mourned and prayed, suddenly an unknown islet arose, not far from the vessel; the crew land, the sacred vessels are carried on shore, and the holy office is celebrated with due solemnity. After mass they return on board ship, and immediately the island begins to tremble, and gradually to sink back into the sea, from which it had risen.

The island had been a kraken! (*Harper's Weekly*, Supplement, 8 April 1871)

We met Archbishop Walkendorf earlier, in Chapter 5 of Olaus Magnus's *Compendious History*, 'Of the Horrible Monsters of the Coast of Norway', with his letter to Pope Leo X: 'and, to this Epistle, was [attached] the head of another Monster, seasoned [preserved] with Salt'. A seasoned head of a kraken, it would appear.

Norwegian Kraken-Islands and Bishop Pontoppidan

It was a common legend amongst the coastal people of Norway that islands close to the coast sometimes appeared and disappeared at random. The supposition, or superstition – much the same thing in the legend – was that the 'floating islands' were 'looked upon, by the common people, as the habitations of evil spirits, which appear at sea for the purpose of confounding their reckoning, and leading them into danger and difficulty'. But, as the same writer noted, and continuing on to Bishop Pontoppidan's perusal of the 'monstrous sea animal':

> That these superstitious notions are occasioned by the appearance of some monstrous sea animal, is the more likely, in as far as real floating islands are never seen at sea, being incapable of resisting the swell and tumult of its waters ...
>
> 'But, according to the laws of truth,' says Pontoppidan, 'we ought not to charge this apostate spirit without a cause. I rather think that this devil, who so suddenly makes and unmakes these floating islands, is nothing else but the kraken, which some seafaring people call Soe-draulen, that is Soe-trolden, or Sea-mischief. What confirms me in this opinion is the following occurrence, quoted by that worthy Swedish physician Dr Urban Hierne [Dr Urban Hjärne (1641–1724)], in his short introduction to an *Enquiry into the Ores and Minerals* of that country:
>
> 'Amongst the rocks about Copenhagen there is sometimes seen a certain track of land, which at other times disappears, and is seen again in another place. Buræus

has placed this as an island in his map. The peasants, who call it Gummers-ore, say that it is not always seen, and that it lies out in the open sea, but I could never find it. One Sunday when I was out among the rocks, sounding the coast, it happened, that in one place I saw something like three points of land in the sea, which surprised me a little, and I thought that I had inadvertently passed them over before. Upon this, I called to a peasant to inquire for Gummers-ore, but when he came we could see nothing of it; on which the peasant said, all was well, and that this prognosticated a storm, or a great quantity of fish,' &c.

'Now,' says the Bishop, 'who is it that cannot discover, at first sight, that this visible and invisible Gummers-ore, with its points and prognostications of fish, cannot possibly be any thing else but the krakken, krabben, or soe-horven, improperly placed in a map by Buræus as an island. Probably the creature keeps himself always about that spot, and often rises up amongst the rocks and cliffs.' ('Remarks on the Histories of the Kraken and Great Sea Serpent', *Blackwood's Edinburgh Magazine*, March 1818)

Our venerable Pontoppidan gave extensive exposure to his views on the kraken in his *Natural History of Norway*. He introduced the 'krakken, krabben, or soe-horven', amongst other names, at the beginning of Section XI of his *History*:

I am now come to the third and incontestibly the largest Sea-monster in the world; it is called Kraken, Kraxen, or, as some name it, Krabben, that word being applied by way of eminence to this creature. This last name seems indeed best to agree with the description of this creature, which is round, flat, and full of arms, or branches. Others call it also Horven, or Soe-horven, and some Anker-trold.

Among all the foreign writers, both ancient and modern, which I have had the opportunity to consult on this subject, not one of them seems to know much of this creature, or at least to have a just idea of it. What they say however of floating islands, as they apprehended them to be, (a thing improbable that they should exist in the wild tumultuous ocean) shall afterwards be spoken of, and will be found applicable without any hyperbole to this creature, when I shall have first given some account of it.

Pontoppidan was one of many writers over the ages who gave accounts of the kraken, either (and mostly) of myth and legend, or (occasionally) as a real phenomenon of some monstrous marine magnitude. But the learned bishop was regarded with esteem as one of the most judicious and 'precise', though, in his self-admittedly *'more enlighten'd age'*, also most naturally sceptical writers on the beast.

Pontoppidan wrote of 'the credulous Ol. [Olaus] Magnus', concerning Magnus's account 'of the Whale being so large, that his back is looked upon as an island; and that people might land, light fires, and do various kinds of work upon it, is a notoriously fabulous and ridiculous romance'. But the *Swedish* archbishop of *Carta Marina* fame lived in the pre-Enlightenment sixteenth century that the *Danish*-born bishop excused as 'that dark age, when that author wrote', compared with his own more rational eighteenth-century *'enlighten'd age'*.

Olaus Wormius, also, who is generally truthful enough, relates having seen, about the year 1643, one of these enormous monsters, and states that they resemble an island far more than an animal. He expresses his belief that there are but few krakens in existence, and curiously enough adds, that while they are themselves immortal, the medusæ are nothing more than the eggs and the spawn of these monsters.

Other writers of the same century confirm his statement, and believe in the immortality of the kraken – a faith which was not even shaken when in 1680 the carcass of one of these monsters was for the first time discovered in the Gulf of Newangen, in the parish of Astabough [Ulvangen fjord, Alstadhoug parish, mid-Norwegian coast]. His arms had become entangled in the countless cliffs and rocks which characterize the dangerous coast of that neighborhood, and the animal had died there, unable to extricate itself. When putrefaction commenced in the enormous mass, the odor became so offensive for miles and miles that serious fears of a pestilence were entertained.

Fortunately, the waves came to the aid of the frightened people, tearing off piece after piece, and carrying it into the ocean; and when the last remnant had been washed away, an official report of the whole event was drawn up by a clerical dignitary, and is still to be found in the government archives at Drontheim [Trondheim].

A similar case occurred on the Newfoundland Banks, where polypi abound in such numbers that the fishermen of all numbers, who congregate there in the season, use every summer nearly two millions as bait, with which to catch codfish. Toward the end of the last century a monstrous specimen of this class died on these banks beyond Pine Light, and here, also, the mass of putrefying matter was so enormous, and the odor so intolerable for a great distance, that the grave apprehension of an epidemic drove the fishermen from the neighborhood till the currents had carried off every trace of the terrible animal.

Of all the authors, however, who have given us more or less detailed accounts of their experience with the *soetrolden*, or sea-scourge, as the Swedes call it, Pontoppidan is by far the most precise in his statements ... Such is the account found in the Natural History of the learned bishop, who, no doubt, wrote what he conscientiously believed to be true, although he can not quite disguise his own skepticism in regard to some of the facts mentioned ... ('The Kraken', *Harper's Weekly*, Supplement, 8 April 1871)

Pontoppidan's account of the kraken followed from his introductory remarks in Section XI of his *History*, beginning Section XII:

Our fishermen unanimously affirm, and without the least variation in their accounts, that when they row out several miles to sea, particularly in the hot summer days, and by their situation (which they know by taking a view of certain points of land) expect to find 80 or 100 fathoms water, it often happens that they do not find above 20 or thirty; and sometimes less. At these places they generally find the greatest plenty of fish, especially cod and ling.

Their lines, they say, are no sooner out than they may draw them up with the hooks all full of fish; by this they judge that the kraken is at the bottom.

They say this creature causes those unnatural shallows mentioned above, and prevents their sounding. These the fishermen are always glad to find, looking upon them as the means of their taking abundance of fish. There are sometimes twenty boats or more got together, and throwing out their lines at a moderate distance from each other; and the only thing they then have to observe is, whether the depth continues the same, which they know by their lines, or whether it grows shallower by their seeming to have less water.

If this last be the case, they find that the kraken is rais-ing himself nearer the surface, and then it is not time for them to stay any longer; they immediately leave off fishing, take to their oars, and get off as fast as they can. When they have reached the usual depth of the place, and find themselves out of danger, they lie upon their oars, and in a few minutes after they see this enormous monster come up to the surface of the water; he there shows himself sufficiently, though his whole body does not appear, which, in all likelihood, no human eye ever beheld, (excepting the young of this species, which shall afterwards be spoken of;) its back or upper part, which seems to be in appearance about an English mile and a half in circumference, (some say more, but I choose the least for greater certainty,) looks at first like a number of small islands, surrounded with something that floats and fluctuates like sea-weeds.

Here and there a larger rising is observed like sand-banks, on which various kinds of small fishes are seen continually leaping about till they roll into the water from the sides of it; at last several bright points or horns appear, which grow thicker and thicker the higher they rise above the surface of the water, and sometimes they stand up as high and as large as the masts of middle-sized vessels. It seems these are the creature's arms, and, it is said, if they were to lay hold of the largest man-of-war, they would pull it down to the bottom.

After this monster has been on the surface of the water for a short time, it begins slowly to sink again, and then the danger is as great as before; because the motion of his sinking causes such a swell in the sea, and such an eddy or whirlpool, that it draws everything down with it, like the current of the River Male. ('Marvels in Marine Natural History', *The Eclectic Magazine*, Vol. 8, 1846, extracted from Pontoppidan's *Natural History of Norway*)

Pontoppidan was a man of the post-scientific revolution and Enlightenment empiricism that required experiential evidence of natural phenomena – 'the best instructor,' as he called it – to ascertain their real nature. For the kraken he relied on 'what has been related to me by my correspondents, and what I have otherwise collected by an industrious enquiry and examination into every particular, concerning which I could receive intelligence'. Sceptic to the core, he concluded his kraken accounts with a final (and rather open-ended) rejoinder:

If I was an admirer of uncertain reports, and fabulous stories, I might here add much more concerning this and other Norwegian Sea-monsters, whose existence I will not take upon me to deny; but do not chuse, by a mixture of uncertain relations, to make such accounts appear doubtful, as I myself believe to be true and well attested. I shall therefore quit the subject here, and leave it to future writers on this plan, to complete what I have imperfectly sketched out, by further experience, which is always the best instructor.

Henry Lee (1826/27–88) was a famous nineteenth-century doubting Thomas of cryptozoology, but more of the sea serpent than of the kraken-cuttle-calamary-giant squid. In his *Sea Monsters Unmasked* (1883) he wrote about Pontoppidan's own limitations, that 'when he [Pontoppidan] wrote, science was only slowly recovering from neglect of many centuries duration'. That 'Pontoppidan was not a fabricator of falsehoods; but, in collecting evidence relating to the "great beasts" living in "the great and wide sea," was influenced, as he tells us, by "a desire to extend the popular knowledge of the glorious works of a beneficent Creator."' And that: 'He gave too much credence to contemporary narratives and old traditions of floating islands and sea monsters, and to the superstitious beliefs and exaggerated statements of ignorant fishermen; but if those who ridicule him had lived in his day and amongst his people, they would probably have done the same ...'

A tolerant view of 'the Norwegian bishop' whose kraken commentaries Lee then went on to quote rather extensively; he believed Pontoppidan to have been, for his time, 'a conscientious and painstaking investigator'. Lee paid considerable homage to Pontoppidan's modest claim that he would shed such light as he could on 'this creature ("the Kracken") ... the largest and most surprizing of all the animal creation', but that he, Pontoppidan, thought 'perhaps much greater light in this subject may be reserved for posterity'. That 'much greater light', Lee affirmed, 'has been thrown upon it by the discoveries of the last few years', so that:

> ... seen in the clearer atmosphere of our present knowledge, the great sea-monster which loomed so indefinitely vast in the mist of ignorance and superstition, stands revealed in its true form and proportions ... and we recognise in the supposed Kraken, as the Norwegian bishop rightly conjectured that we should, an 'animal of the Polypus (or cuttle) kind, and amongst the largest inhabitants of the ocean.' (From *Sea Monsters Unmasked*)

Hans Egede's Greenland *Hafgufa*

In the northern seas bordering the Arctic, from Norway to Greenland, there was in medieval times believed to exist a massive sea monster that in Icelandic was called *Hafgufa* (Icelandic: *'haf'*: sea; *'gufa'*: steam or vapour or mist – like a whale's spout). *Hafgufa* has also been translated in English as 'Sea-Reek' by the eminent Icelandic language scholar and translator Hermann Pálsson (1921–2002), lecturer and later professor of Icelandic studies at Edinburgh University from 1950 till 1988. 'Reek' was probably not a coincidental word choice for an Icelandic scholar who taught and lived in a city – Edinburgh – that was and still is familiarly called *Auld Reekie*. The meaning of 'reek' derives from the Old Norse and subsequently Scottish dialect word for 'smoky', which Edinburgh used to be. A traditional Hogmanay greeting remains to this day, 'Lang may yer lum reek!' (as in, 'Long may your chimney smoke!', meaning, may you always be able to afford enough fuel for your fireplace; so, 'Long may you prosper!') And thereby hangs the etymological tale of old *Hafgufa*, the 'Sea-Reek'.

The Danish Lutheran missionary Hans Egede spent fifteen years in Greenland, between 1721 and 1736. His mission was not solely dedicated to illuminating the minds of 'Heathens', as his vocation called him to do. He travelled extensively around the country, learned the local language and customs, and compiled copious notes of his observations about Greenland's natural history, published as *A Description of Greenland* in 1757, a year before his death on 5 November 1758.

In one section of the *Description*, Egede alights on the subject of local Greenlandic sea monsters, three of which he finds mentioned in the *History of Greenland* (*Gronlandia*

Antiquæ, 1706), by the Icelandic historian Tormod Torfæus (1636–1719).

> As for other sea monsters and wonderful animals, we find in Tormoder's [*sic*] *History of Greenland*, mention made of three sorts of monsters … But none of them have been seen by us, or any of our time, that ever I could hear, save the most dreadful monster, that showed itself upon the surface of the water in the year 1734, off our new colony in 64° [north latitude].

The 'most dreadful monster' Egede saw 'in the year 1734, off our new colony in 64°' was, as related earlier, the sea serpent. Here he goes on to pick out and describe the third of Tormod's *Gronlandia Antiquæ* sea monsters: the most terrible of the trio for its utter, voracious kraken-monstrousness:

> The third monster, named Hafgufa, is so terrible and frightful, that the author [Tormod] does not well know how to describe it; and no wonder, because he never had any true relation of it: its shape, length, and bulk, seems to exceed all size and measure. They that pretend to have seen it, say, it appeared to them more like a land than a fish, or sea animal. And as there never has been seen above two of them in the wide open sea, they conclude, that there can be no breed of them; for, if they should breed and multiply, all the rest of fishes must be destroyed at last, their vast body wanting such large quantity of nourishment.
>
> When this monster is hungry, it is said to void through the mouth some matter of a sweet scent, which perfumes the whole sea; and by this means it allures and draws all sorts of fishes and animals, even the whales to it, who in whole droves flock thither, and run into the wide opened

swallow of this hideous monster, as into a whirlpool, till its belly be well freighted with a copious load of all sorts of fishes and animals, and then it shuts the swallow, and has for the whole year enough to digest and live upon; for it is said to make but one large meal a year.

This, though a very silly and absurd tale, is nevertheless matched by another story, every whit as ridiculous, told by my own countrymen, fishermen in the Northern part of Norway. They tell you, that a great ghastly sea monster now and then appears in the main sea, which they call Kracken, and is no doubt the same that the islanders call Hafgufa, of which we have spoken above. They say, that its body reaches several miles in length; and that it is most seen in a calm; when it comes out of the water, it seems to cover the whole surface of the sea, having many heads and a number of claws, with which it seizes all that comes in its way, as fishing boats with men and all, fishes and animals, and lets nothing escape; all which it draws down to the bottom of the sea.

Moreover they tell you that all sorts of fishes flock together upon it, as upon a bank of the sea, and that many fishing boats come thither to catch fish, not suspecting that they be upon some such a dreadful monster, which they at last understand by the intangling of their hooks and angles in its body; which the monster feeling, rises softly from the bottom to the surface, and seizes them all; if in time they do not perceive him and prevent their destruction, which they may easily do, only calling it by its name, which it no sooner hears, but it sinks down again as softly as it did rise.

One of the old Norse-Icelandic heroic or legendary sagas (*fornaldarsögur*), from the thirteenth century, is Örvar-Odd's saga, written by an anonymous Icelander about the life and exploits of its eponymous hero Örvar-Odd. (The Icelandic scholars and academics Paul Edwards and Hermann Pálsson translated the name as 'Arrow-Odd' in their English version of the 'medieval novel', published in 1970.)

Fast-leaping past the many battles and vicissitudes of our hero, it happened that he came to be on a voyage in the Greenland Sea in the company of his son, Vignir. There they espied two rocks that emerged above the surface of the water which they sailed between towards a large island 'covered with heather'. Five men went on the 'heather-back' island to look for water, shortly after which 'the island foundered and they were all drowned'. The two rocks also disappeared. Odd 'asked Vignir if he could explain' the disappearances, which he did:

> I'll tell you about it: these were two sea-monsters, one called 'sea-reek,' [the *hafgufa*] and the other 'heather-back.' [*lyngbakr*] The sea-reek's the biggest monster in the whole ocean. What it does is to swallow both men and ships, and whales too, and anything else it can get. It stays underwater for days, and then it puts up its mouth and nostrils, and when it does it never stays on the surface for less than one tide. Now that sound we sailed through [between the rocks] was the space between its jaws, and its nostrils and lower jaw were the two rocks we saw in the sea. The island that foundered was the heather-back. (From *Arrow-Odd: A Medieval Novel*, translated by Paul Edwards and Hermann Pálsson, 1970)

Another medieval work of Old Norse literature that included our *hafgufa* was *Konungs skuggsjá* (*The King's Mirror*), from the mid-thirteenth century (translated into

English, most notably by Laurence Marcellus Larson, professor of history at the University of Illinois, and published in 1917). The narrator described: 'a fish ... which it is scarcely advisable to speak about on account of its size, which to most people will seem incredible ... Most often in our tongue we call it *hafgufa* [Prof. Larson translated it as "kraken"].'

The *hafgufa*-kraken-'fish' is said to feed by stretching up its neck 'with a great belching', following which there 'comes forth much food' which attracts shoals of other fish towards it, 'believing they shall obtain their food and good eating'. But the canny *hafgufa*, keeping his great maw open with so many fish feeding therein, when its mouth is full, 'then it locks together its jaws and has the fish all caught and enclosed ...'

And if that great gulp isn't a pretty precise description of a humpback whale feeding, it comes very close. But before ships crossed the seas as commonplace and seafarers saw with real eyes the real sea creatures round about them, the medieval eye's mind was more familiar with the mythical monsters and heroes ashore and afloat that the Norse saga-narrators spun into their fabulous *fornaldarsögur*. A great humped lump surfacing and disappearing slowly beneath the waves could very understandably be the leviathan *lyng-baker*, a great whale which the Norsemen knew from their longboat voyages.

In those mystical times of Old Norse yore and lore centuries before the Enlightenment of empirical scientific method and the Age of Reason, *hafgufas* and 'great ghastly sea-monster' krakens were not just fabulous; they were real. But the point wasn't whether they were *actually* real. The point was that, in those saga-storied times, they were imaginatively, thrillingly – *terrifyingly* – so.

... It is very different with Augustus of Bergen [Karl-Augustus von Bergen, German anatomist and botanist, 1704–59], a man of critical mind, who, not having seen a kraken himself, collected all the Scandinavian accounts of which he heard, and, after examining them carefully, came to the conclusion that there does exist a gigantic polypus – though far from boasting of the dimensions usually attributed to the monster – that it is provided with arms, that it emits a strong odor, that it shows at times long tentacles, and only appears in summer-time and during calm weather. It is remarkable how fully the conclusions of this learned naturalist have been confirmed by modern discoveries.

The great Linné [Carl Linnaeus (1707–78), 'the father of modern taxonomy'], a Swede in heart as in race, seems to have been troubled with strange doubt concerning this pet monster of his countrymen; for, after having solemnly introduced the kraken into his Swedish fauna, and after speaking of it even more fully in his great work, *The System of Nature*, he suddenly drops him in the seventh edition, and never more says a word of the gigantic polypus.

This did not have much effect, however, on the sailors of his and of other lands, as they were not much given to reading Latin works; and in Sweden, as well as in France, the faith in the kraken remained as general and as firm as before. Countless votive offerings adorn to this day the little chapels that rise high above the iron-bound coast, with their tiny turrets and tinkling bells; but none more weighty in precious metals, none more faithfully offered to the Lord of the Sea, than those which speak of the delivery from the dread kraken.

One of these – in the Church of 'Our Lady of the Watch at Marseilles' – is accompanied by a touching recital of a fearful combat with the monster on the coast of South Carolina; and another, hung up in the chapel of St. Thomas, at St. Malo, testifies to the escape of a slave-ship from the arms of a gigantic polypus at the very moment when it was leaving the port of Angola.

In 1783 a whaler assured Dr. Swediaur [Dr François-Xavier Swediaur, Viennese-born physician, scientist and philosopher (1748–1824)] that he had found in the mouth of a whale a tentacle of twenty-seven feet length. The report was inserted in a scientific journal of the day, and there read by Deny Montfort [Pierre Denys de Montfort (1766–1820), a French naturalist with specific interest in giant octopuses inspired by this account of a 27ft-long tentacle], who at once determined to obtain more ample information on the subject.

It so happened that just then the French government had sent for a number of American whalers, in order to consult with them as to the best means by which the French fisheries could be revived. These men were staying at Dunkirk; and here Montfort questioned them, and, upon inquiry, it appeared that two of them had found feelers, or horns, of such monstrous animals. Ben Jonson [British dramatist (1572–1637)] saw one in the mouth of a whale, from which it hung to the length of thirty-five feet; and Reynolds [possibly Sir Joshua Reynolds, English painter (1723–92)] another, floating on the surface of the sea, forty-five feet long, and of reddish slate-color.

But of all the reports which he heard, the following was the most minute, and yet also the most extraordinary:

Capt. Dens' Anchertroll Horror Off West Africa

Captain John Magnus Dens, a Danish sailor of high character and established uprightness, deposed that, after having made several voyages to China in the service of the Gottenburg Company, he had once found himself becalmed in the fifteenth degree of south latitude, at some distance from the coast of Africa, abreast of St. Helena and Cape Nigra [southern Angola]. Taking advantage of his forced inactivity, he had determined to have his ship cleaned and scrubbed thoroughly, and for that purpose a few planks were suspended on the side of the vessel, on which the sailors could stand while scraping and calking the ship.

They were busy with their work, when suddenly an *anchertroll* – so the Danes call the animal – rose from the sea, threw one of its arms round two of the men, tore them with a jerk from the scaffolding, and sank out of sight in a moment. Another feeler [tentacle] appeared, however, and tried to grasp a sailor who was in the act of ascending the mast; fortunately the man could hold on to the rigging, and as the long feeler became entangled in the ropes, he was enabled to escape, though not without uttering most fearful cries. These brought the whole crew to his assistance; they quickly snatched up harpoons, cutlasses, and whatever they could lay hands on, and threw them at the body of the animal, while others set to work cutting the gigantic feeler to pieces and carrying the poor man to his berth, who had swooned from intense fright.

The monster, with five harpoons thrust deep into its quivering flesh, and holding the two men still in its huge arms, endeavored to sink; but the crew, encouraged by their captain, did their utmost to hold on to the lines to which the harpoons were fastened. Their strength was, however, not sufficient to struggle with the marine giant, and all they could do was to make fast the lines to the ship, and to wait till the forces of the enemy should be exhausted. Four of the ropes snatched, one after the other, like mere threads, and the harpoon of the fifth tore out of the body of the monster with such violence that the ship was shaken from end to end; thus the animal escaped, with its two victims.

The whole crew remained overcome with amazement; they had heard of these monsters, but never believed in their existence; and here, before their eyes, two of their comrades had been torn from their side, and the third, overcome with fright, died the same night with delirium. The feeler which had been separated from the body remained on board as an evidence that the whole had not been a frightful dream; it measured at the base as many inches as their mizzen-mast, was still twenty-five feet long, and at the pointed end provided with a number of suckers, each as large as a spoon. Its full size must have been far greater, however, as only part of it had been cut off, the animal never even raising its head above the surface.

The captain, who had witnessed the whole scene, and himself thrown one of the harpoons, ever afterward considered this encounter the most remarkable event of his checkered life, and calmly asserted the existence of the kraken. ('The Kraken', *Harper's Weekly*, Supplement, 8 April 1871)

Capt. Dens' account of the kraken's attack on his ship was published originally in French in the second volume of Denys de Montfort's *Histoire Naturelle Générale et Particulière des Mollusques* (Paris, 1801/02). Plate XXVI in that volume, on page 256 – 'Le Poulpe Colossal' – showing a giant octopus attacking a sailing ship, is probably the most widely reproduced image of a kraken-attack.

All these ancient accounts, the Norwegian legends, the reports of sailors of many nations, and the minute descriptions of Sicilian divers, who spoke of polypi as large as themselves, and with feelers at least 10ft long, could not fail to make an impression upon men of science, and the most discreet among them came to the conclusion that there must be some truth amid all those fables.

From Kraken to *Architeuthis dux*

It was, however, reserved to our century to strip the facts of all exaggeration, and to establish the existence of such monsters beyond all controversy. A kind of mollusc, called cephalopods, was found in various seas, whose peculiar formation and strange appearance sufficiently explained the marvels told of the kraken. An elongated sack in the form of an egg, or a cylinder, from which protrudes at one end a thick, round head, with a pair of enormous flat eyes; on this head, at the summit, a kind of hard, brown beak, after the manner of a parrot's bill, and round the beak a crown of eight or ten powerful, long arms – this is the polypus, or octopus, which passed of old for a kraken ...

The cephalopodes on European and American coasts are generally only of small size, although in the Mediterranean and the Adriatic seas some have been found of larger dimensions, and others still greater are kept in museums. In the open sea, however, vessels have encountered genuine giants of the kind, and these are, no doubt, the true representatives of the kraken.

Rang met one of the size of a ton, and of reddish color; while Pennant [Thomas Pennant (1726–98), Welsh

Le Poulpe Colossal. (*Histoire Naturelle Générale et Particulière des Mollusques*, by Denys de Montfort, Paris, 1801/02)

naturalist and author; in *British Zoology* (1776)] saw in the Indian seas an eight-armed cuttle-fish, with arms of fifty-four feet in length and a body of twelve feet in breadth;

This depiction of a giant octopus/kraken attacking a ship first appeared in the 'Amphibious Carnivora' section of the 'Mammalia' volume XXV of Sir William Jardine's *The Naturalist's Library*, 1839. It referred in the text specifically to 'the Colossal Cuttle-fish' and its attack on Dens's vessel 'in the African Seas (off the coast of Angola) by a monster of this kind'.

thus making it extend, from point to point, one hundred and twenty feet.

[Pennant, in his description of the eight-armed cuttle-fish, mentions, that he has been well assured by persons of undoubted credit, that in the Indian seas this species has been found of such a size as to measure two fathoms (12ft) in breadth across the central part, while each arm was nine fathoms (54ft) in length. He further states, that the natives of the Indian isles, when sailing in their canoes, always take care to be provided with hatchets, in order to cut off immediately the arms of such of those animals as happen to fling them over the sides of the canoes, lest they should pull it under water, and sink it. ('Remarks on the Histories of the Kraken and Great Sea Serpent', *Blackwood's Edinburgh Magazine*, March 1818)]

A naturalist of Copenhagen, who has made the study of these animals his specialty – Steenstrup [Prof. Johannes Japetus Smith Steenstrup (1813–97)] – had occasion to examine one of these monsters in 1855 on the coast of Gothland, where it had been caught by fishermen. It required several carts to carry the body off; and the hind part of the mouth, which he saved from destruction, still had the size of an infant's head ... ('The Kraken', *Harper's Weekly*, Supplement, 8 April 1871)

On 26 November 1854 the polymath Danish natural scientist Johannes Steenstrup gave a presentation at the Danish Natural History Society. Steenstrup first summarised historical depictions and descriptions of a marine creature characterised as a 'sea monk', ostensibly for its putative, though, in fact, rather far-fetched resemblance to a robed medieval monk. His conclusion was: 'The Sea Monk is firstly a cephalopod' – in other words, a squid. He showed his audience a jar containing the preserved jaw-beak (around 10–12cm in size) of a massive creature that had washed ashore 300 years before at Aalbækstrand on the coast of Denmark, at the southern extremity of the Skagen peninsula, on the Øresund strait between Denmark and Sweden.

The size of the Øresund 'sea monk's' beak convinced Steenstrup that 'the stranded animal must thus belong not only to the large, but to the really gigantic cephalopods, whose existence has generally been doubted'. And so the giant squid, which Steenstrup was the first to investigate in any scientific detail, was first given its scientific moniker of *Architeuthis dux*, though through some pretty muddled, and muddied, taxonomic waters for quite a while, which became a natural updated doppelganger of the kraken.

Even the kraken-*Architeuthis*'s smallest relatives caused sensations of sucky shock to someone grabbed by one.

> William Buckland, the great naturalist's [i.e. Francis (Frank) Trevelyan Buckland's] son, and an excellent observer himself, took pains to examine the varieties known to the British coast, and allowed one small specimen to grasp his hand and arm. He describes the feeling to be such as if a hundred tiny air-pumps had been applied at once, and little red marks were left on the skin where the suckers had been at work.
>
> 'The sensation,' he says, 'of being held fast by a (literally) cold-blooded, soulless, pitiless, and voracious sea-monster almost makes one's blood run cold. I can now easily understand why they are called man-suckers; only the natives of the Chinese and Indian seas have such a horror of them – for in those climates they are seen large and formidable enough to be dangerous to any human being who may be so unfortunate as to be clutched by them.' ('The Kraken', *Harper's Weekly*, Supplement, 8 April 1871)

The Colossal Connemara Calamary Caper

If ever an Irish ex-fisherman grandfather wanted a story to tell his grandchildren round the peat fire of a winter's evening, the exploits of two Connemara fishermen one day in April 1875 would have given more than enough material to entertain – and enthrall and terrify – the youngsters. Not content with simply encountering a very large 'cuttle' that was alive and tentacling menace in ten different directions, they decided to pursue the beast – to obtain juicy chunks of it to use 'as bait for coarse fish'!

*Capture of an enormous Cuttle-fish off Boffin Island,
on the Coast of Connemara*

On Monday last [26 April 1875] the crew of a curragh [a
large kind of coracle made with wooden ribs, and covered with tarred canvas], consisting of three men, met
with a strange adventure north-west of Boffin Island,
Connemara. The capture of a cuttle-fish sounds little
of an exploit. Ordinarily the fish is of small size, a few
inches in circumference, with projecting arms, studded
with suckers, by which it retains its prey – the body containing a dark fluid, which it emits on being startled, and,
blackening the surrounding water, so eludes its enemy.

Very different indeed from this ordinary type was the
creature in question. Having shot their spillets (or long lines)
in the morning, the crew of the curragh observed to seaward
a great floating mass surrounded by gulls; they pulled out,
believing it to be a wreck, but, to their great astonishment,
found it to be a cuttle-fish, of enormous proportions, and
lying perfectly still, as if basking on the surface of the water.

What rarely enough occurs, there was no gaff or spare
rope, and a knife was the only weapon aboard. The cuttle
is much prized as bait for coarse fish, and, their wonder
somewhat over, the crew resolved to secure at least a portion of the prize. Considering the great size of the monster,
and knowing the crushing and holding powers of the arms,
open hostility could not be resorted to, and the fishermen
shaped their tactics differently. Paddling up with caution,
a single arm was suddenly seized and lopped off.

The cuttle, hitherto at rest, became dangerously active
now, and set out to sea at full speed in a cloud of spray,
rushing through the water at a tremendous rate. The
canoe immediately gave chase, and was up again with the

enemy after three-quarters of a mile. Hanging on to the rear of the fish, a single arm was attacked in turn, while it took all the skill of the men to keep out of the deadly clutches of the suckers. The battle thus continued for two hours, and while direct conflict was avoided, the animal was gradually being deprived of its offensive weapons.

Five miles out on the open Atlantic, in their frail canvas craft, the bowman still slashed away, holding on boldly by the stranger, and steadily cutting down his powers. By this time the prize was partially subdued, and the curragh closed in fairly with the monster. The polished sides of the canoe afforded slender means of grasp, and such as remained of the ten great arms slashed round through air and water in a most dangerous but unavailing fashion. The trunk of the fish lay alongside, fully as long as the canoe, while, in its extremity, the mutilated animal emitted successive jets of fluid which darkened the sea for fathoms round. The head at last was severed from the body, which was unmanageable from its great weight, and sank like lead to the bottom of the sea ...

Of the portions of the mollusk taken ashore, two of the great arms are intact, and measure eight feet each in length and fifteen inches round the base. The two tentacles attain a length of thirty feet. The mandibles [beak] are about four inches across, hooked, just like the beak of an enormous parrot, with a very curious tongue. The head, devoid of all appendages, weighed about six stone [84lb; 38kg], and the eyes were about fifteen inches in diameter.

Doubtless this account may sound exaggerated, but I hold such portions of the fish as are fully sufficient to establish its enormous size, and verify the dimensions above given. – *Thomas O'Connor, Sergeant, Royal Irish Constabulary; Boffin Island, Connemara, April 28, 1875.* (*The Zoologist*, June 1875)

Newfoundland Visitors at Portugal Cove and Trinity Bay

Portugal Cove

In the 1870s and '80s there was a veritable carnival of colossal calamaries sighted, encountered and even grappled with on and off the coasts of Newfoundland. One of the most notable amongst such visitations occurred in October 1873. It concerned two fishermen (or maybe just one) and one of their sons (or not, maybe) from Portugal Cove, on Conception Bay, just across the peninsula from Newfoundland's main city of St John's, and their intimate confrontation with a live and decidedly 'animated' visitor to the bay: a 'great Devil-Fish', otherwise known, in the day, as a giant cuttle or calamary. An eminent Newfie 'Presbyterian clergyman, essayist, historian and naturalist' of the time, the Irish-born Rev. Moses Harvey (1820–1901), related 'in a graphic and thrilling narrative' his personal involvement with the events of that day:

How I Discovered the Great Devil-Fish, by Rev. M. Harvey

... On the 26th of October, 1873, two fishermen named Theophilus Piccot [*sic* – Picot] and Daniel Squires were out in their fishing boat, off the cove, catching herring. The son of the former, a boy of twelve, had charge of the helm. When near Belle Isle they saw a bulky object floating on the surface of the water. Supposing it to be a portion of a wreck, they rowed towards it, and one of them struck at it with his boat-hook. Instantly the seemingly dead mass became animated. It reared itself above the waves, presenting a most ferocious aspect, and displaying to the horrified fishermen a pair of great eyes, gleaming with rage, and a horny beak, with which it struck the gunwale of the boat.

The next instant a long, thin, corpse-like arm shot out from the head, with the speed of an arrow, and coiled itself round the boat. It was immediately followed by a second arm, much stouter but shorter, and both, in some mysterious way, glued themselves to the boat, which presently began to sink. The terrible monster then disappeared beneath the surface, dragging men and boat with it. The terror-stricken fishermen were completely paralyzed, and thought their last hour had come. The water was pouring into the boat as it sank lower and lower, and in a few seconds all would have been over with the unfortunate men.

Quick as lightning, however, the boy Piccot took in the situation, and, seizing a small tomahawk that fortunately lay in the bottom of the boat, the brave little fellow dashed forward, and with two or three quick blows cut off both arms as they lay over the edge of the boat. The creature did not attempt to renew the fight. He discharged some two or three gallons of an inky fluid, which emitted a strong odour not unlike musk, and darkened the water for many yards around. Then the huge slimy mass seemed to slide off, and the hideous, threatening beak disappeared.

The terrified men only saw the extremity of the tail above the surface as the creature disappeared, and they declared that to them it seemed 6ft. or 7ft. across. Fearing pursuit from the monster, they rowed shoreward for their lives, but not before Tom Piccot had secured the amputated arms, which he brought home as trophies of the combat.

It did not occur to Tom that he had done anything remarkable. He threw down the shorter arm outside his door, where, unfortunately, it was soon devoured by hungry dogs. The long, thin arm, however, he carefully preserved. He had an idea that it might be converted into a rope for mooring his boat! The clergyman of the village heard of the occurrence and recommended him to bring it to me, as I was 'crazy after all kinds of strange beasts and fishes.'

Next day Tom presented himself at my door in St John's, asking if I 'would buy the horn of a big squid.' He told me the whole story in a few brief words, merely remarking, in a casual way, that he thought 'he had done for the big squid.' How eagerly I closed the bargain may be imagined. Tom went away a happy boy with the reward I gave him. He was not happier than myself, however, for I was now the possessor of one of the rarest curiosities in the whole animal kingdom. (*Wide World Magazine*, March 1899)

The naturalist Reverend apparently high-tailed it over to Portugal Cove where he 'found the two fishermen but partially recovered from the terror' of their confrontation: 'They still shuddered as they spoke of it … They affirmed that the length of the loathsome, slimy brute was not less than 60ft., and that the head 'was as big as a six-gallon keg.' … but of course by the length they meant the outspread arms as well as the body; and I shall show presently that they were not very far beyond the mark.'

There is no doubt that a giant squid brawled with the Portugal Cove fisherman Theophilus Picot in October 1873. And that one of its tentacles (the one not 'devoured by hungry dogs'), measured by Rev. Harvey at 19ft in length, was preserved for posterity. And that the creature was subsequently estimated to have been 'no less than 60ft.' long. Moreover, that the Rev. Harvey came into possession of bits from another similar animal hauled ashore at Logy Bay, near St John's, a few weeks later, in the net of four local herring fishermen.

The men gave me a graphic account of the capture. Four of them were engaged in a boat hauling in a large herring-net. They found it unusually heavy as they drew it towards the boat, and concluded that they had a specially fine haul of herring. As the mass came nearer the surface, however, they were startled at its violent convulsive movements, which threatened to burst the net or carry it away. Their united strength was called for, and when the contents of the net came into view, they were horrified to see a pair of large, cruel eyes glaring at them, and a confused mass of ghostly white arms wriggling in the meshes of the net and struggling to get free. Two of these arms – evidently the tentacles – shot out a certain length, through a rent in the net, quivered for a moment in the air, but, fortunately, failed to reach the boat, and were quickly withdrawn.

The men were now thoroughly alarmed, and thought of letting the net go altogether; but finally they decided on killing the struggling monster. One of them drew his sharp fish-splitting knife and, watching his opportunity, made a rapid cut behind the eyes and severed the central mass or head, with the ten arms attached, from the body. Unfortunately the knife touched and destroyed the eyes, leaving only the sockets, which I afterwards found on measurement to be each 4in. in diameter. The convulsive movements now ceased, and the men had no further trouble in landing their prize.

... The courage of the men in grappling with an unknown monster must be admired; and one of them

afterwards informed me confidentially that they had such
a bad half-hour with it that money would not induce him
to take part again in capturing such a horrible beast.

Rev. Harvey was not shy about conflating the evidence
of 'his' devil-fish and the sea serpent as one and the same
critter, and his kinship with other 'high [actually, higher]
authorities' on the matter:

Here I may say that I firmly believe that the devil-fish
and the sea-serpent are identical, and should this theory
be sustained, it would follow that I have been successful
in unmasking both ... I have long held this opinion; and
such high authorities as Dr. Andrew Wilson [Scottish
zoologist and 'prolific author'; 1852–1912] and Mr. Henry,
F.L.S. Lee [of *Sea Monsters Unmasked* authorship], also
hold this theory.

The specific details of those incidents, however, as col-
ourfully chronicled by Rev. Harvey a quarter of a century
after they happened, including how many fishermen were
actually in the Portugal Cove boat, amongst others (not
least Harvey's misspelling of Picot's name as 'Piccot'), have
been controversial. A long letter about the events, including
Picot's 'description of this great squid, cuttle or devil-fish',
was published in the February 1874 issue of *The American
Naturalist*, from 'Mr. Murray, of the Canadian Geological
Survey': it only mentioned one fisherman in the boat, Picot.
No mention of one tentacle being 'devoured by dogs',
hungry or otherwise.

A meticulous investigator of such anomalies, other mon-
ster-myths and paranormal lore and legends, Garth Haslam,
lays out the inconsistencies of the 'Theophilus Picot and

the Giant Squid' story on his website anomalyinfo.com ('Anomalies: The Strange & Unexplained'), established by him in 1996. According to Haslam's forensic examination of the details, the Rev. Moses Harvey might well have deliberately or mistakenly (or both) distorted elements of the events, including his pivotal role in them, possibly for self-aggrandisement.

But the terror of the Portugal Cove fisherman (or men – or men and a boy) in his (or their) colossal cuttle-scuffle on the waters of Conception Bay in October 1873 was not only singular in the annals of the great calamary but also, surely, real. And our Rev. Harvey, for all or any of his factual peccadilloes, did tell a pretty good story – thrilling, even!

Trinity Bay

Some years after the Portugal Cove sensation, another 'great devil-fish' was stranded on the rocky shore of Trinity Bay, at Catalina, on the east coast of Newfoundland. Fishermen took it alive out of the water (but only after it had tired and calmed down from being stranded by the ebbing tide); 'the monster' died soon thereafter. It was eventually sold to the New York Aquarium for exhibition there in 'a large glass tank … prepared for its reception'. *The Penny Illustrated Paper and Illustrated Times*, of London, and *Harper's Weekly* both ran articles about the event with similar sketches to illustrate the flailing beast:

The Great Devil-Fish

Many people whose knowledge of the cuttle-fish is confined to the dwarfish *octopi* which are among the chief attractions of our English Aquariums may, not unnaturally, have been led to look with incredulity upon the

The giant squid. (*Ocean Wonders – A Companion for the Seaside*, by William Emerson Damon, 1879)

wondrous story of the combat between a man and a devil-fish, as vividly related by Victor Hugo in his 'Toilers of the Sea.' But the engraving on our front page ['The great Atlantic devil-fish aground on the Newfoundland coast'] may disabuse them of their disbelief. With Mr. Henry

Lee, the popular naturalist, we are of opinion that there are more things in the ocean depths than are dreamt of in the philosophy of many. Leaving Mr. Lee to dwell at length on the fruitful theme in his forthcoming work on 'The Great Sea Serpent,' return we to 'our muttons' in the shape of the monster of the deep pictured in our present Number, from the drawing of an American Artist.

This huge devil-fish (whose death throes are vigorously delineated) is the latest and most remarkable addition to the New York Aquarium. We are assured it is the largest that has ever been seen; and, while to the student it is a choice object of examination, to the uneducated public it is a most horrible looking creature.

On Sept. 22 last a heavy equinoctial gale swept the shores of St. John's, Newfoundland, and this wanderer was driven ashore in an exhausted condition at Catalina, on the northern shore of Trinity Bay. The tail had got fast on a rock as it was swimming backward, and it was rendered powerless. In its desperate efforts to escape, the ten arms darted about in all directions, lashing the water into foam, the thirty-foot tentacles in particular making lively play as it shot them out and endeavoured to get a 'purchase' with their powerful suckers, so as to drag itself into deep water. It was only when it became exhausted and the tide receded that the fishermen ventured to approach it. It died soon after the ebb of the tide, which left it high and dry on the beach. The fishermen took possession of the 'treasure trove,' and the whole settlement gathered to gaze in astonishment at the monster.

The two men loaded their little craft with the body of the gigantic cuttle, and arrived with it at St. John's on Sept. 26, in a perfectly fresh condition. As soon as the news spread an eager desire to see the monster was awakened, and the fishermen were advised to exhibit it before the public. The Government granted the use of the drill-shed for the purpose, and on the floor, supported by boards, the creature was laid out in all its gigantic proportions. The lucky fishermen reaped a golden harvest and found the big squid by far the best catch they had ever made.

This scene was very curious. There lay the cuttle with its ten arms stretched out, two of them 30 ft. in length, having rows of powerful suckers an inch in diameter at their broadened extremities. The other arms, eight in number, were entirely covered in suckers on the under side, and were 11 ft. in length. The body is 10 ft. in length and nearly 7 ft. in circumference, and terminates in a caudal [tail] fin 2 ft. 9 in. across. When taken from the water the colour of the squid was a dusky red, but that has disappeared, and the body and arms are now perfectly white.

There is the usual horny beak, the parrot-like mandibles of which project from a membraneous   bag in the centre of the mass which constitutes the head, and from which the ten arms radiate. Certainly, the idea of being clutched in those terrible arms, from which there could be no escape when once they had closed, and then torn and rent by the formidable beak, is enough to send a shuddering thrill through the stoutest heart. The devil-fish possessed a pair of huge staring eyes, the sockets being eight inches in diameter. Their expression, when the creature was alive on the beach, is said by the fishermen to have been peculiarly ferocious. (*The Penny Illustrated Paper and Illustrated Times*, London, 17 November 1877)

The 'Devil Fish' Attack on the Schooner *Pearl*

One of the most frightening narratives of an ostensibly true confrontation between a monstrous 'great calamary' and a small sailing craft was variously reported in 1874, including, and probably first, as a 'strange story ... communicated to the Indian papers'. *The Times* ran the story on 4 July 1874. It was cited by an article in *Boys' Life* of May 1983 ('How Giant is the Giant Squid?') as: 'Possibly the best documented attack by a [giant] squid.' The witness to the great calamary's annihilation of the small trading schooner *Pearl*, in the southern Bay of Bengal, was a nearby steamship, the *Strathowen*, which picked up the survivors, including the *Pearl*'s master, Capt. James Floyd, who gave a first-hand account of the mêlée:

Fate of the Schooner Pearl – *Frightful Scene in the Indian Ocean – A Devil Fish Swallows a Schooner*

The following strange story has been communicated to us by James Floyd, late master of the schooner *Pearl*:

We had left Colombo [Ceylon/Sri Lanka] in the steamer Strathowen, and rounded Galle, and were well in the Bay [i.e. to the east of Sri Lanka in the southern Bay of Bengal], with our course laid for Madras, steaming over a calm and tranquil sea. About an hour before sunset on May 10th, we saw on our starboard beam, and about two miles off, a small schooner lying becalmed; there was nothing in her appearance or position to excite remark, but as we came up with her, I lazily examined her with my binocular, and then noticed between us, but nearer her, a long, low swelling, lying on the sea, which from its color and shape I took to be a bank of seaweed.

The devil-fish taken on the Newfoundland coast, now in the New York Aquarium. (*Harper's Weekly*, 3 November 1877)

Céphalopode géant capturé sur la côte de Terre-Neufe ('Giant cephalopod captured on the coast of Newfoundland'). (*L'illustration européenne*, 1877–78)

The great Atlantic devil-fish aground on the Newfoundland coast.
(*The Penny Illustrated Paper*, 17 November 1877)

As I watched, the mass hitherto at rest on the quiet
sea, was set in motion. It struck the schooner, which
visibly reeled and then righted; immediately afterwards
the masts swayed sideways, and with my glass I could

clearly discern the enormous masts and hull of a schooner coalescing – I can think of no other term. Judging from their exclamations, the other gazers must have seen the same appearance. Almost immediately after the collision and coalescence, the schooner's masts swayed toward us, lower and lower; the vessel was on her beam end, lay there a few seconds, and disappeared, the masts righting as she sank, and the main exhibiting a reversed ensign [signal of distress] struggling toward its peak.

A cry of horror arose from the lookers on; and, as if by instinct, our ship's head was at once turned toward the scene, which was marked by the forms of those battling for life – the sole survivors of the pretty little schooner which only twenty minutes before had floated bravely on the smooth sea.

As soon as the poor fellows were able to tell their story they astounded us with the assertion that their vessel had been submerged by a gigantic cuttle-fish or calamary, the animal which, in a smaller form, attracts so much attention in the Brighton Aquarium as the octopus. Each narrator had his version of the story, but in the main all the narrative tallied so remarkably as to leave no doubt of the facts.

As soon as he was at leisure, I prevailed on the skipper to give me his written account of the disaster, and I have now much pleasure in sending you a copy of his narrative:

Capt. Floyd's Narrative

'I was lately the skipper of the *Pearl* schooner, 150 tons, as tight a little craft as ever sailed the seas, with a crew of six men. We were bound from the Mauritius to Rangoon in ballast to return with paddy [rice], and had put in at Galle for water. Three days out we fell becalmed in the bay (lat. 8 deg. 50 min. N., long. 84 deg. 05 min. E.). On

May 10th about 5 p.m. (8 bells [4 p.m.] I know had gone),
we sighted a two-masted screw [steamer] on our port quarter, about five or six miles off; very soon after, as we lay
motionless, a great mass rose slowly out of the sea, about
half a mile off on our larboard [port] side, and remained
spread out as it were and stationary; it looked like the back
of a huge whale, but it was sloped less, and was of a brown-
ish color; even at that distance it seemed much longer than
our craft, and seemed to be basking in the sun.

"'What's that?" I sung out to the mate. "Blest if I knows;
barring its size, color and shape, it might be a whale,"
replied Tom Scott. "And it ain't the sea serpent," said one
of the crew, "for he's too round for that 'ere crittur."

'I went into the cabin for my rifle, and as I was preparing to fire, Bill Darling, a Newfoundlander, put up his
hand. "Have a care master; that 'ere is a squid, and he'll
capsize us if you hurt him." Smiling at the idea, I let fly
and hit him, and with that he shook, there was a great
ripple all around him, and he began to move.

'"Out with all your axes and knives," shouted Bill,
"and cut at any part of him that comes aboard; look alive,
and Lord help us!" Not aware of the danger, and never
having seen or heard of such a monster, I gave no orders,
and it was no use touching the helm or ropes to get out of
the way. By this time three of the crew, Bill included, had
found axes, and one a rusty cutlass, and all were looking
over the ship's side at the advancing monster.

'We could now see a huge oblong mass moving by jerks
just under the surface of the water, and an enormous train
[wake] following. The oblong body was at least half the
size of our vessel in length, and just as thick; the wake or
train might have been 100 feet long. In the time that I have
taken to write this the brute struck us, and the ship quivered

under the thud. In another moment, monstrous arms like trees seized the vessel, and she heeled over; in another second the monster was on board, squeezed in between the two masts, Bill screaming, "Slash for your lives!"

'But our slashing was of no avail, for the brute, holding on by his arms, slipped his vast body overboard and pulled the vessel down with him on her beam ends. We were thrown into the water at once; and just as I went over I caught sight of one of the crew, either Bill or Tom Fielding, squashed up between the mast and one of those awful arms. For a few seconds our ship lay on her beam ends, then filled and went down. Another of the crew must have been sucked down, for you only picked up five. The rest you know. I can't tell who ran up the ensign.' (*Sacramento Daily Union* [California], 31 July 1874)

The *Alecton*'s Capture of (Part of) a Giant Squid

On 30 November 1861 a French warship, the steam corvette *Alecton*, commanded by Lieutenant Frédéric Bouyer, was passing between the Canary Islands and Madeira en route from the French naval base at Toulon to the French South American colony of Cayenne (French Guyana). What happened that day he and M. Sabin Berthelot, the French Consul at the Canary Islands (the *Alecton*'s next port-of-call), 'communicated to the Paris Academy of Sciences, through M. Vaillant': no less than the rendezvous with and capture of (part of) a 'giant Calamary', a 'monster ... found floating at the surface of the water'. The narrative has gone down in giant squid chronicles as one of the most graphic accounts of our human interaction with the successor to the great kraken.

The story has been told diversely in reconstructed formats. The most faithful was a script by the French naturalist Armand Landrin in his *Les Monstres Marins* (translated in English by W.H. Davenport Adams and published in 1875 as *The Monsters of the Deep: and Curiosities of Ocean Life*), which he borrowed virtually verbatim from Capt. Bouyer's own account of the voyage, *La Guyane française; notes et souvenirs d'un voyage executé en 1862–1863*, published in 1867, as follows:

M. Bouyer was leaning on the bulwark of his vessel, lost in thought, when his reverie was suddenly interrupted by a sailor.

'Captain,' he said, 'the look-out man signals a wreck, away on the larboard [port side].'

'It is a canoe capsized,' says another.

'It is red, and resembles a dead horse,' says a third.

'It is a mass of sea-weed,' says a fourth.

'It is a cask,' says a fifth.

'It is an animal; look at its feet,' says a sixth.

I directed myself immediately towards the object signalled, which was so differently judged by different men, and I recognised it as the giant poulpe, whose existence seemed relegated into the regions of fable. Thus, then, I found myself in the presence of one of those fantastic creatures which the sea sometimes upheaves from its depths, as if to hurl a defiance at the incredulity of naturalists. The opportunity was too unexpected, and too felicitous, not to tempt me. So I quickly resolved to capture the monster, with the view of examining it more thoroughly.

Immediately all on board are astir; the muskets are loaded; the harpoons thrust into their handles; running knots are made ready; every arrangement for this novel chase is concluded. Unfortunately the sea rolled very heavily, and each time the billows caught us on the broadside, the *Alecton* rolled in so disorderly a manner as to impede our evolutions; while the animal itself, though keeping always on the surface of the water, moved to and fro with a kind of instinct, as if desirous of avoiding our vessel.

After several manœuvres, we contrived to pour into it a score of bullets; but to these it appeared insensible. I then got near enough to launch a harpoon, as well as a noose, or slip-knot; and we were preparing to multiply the number of its bonds, when a violent movement, either of the harpoon or of the ship, started the harpoon, which had not got firm hold in the monster's viscid skin. At the same time, the part of the body which our rope had entangled was torn away, and we hauled on board but a fragment of the extremity.

We now found that it was a colossal *encornet* [squid]; its body measuring five to six feet in length; the tentacles, eight in number*, were of the same dimensions. (*The form of the animal attacked by M. Bouyer is that of a calamary, which is a decapod, yet it is only the poulpes which possess eight arms of equal length. It is probable, therefore, that it had lost its two larger arms in some submarine contest, and that it was its mutilated condition which prevented it from diving rapidly, or ejecting its inky discharge, according to the custom of frightened cephalopoda.) [To which the translator of M. Landrin's work appended the sarcastic remark: 'Credat Judæus Apella!', part of a quote from one of the *Satires* of the Roman poet Horace, meaning, 'Apella the Jew might believe it!', which is followed by 'Non ego': 'Not I.' It echoed a stereotype of that time that Jews were credulous, meaning to dismiss any aforesaid notion as ridiculous.]

Its colour, a brick-like red; its body greatly swollen towards the centre; its eyes, flat, glaucous, large as saucers, fixed. In the combat, which lasted three hours, it vomited foam, blood, and viscous matter which diffused abroad a strong *odour of musk.*

Both officers and sailors begged of me to launch a boat, and give them another opportunity of garroting the monster, and bringing it alongside. They might, perhaps, have been successful, if I had yielded to their petition; but I feared lest in this bodily encounter the animal might launch one of its long and many-suckered arms against the side of the canoe, might capsize it, or choke some of my men in its formidable thongs [*fouets*: i.e. whip-like arms], which are charged, it is said, with electric and paralyzing effluvia. And as I was unwilling to expose the lives of my men to satisfy a vain curiosity, I thought it right to control the feverish ardour which had seized upon all of us during this eager pursuit, and gave orders for its abandonment.

The mutilated monster was now fleeing from us; and without appearing to be gifted with any great swiftness of movement, dived several fathoms, and came up on the other side of the ship, whenever we succeeded in bearing down upon it.

The portion of its club-shaped extremity which we had on board weighed fourteen kilogrammes. It is a soft substance, with a strong odour of musk. The part corresponding to the dorsal spine is comparatively hard. It broke easily, and the fracture was white as alabaster. The whole animal, according to my estimate, must have weighed from two to three tons. (!) It breathed noisily; but I did not observe that it ejected any of the inky fluid by means of which the little cuttle-fish about

Newfoundland disturb the transparency of the water to escape their enemies.

The seamen told me that they had seen, to the south of the Cape of Good Hope, some similar poulpes, though of smaller size. They affirm that the animal is a bitter enemy of the whale; and in fact, we may ask, why should not this creature, which seems a rude, half-finished outline or sketch, attain to gigantic proportions? There is nothing to stop its growth; neither bone nor carapace: *a priori*, we can see no limits to its development.

However this may be, this horrible fugitive from the menageries of old Proteus long pursued me, like a nightmare, in my dreams. Long did I see fixed upon me that vitreous, sickly glare, and those eight arms, which entwined me in their serpent-like folds. Long did I preserve the recollection of the monster encountered by the *Alecton*, at two o'clock in the afternoon of the 30th of November 1861, at forty leagues from Teneriffe.

Since with my own eyes I have seen this strange animal, I no longer dare to regard with incredulity the stories of earlier navigators.

I suspect that the sea has not said its last word, and that it holds in reserve some scions of extinct races, some degenerate descendants of the trilobites; or rather, that it elaborates in its ever-active crucible some unrevealed model, to become the terror of seamen, and the subject of mysterious ocean-legends.

THE END

The giant squid being taken by the *Alecton* near the Canary
Islands in 1861.

The
History
Press

 The destination for history
www.thehistorypress.co.uk